Mirrabooka Magic

Also by Maggie McGuinness

Planet Single (A Romantic Comedy)

Mirrabooka Magic

Maggie McGuinness

Published by WordWise Publishing
www.wordwise.com.au

ISBN: 978 0 64505 170 4

Dedication

Dedicated to Missy and Tilly, the two beautiful cattle dog rescues who provided the real-life inspiration for Ruby Roo

Chapter 1 – Going home

The decision to jump proved almost fatal.

The big kangaroo had been sitting on the edge of the road for several minutes, twitching its nose and eyeing off lush green grass on the far side. Why it chose that particular moment to push off with its powerful haunches and leap down the embankment is anybody's guess.

The driver of the vehicle swinging around the sharp corner had no time to consider marsupial decision-making processes. Faced with a large kangaroo in mid-air, all Juliet could do was follow the instruction that had been drilled into her brain ever since she became old enough to drive on Australian country roads: stay straight and brake. She knew that swerving to avoid a kangaroo, wallaby, wombat or any of the other creatures that liked to turn up at short notice was a recipe for disaster.

Luckily, on this occasion, she'd been concentrating on the tight turn and reacted fast, stepping hard on the brakes of the SUV with a squeal of rubber on asphalt, and easing off when the tail-end began to slew sideways. That gave Skippy the split second he needed to land and then take off in another huge bound, clearing the gravel edge of the road and some fallen branches and bouncing away into the scrub.

Juliet drove slowly to a straight stretch of road and pulled over, heart pounding.

"Whoa! That was close! Just as well I took the corner nice and slow. Are you okay, Ruby?" She turned to look at her passenger in the back seat.

Ruby – full name Ruby Roo, but often called Ruby, Roo or Roo-dog for short – was a red heeler or, to use the breed's official name, an Australian cattle dog. An intelligent and agile dog with a strong and sometimes stubborn personality, she was typical of the breed and fiercely loyal to her owner. Hearing Juliet's voice, she stood up and looked around, pricking up her ears. Her peaceful snooze had been interrupted by the sudden stop, and only her doggie seatbelt harness had stopped her from sliding in an undignified heap onto the floor. Everything seemed to be in order now though, and she reached forward as far as she could to give her owner's arm a reassuring nudge.

Juliet twisted further in her seat to pat the dog's thick red fur, her spirits lifted as always by the alert and adoring look in Ruby Roo's amber eyes.

"Right, let's get back to it. We just have to watch out for kangaroos or any other bush creatures with a death wish. You tell me if you see one, okay?"

The dog wagged her tail in agreement and sniffed at the air through the part-open window as the car pulled back onto the road. She felt a surge of excitement – something was telling her they were nearly home. Perhaps it was the tangy smell of the eucalypts, or the chimes of the bellbirds – or perhaps it was the relief she could sense radiating from every atom of her owner's body.

Home. After seven hours of driving, starting off in the chaos and noise of the inner city, they had almost reached the far eastern point of the state of Victoria, Australia. On that corner of the country, where the Tasman Sea stretched from mainland Australia across to New Zealand, the little town of Mirrabooka was nestled on a peninsula between a big saltwater inlet and the ocean, part of a coastline of wild and rugged beauty. Mirrabooka was where Juliet and her sister, Isabella, had grown up, enjoying an idyllic childhood of swimming in the surf and exploring the bush and the beaches.

Juliet was desperate to get back home – to her real home, that is. She'd spent the past two years in the city, moving there to be with a man she'd thought would be her future. Her house in Mirrabooka had become a holiday home for those years, but she'd only visited it a few times. Ronan loved the buzz and the nightlife of the city and didn't like the long drive to the coast.

Having little to do with his own family, Ronan didn't understand Juliet's strong family bonds and he never made an effort to get along with Isabella or her husband, Byron, or show interest in their two-year-old daughter, Clementine. Juliet had hoped they'd all warm to each other with time, but that had never happened. Now she could see that she'd missed out on far too much of Clemmie's babyhood because of her efforts to keep Ronan happy. Well, she could make up for lost time now she was going home for good.

Everything had fallen apart back in the city two days ago. She'd discovered that Ronan was cheating on her and had confronted him about it, and they'd had a huge argument. Then he did something she'd never forgive him for – something even worse than the infidelities.

Juliet had stormed out of their inner-city terrace house, taking Ruby Roo with her, and stayed the night with a sympathetic friend. She only returned the next day to pack up her belongings, and then she and Roo had jumped in the car and headed east without a backward glance.

The drive had given her hours to analyse the relationship and its demise, and to realize that Ronan, as well as being dishonest and unfaithful, was utterly selfish. Basically, he thought everything should revolve around him, Juliet could now see.

As the wheels of the car whirred across mile after mile of highway, taking its passengers past the broad city outskirts and then through green grazing land and rolling hills, Juliet's head was crowded with scenes from her two years with Ronan. Why had she put up with him all that time? Isabella and Byron had never liked him, although they'd never admitted it. Come to think of it, her friends hadn't seemed to like him much either. Was she the only person who couldn't see what an unpleasant egomaniac he really was?

After hours of such thoughts, Juliet's brain was completely frazzled, and she had to call a halt to the self-recriminations. She pictured instead scenes of home – the vast expanse of golden sand, the cold, clear water of the surf, and the sea birds soaring and gliding on the ocean breeze. Those images saw her through the next leg of the drive but, by the time they finally reached the tiny hamlet on the highway with the turnoff to Mirrabooka, Juliet was exhausted. She made a final attempt to gather her strength, knowing she had to keep a grip on her emotions a bit longer. Once she was back in her own beloved cottage, she could fall in a heap and cry over broken dreams.

After turning off the highway, there were only about twenty minutes of the journey left, but most of it was on narrow, winding roads through the bush. Juliet had to force herself to focus on the many tight corners, and it was just as well she did, or the kangaroo would not have lived to hop through another day.

She felt the SUV surge down a hill. "Easy does it," she whispered to herself. Juliet knew every twist and turn in this stretch of road. There was the first glimpse through the trees of the smooth, dark water of the inlet that stretched inland for miles, all the way from the ocean to the foothills of the ranges.

There was the part of the road that sometimes flooded, where she'd once tried to drive through the floodwater in her old Volkswagen Beetle and got stuck, having to be hauled out backwards by a tow-truck. Her friend Tom still loved to remind her about that.

And then, finally, there was the sign saying 'Mirrabooka – 5 kms' that always made her stomach flutter with excitement.

Ruby Roo sniffed at the air again. Now it held the salty freshness of the ocean as well as the tangy fragrance of the forest. She gave a little whine – there was *definitely* something exciting going on.

"We've made it, Roo-dog! Home at last." Juliet sighed with relief as they reached the outskirts of the quiet coastal village.

She hadn't told anyone she was coming home – not even Isabella. She was too tired and emotionally shattered to talk to anybody yet. All she wanted to do was look out to sea and fill her lungs with that fresh salty air, then drop her bags on the floor of the mud-brick cottage and crawl under her big, soft quilt.

Juliet turned the car off the main road just before they reached town, heading along a bumpy dirt track that led to one of her favourite places – the tip of the thin finger of land that separated the ocean from the saltwater inlet. Arriving at the small parking area, she noticed with relief it was empty and there didn't seem to be any bushwalkers admiring the view, so it looked like she would have the solitude she craved.

She climbed stiffly down from the front seat and opened the rear door, quickly slipping the harness off the impatient dog.

"Good girl. Out you get."

Ruby Roo leapt down with glee, did a few joyful circuits of the grassy area and then bounced into the undergrowth, disturbing a flock of wrens that took off in a blur of blue and brown wings.

Smiling at the dog's happiness, Juliet left her to investigate the surroundings and walked over the grass to the rocky outcrop that jutted into the water, where pink granite glowed with a soft warmth in the late afternoon sun. She stepped down onto the rocks at the edge and noticed with satisfaction the clean, clear water of the incoming tide flowing around them. A shoal of tiny fish darted past the rocks, perhaps spooked by Juliet's arrival or, more likely, by the two pelicans cruising serenely along the channel.

To her left, the inlet shone like a mirror, bordered by the ranges that sloped down to the sea, where a faint pink haze hinted at the sunset that wasn't far away. To her right, a graceful arc of golden surf beaches stretched as far as she could see, broken only by the choppy entrance – a channel running through the sand of about fifty yards wide – where the inlet met the sea. The entrance looked unassuming enough that afternoon, but it could be treacherous to unwary boat drivers.

On this afternoon, however, all was serene, and the only boats in sight were dotted around some of the islands and the channels of the inlet, where their occupants would have been enjoying peaceful conditions for fishing. Juliet scanned the vessels and was pleased to see that her friend Tom's boat was anchored at his favourite bream-fishing spot.

Tom was the local doctor, who'd gone to school with Juliet. They'd been great friends ever since grade one when he'd dared her to climb the cliff alongside Little Beach with him. The fact that she'd not only accepted the dare but had beaten him to the top had impressed him no end. He was one of Juliet's closest friends and she was looking forward to seeing him again, but their reunion would have to wait a while – right now she needed home, and sleep.

She gazed once more at the lines of surf, watching the waves surge up the beach and slide back, leaving only a jagged pattern of white foam fingers on the shoreline. She sighed with contentment as her eyes soaked up the glorious, familiar view, all her troubles momentarily forgotten.

The boom and swoosh of the surf was music to Juliet's ears, and she could hear it night and day from her cottage, which was only a short walk from the beach. Growing up in the town, the surf had formed a constant soundtrack to her life, its music becoming part of her soul. Whenever Juliet was away from the ocean, she always had a vague feeling that something was missing, and the incessant hum and blaring horns of city traffic had been a poor replacement.

Ruby Roo trotted onto the rocks and nudged Juliet's hand with her nose.

"I agree, Roo, it's time to go home. We'll come back here tomorrow."

She gave a last fond glance towards Tom's boat and headed back to the car, driving slowly for a few minutes up another dirt track that led to a pretty mudbrick cottage set among tall trees. She parked near the front veranda and switched the ignition off with relief. In the quiet of the bush, she could still hear the mutter of the surf, and now there were the chimes of bellbirds as well – her second-favourite sound in the whole world.

She gazed at her home, with its timber front steps, wide verandah and corrugated iron roof, and realized with a rush how utterly exhausted she was. Even opening the car door was going to need a surge of energy. Ruby Roo whined with impatience to be out and exploring the familiar territory.

"Come on, move it!" Juliet said to herself, climbing down and letting out the dog, who showed no signs of flagging energy whatsoever. Ruby leapt down and dashed around the bush block in a blur of red fur, her nose hard at work sniffing all the enticing bushy scents. Juliet grabbed a couple of bags from the car and walked up the few stairs and across to the front door, thinking how neat and tidy it all looked. Isabella and Byron had done a great job of looking after the cottage while she'd been away, even though they lived on the far side of the inlet.

Those two years in the city had been a rollercoaster ride of highs and lows. Her first novel had been published and became an immediate success, and Juliet had found herself labelled 'best-selling author' at the age of only twenty-six. She'd been drawn up into an exciting whirlwind of publicity, with a busy program of readings, signings and interviews. Some of it had been great fun, but often it was too hectic for her liking. Just living in the city had been a challenge, and she'd often longed for the beauty and serenity of home. At least she'd had Ronan to show her around. He was also a writer, although he didn't like his work to be compared to hers. He liked to stress that he wrote *literary* fiction, as opposed to Juliet's popular fiction that appealed to the masses, which was why his sales figures were so much lower. He had excuses for everything, really, Juliet mused as she unlocked the door and stepped inside, dropping the bags on the floor. He'd certainly had plenty of excuses for cheating on her.

"I'm sorry, babe," he'd said. "But monogamy kills my creativity. You know what I mean?"

"No. Not at all," she'd replied.

The thought of sharing that precious intimacy with anyone else appalled Juliet. She had loved Ronan, and thought he loved her. Either she'd been badly wrong, or they had very different ideas about the definition of the word.

"I do love you!" he'd protested. "But I can't tie myself down to one woman. I thought you would understand, but you're so naïve! You can't shake off that boring, small-town mentality, can you?"

That had stung. She already felt out of place in the fast, brittle world of the city – she didn't need Ronan to remind her how unsophisticated she was.

Well, no matter. She'd left that world now, for good. She'd already signed the contract for her second novel and received a nice advance for it, and yesterday had rung her agent to say she was going home to focus on finishing it and starting the third one in the series. That was the official story, anyway. The agent certainly didn't mind; the sooner the next book was completed the better. The publishers were licking their lips at the thought of Juliet Cooper's follow-up best seller.

In reality, Juliet knew she'd come home to let her heart be comforted by the murmur of the ocean and the stillness of the bush. This was where her bruised soul could start to heal, and where she would be surrounded by people who really did care about her. And, while Mirrabooka was working its gentle magic on her, yes, she would write. She would throw herself into her work and hope it might dull the pain of betrayal, loss and loneliness. Love? That was a game fraught with danger, and she'd had enough of it.

Chapter 2 – An angry angel

Finn McLaren walked along a dusty track and cursed the flies that buzzed around his face in the late autumn sunshine. He'd decided to walk into town to kill time and get some exercise but had underestimated how long it would take. The groceries he carried home in a backpack were heavy, even though the store hadn't been able to supply half the stuff he'd wanted. He cursed the flies some more, and then he cursed the train of circumstances that had led him to be in the middle of nowhere, and then he cursed the lack of city conveniences he still couldn't get used to. If it wasn't mobile phones dropping out of range and internet access that seemed to depend on the alignment of the planets, it was an apparent conspiracy that whatever he particularly wanted to buy would not be available that day. That's what happens when you're living out in the sticks with one general store, he grumbled to himself.

Well, he'd be back in the city in a few months, able to buy everything he could possibly want in the big supermarkets and enjoy all the comforts of his plush, modern home. Mind you, he'd need to move into something more modest soon. He was still paying an exorbitant amount for the apartment that his fiancée – now ex-fiancée – had insisted they move into, although Sophia's desire for it had never translated into helping pay the rent. He'd never much liked the big, showy apartment anyway, and it was far too big for one person.

Deep in thought about his eventual return to the city, he turned into the driveway of the bush block that was home for his sojourn in the back of beyond.

He glimpsed something moving around in the shrubs in front of the cottage he'd rented and wondered what it could be. The kangaroos and wallabies didn't come this close; not in daylight, anyway. It was definitely an animal though, and he glimpsed red fur – perhaps it was a dingo? Whatever it was, the creature was nosing around his front veranda. Dingoes were dangerous, weren't they? They certainly weren't something he had to deal with in the city, so he decided to err on the side of caution.

"Hey! Get out of there!" He picked up a clod of dirt and threw it on impulse, more in frustration about his current predicament than any real desire to hit the animal. His aim was usually terrible, anyway. Although he'd always been a good footballer, due to his fitness and running speed, ball sports were not really his forte. This time, however, some fluke of fate made his aim true and the clod smacked the 'dingo' right on the nose.

The animal yelped in fright and looked confused, and not dangerous at all. In fact, it looked a lot less like a dingo and more like someone's pet dog, and that someone was running down the steps of the cottage next door and stepping over the low side fence, heading straight towards him.

'Hey!" yelled the most beautiful woman he'd seen in the last three hundred miles.

She whistled to the dog, who ran to her side, and soothed it with lots of pats, then straightened up her slim figure, clad in faded jeans and a white blouse, and turned towards him. Glorious honey-blonde hair cascaded around a face of classic beauty that belonged to a painting on a gallery wall. The woman looked like a vision . . . an angel . . . an *angry* angel. Her blue eyes were as hard as flint.

"Why did you do that? You hurt her!" She stared at Finn in a way that made him hot with shame.

"Oh, I'm sorry. I thought it was a dingo! I'm Finn . . . I mean Fred. Fred Murray. I've rented the cottage for a few months – arranged it with Isabella. I'm from Melbourne . . . a lawyer, a barrister actually, although I'm having a kind of sabbatical right now," he garbled, most uncharacteristically. Normally, he was a man who considered words carefully before he spoke, especially in court, where they were tools used with skilled accuracy. Now, though, his words were like the ramblings of a child. A naughty child.

The angry angel was still looking at him as though he'd crawled out from under a rock.

"Lawyer and dog-botherer, I see," she said, hands on hips. The dog's eyes were fixed on him too, with an intense and intimidating stare.

He stood in front of her, feeling foolish, while she looked him up and down.

"Right. Um. I'm sorry about that. I didn't mean to hit it. Normally I'm a terrible shot—" he tried to explain.

"Oh, so you chuck things at lots of innocent creatures do you, but only hit a few? Well, that's just great. What is it with you men who lash out all the time? You . . . you . . . selfish, violent, *city* guys who can't even tell a dog from a dingo and have anger management issues. What are you? Some kind of sadistic psycho? This is *my* dog; her name is Ruby Roo and she's usually quite friendly. Until she decides to attack someone, and nearly rips their leg off with her very sharp teeth. She's got recent form at that. And the next time you hurt her, she gets a go at *your* leg, okay?"

The woman was full-on shouting at him now, with her eyes full of tears, and she looked close to losing it completely. Finn, who for the time being was going under the name of Fred – when he remembered, at least – was used to dealing with emotional meltdowns. As a criminal lawyer, he often dealt with people who were affected by, or had allegedly instigated, distressing events. This woman was traumatised, and not just about the dog.

"I'm very sorry," he said quietly. "I really am."

He looked straight at her, and she stared back at him, taking a couple of deep breaths. Her face softened a little, and it almost seemed to Finn that they'd met somewhere before and were both on the verge of recognising each other. The veil of anger had only lifted for a few fleeting moments, however. It swiftly dropped again, and her expression turned back to a glare.

"Huh. I should hope so." The woman narrowed her eyes, and the dog gave a quiet snarl with a curl of the lip revealing teeth that did indeed appear sharp. The two of them turned and stalked away.

"Oh, in case you think I'm rude . . ." She stopped abruptly and looked back to glower some more. "I'm Juliet. I live over there, I own that cottage you've rented, and I'm a member of the Animal Lovers' Society."

She stepped back over the low fence and marched through the native bush garden, with the red dog loping beside her. They strode across the driveway, then ran up the steps and across the veranda, disappearing from sight with a bang of the door.

"Oh, that's terrific," Finn muttered to himself. "The absent landlord – now my neighbour – has returned, and she happens to be a gorgeous woman who thinks I'm some sort of weirdo who likes hurting animals."

He eased the heavy backpack to the ground and stood looking after the woman and the dog while he stretched his back for a moment. Had he met her before? No – he would definitely have remembered her striking looks. How odd that he'd felt some sort of connection with her for a second or two.

It didn't matter what she thought of him, anyway. Did it? He'd had quite enough trouble with women for the time being. His decision to go to the country had caused big problems with the woman he'd left behind in the city, triggering a huge argument that made the differences between them painfully obvious. There was a chasm between the two of them that would never be breached, Finn had realized, as Sophia had yelled, slammed doors and thrown things around the apartment.

That made two beautiful women shouting at him in just a few weeks, he mused – most unusual. There was a big difference, though, between the two episodes. Although Sophia was also a stunning woman, with exotic looks and a curvy body that turned heads wherever she went, she had looked ugly during that argument – her face contorted with rage and the sarcastic words she'd been berating him with.

Juliet, however, had still looked beautiful despite her outrage, and had seemed so hurt and vulnerable he'd wanted to take her in his arms and comfort her. But that was ridiculous, he didn't even know her, and it completely went against his recent resolve. He'd driven for hours to get to this godforsaken town, telling himself mile after interminable mile that he'd had enough of women. They were a distraction to his career and too much trouble. He was happy to be single now and for the foreseeable future, so that he could consider his own needs rather than always running around looking after someone else's.

He just hadn't expected such an angelic-looking woman to appear out of nowhere and immediately snatch at his heart like that. And it wasn't only because she was beautiful, although her looks had certainly taken his breath away. There was something else. She seemed . . . real, somehow, with her tangled hair and blue shadows under tired eyes. He wanted to see her smile, so those eyes could light up with joy. He wanted to see her relaxed and carefree – not looking as though she carried the weight of the world on her shoulders. She seemed unaware of her beauty; natural in a way that Sophia could never be.

Sophia! Just thinking about her sent a chill across his shoulder blades, like a cloud had covered the sun and a wind sprung up from the shadows. He hoisted the backpack onto his shoulder and trudged up the dusty steps to his own front door.

*

What a horrible man! Juliet resolved to keep her dog away from that side of the fence, so there would be no more risk of attack by that lunatic from the city. And she would stay away from him too. How dare he hurt an innocent creature!

She got food and water for Ruby Roo and was still muttering indignant thoughts as she flung open the windows of her cottage to let the refreshing, salty breeze sweep in. While Ruby finished her snack and curled up in her basket with a happy sigh, Juliet stripped off her shirt and jeans, found her favourite old flannel PJs and crawled into bed, letting the soft quilt wrap around her. Other indignant thoughts would have to wait.

Now Juliet could truly relax, for the first time in months. She lay on her back and stretched her legs, pointing her toes and then relaxing them, feeling her body let go of some of the tension that seemed to have tied her muscles in knots. She was just *so* tired, and her body felt like it was still in the car, being carried along at high speed. She concentrated on letting the tension ebb away, feeling her muscles loosen and her racing thoughts begin to settle. Her shoulders relaxed, and she stretched her arms out wide, reaching out with her fingertips, as a blessed drowsy feeling began to overtake her.

Just as her thoughts were drifting into the welcoming mist of sleep, an image lodged in her mind. It was a tall man with a lean build, black hair, and intense dark eyes, looking at her with concern. It almost felt like she already knew him, and that he was someone special to her.

Oh, there you are! she thought in her drowsiness, feeling a sudden burst of happiness, until the conscious part of her brain remembered who he was and what he'd done. She tensed up again for a moment, feeling her heartbeat quicken, but then forced herself to calm down.

Let it go, stop worrying, Roo's fine.

A contented snuffle from the dog's basket confirmed that fact, and Juliet abandoned herself to oblivion. The two of them were asleep within seconds.

*

"Didn't you read my text message, you dimwit? Or the email I sent with all the details?" Juliet's sister, Isabella, poured tea from a white ceramic pot while Juliet sliced a banana cake that she'd baked that morning.

The two sisters were enjoying the afternoon sunshine, sitting on the decking behind Juliet's cottage, with Ruby Roo stretched out on the wooden boards beside them. The house was on top of a small ridge, and a glorious stretch of the Tasman Sea was spread out before them, sparkling like a sapphire in the sun. Although winter wasn't far away, the area was enjoying a late burst of warm weather, and all three of them were making the most of it. The deck was sheltered by the trees and the higher, surrounding ridges, but the whitecaps dancing on the water hinted at a stiff sea breeze away from shore.

Isabella, expecting her second child, sat back with her feet propped up on a stool.

"I told you I'd let the rental cottage to some bloke from the city who wanted a peaceful retreat. Three whole months! That's a nice bit of income for you this time of year. I can't believe you shouted at him!"

"I know! I feel like a fool," Juliet said. "I did see your messages, but then I completely forgot about them – until I was already in mid-rant. I've been a bit distracted lately, Izzy."

"Of course," her sister murmured. "I'm so sorry about what happened with Ronan. It must have been awful."

"It was. I'd suspected something was wrong for ages, but when I got home from the last book tour, I just knew it. He was swinging between being emotionally detached and then really critical of me – even more than usual – with sarcastic putdowns in the guise of 'jokes'. The worst thing was that he kept accusing me of being paranoid and telling me I was imagining things. Sometimes I wondered if he was right and I was going crazy, but deep down I knew there had to be a reason for the mysterious messages and calls, and his evasiveness. Of course, there was, but it wasn't the excuses he was giving me. He kept lying, over and over again, and getting really angry if I asked him what was going on."

"How did you find out the truth?"

Juliet hesitated, her fingers tightening on the mug until they showed white around the edges. "I snooped. I hate myself for having done it, but I got hold of his phone and I read the emails and text messages."

"You only did it because you had good reason to doubt him," her sister said gently. "You needed some evidence, so you knew where you stood and could take control, instead of letting him steer the ship."

"I know. But I feel awful about it; dirty, somehow. That's not the sort of person I am." Juliet screwed up her nose and took a sip of her tea. "But anyway, I'm relieved I know the truth now. There wasn't just one other girl – there were a few, over the past six months. It started when my novel hit the bestseller lists and the publicity demands ramped up. I don't think he could handle the book's success, although he wouldn't admit it. He got all shocked and angry at me for checking up on him. Like I was the one at fault! We had a huge fight and it got nasty. He punched a hole in the wall and was yelling at me. I was shouting back, and you know I don't do that. Not usually, that is. I began to feel frightened of Ronan – like I didn't even know him, and I was trapped in a house with a stranger. And then . . . and then . . . it got even worse." Her voice faltered, and her eyes filled with tears.

Isabella reached out and covered Juliet's hand with her own. "You don't have to talk about this. Not now – or not ever – if you don't want to. I hate seeing you so upset."

"It's okay. I want to tell you about it, and then maybe I can start to put it behind me. What he did was . . . Oh! It was horrible. He kicked Ruby Roo, really hard. He hurt her. I'll never forgive him for that."

"He kicked her? No! Why would he do that?" Isabella put her hand to her mouth.

"I'd told him it was over, and I was leaving. I walked away to get my car keys, but he went after me, telling me I was being stupid, and I had to stay. He grabbed my arm and wrenched at it, and I cried out and tried to pull away, but then he twisted it even more. He was so angry – I was frightened he might hit me. Roo jumped up and came between us, barking at him, and he let go of my arm but then took aim and kicked her in the ribs, as hard as he could. She yelped and dropped to the floor, but then she leapt up and went for him."

"Good! Did she bite him?"

"Yes, she grabbed his ankle and was growling and snarling and hanging on tight. She's never done anything like that before. I grabbed her and called her off, but she must have punctured the skin. I could see blood on his jeans."

"Well, he deserved it! Of course, she went for him – she was protecting you. Good dog, Ruby Roo!"

The red dog lifted her head for a moment, thumped her tail three times, and went back to sleep. She was tired today, but it was lovely to let her bruised body lie in the sun and rest.

"Ronan started yelling about her being vicious. He said dogs that bite people get taken away and killed." Juliet stifled the first sob, but another one came, and then there were tears running freely down her cheeks. "He said he'd call the council officer and they'd come and get her. Of course, I took Roo and left immediately, after I told him that if he ever touched me again, I wouldn't call her off, and she could tear him apart, for all I cared. He looked scared then. But he can't really do that, can he? Get them to take her away? I've been worried sick for days. I couldn't bear it if anything happened to her . . ."

Juliet put her face in her hands and cried as though her heart had broken in two, her shoulders shaking with emotion and exhaustion.

Chapter 3 – Isabella to the rescue

Hearing her owner's distress, Ruby Roo shook off her desire to sleep and trotted over, jumping up with her paws in Juliet's lap and nudging her arm with her nose, as if to say, "Hey, it's okay. I'm here."

"Good dog, Roo. You're such a good girl." Isabella patted the dog and put her other arm across her sister's shoulders. "Don't worry, Jules. It'll be alright. We won't let anything happen to her," she murmured, shaken by her little sister's distress.

Isabella wasn't sure what the laws were about dogs that bit people. She knew vicious dogs were sometimes put down, but this wouldn't be classed as a serious attack, would it? But if Ronan made a big enough fuss, could he cause trouble? He could certainly cause plenty of stress for Juliet.

"What if he does make a complaint to the council?" Juliet looked up and sniffed, wiping her face with her sleeve, and twisting around to search her pockets for tissues.

"Well, I'm not really sure. You're a long way away from that council now and there are plenty of people round here who'll vouch for Ruby Roo as a well-behaved—"

Isabella stopped in mid-sentence, shocked into silence for a moment. "What's that?"

Juliet's shirt sleeve had ridden up her arm as she turned to reach into her pockets.

"What? Oh, it's a bruise. I only noticed it this morning. That's where Ronan grabbed me. It really hurt at the time, actually. That's why I cried out and Roo came to the rescue."

"Show me." Isabella's eyes darkened with fury at the thought of what her sister had suffered from that smug, self-obsessed man she'd always secretly detested. When Juliet lifted the sleeve to her shoulder, Isabella saw bruising over several inches of skin; ugly blue and black splotches, with finger-marks clearly showing.

"Oh! Look what he did to you!" Her face paled with shock and anger.

"I know. It's quite a sight, but it looks worse than it feels. Don't worry about me, Izzy. Or Roo. I took her to a vet in town, and they said she's just bruised too." It was the younger sister's turn to feel concerned. "Don't get upset, it might be bad for the baby."

"Bubs is happily doing a few somersaults, right now. He or she is fine," Isabella sat back and rubbed her bump, looking thoughtful. "But, okay – now we have a plan. There won't be a problem with Ruby Roo."

"We do? There won't?" Juliet looked at the woman who was not only her big sister, but also her best friend; the one who'd been there to extricate her from all sorts of scrapes and misadventures when they were young. Not much had changed. From the pleased expression on her sister's face, it looked like – in Juliet's darkest hour – Isabella was coming to the rescue again.

"We certainly do have a plan." Isabella looked smug. "That oaf Ronan has done you a favour, as it turns out, because *that* is evidence of assault. As soon as Byron's back, he's going to take photos of the bruising, and then the two of you are going to the police station to talk to Alan. You're going to have it put on record that Ronan assaulted you."

"Oh, look, it's over now. I'm okay, honestly. I don't want to press charges or anything."

"But you would if he complained about Ruby, right? I know you're a nice person, Jules, and don't want to make a fuss, but he *did* assault you. He hurt you and you felt threatened — that's the truth. So, you go and tell Alan the whole story about how you were being assaulted by Ronan and the dog barked at him. She didn't even bite, she just barked — until he kicked her. And then she only went for him because she was defending you and herself. If he gets nasty and wants to cause trouble, you can make even more trouble for him. Alan will advise you what to do, but I reckon he'll be able to take a statement — even if it's put on hold for now. He'll understand, and you know he has zero tolerance when it comes to domestic violence *and* he's a dog lover."

The local police officer had earned the town's respect over many years of policing with tact and understanding, but he could be as hard as nails sometimes.

"Isabella, you are brilliant." Juliet's careworn face brightened for the first time in days. "I'll do exactly as you say, just as an insurance policy for Ruby Roo. And if Byron will provide moral support when I talk to Alan, that would be great."

"Byron will be so incensed that Ronan kicked your beautiful dog, he'll probably start snapping and snarling as well. But, anyway, there's more!"

"More?" Juliet raised her eyebrows.

"If, for any reason, Plan A doesn't work, we'll go for Plan B," Isabella said happily.

"Of course, Plan B. Which is . . .?" Juliet looked at her sister with a smile.

"The current affairs TV shows! Move over, dodgy tradesmen and welfare fraudsters, here's a story about a heroic dog saving its mistress and then being put on death row by an abusive man who writes self-indulgent books that no one reads!"

Juliet burst out laughing and clapped her hands. "You are more amazing by the second! I love you, Izzy!" She gave her sister a big hug, careful not to squash the precious bump.

"I love you too, gorgeous girl, and thank goodness I'm seeing you smile again. But seriously, that man had better not show his face around here anymore." Isabella's eyes darkened again. "Byron will take care of Ronan if he ever turns up. No one treats our Jules like that and gets away with it. Or poor Roo!"

"Byron!" Juliet smiled again. "Your gentle, pacifist husband will go in for some fisticuffs, will he? I'd like to see that!"

"Well, not exactly – I admit that's not Byron's style. But he's right into herbal medicine now. He could doctor Ronan's food with a concoction that would give him the runs for a week."

"Fantastic!" Juliet laughed. "I wish he would – and I'd prefer a serious gut-ache for at least a fortnight. It would serve him right, the creep! I'll definitely talk to Alan, but then I want to stop thinking about all this for a while. I'm exhausted."

"I'm not surprised. But you're home now and I'm here for you, and Byron too. Mum will visit soon and Clementine's going to be so happy to see you. We haven't told her yet that you're back. We're making it a surprise." Isabella's face lit up when she said her daughter's name.

"Well, I hope she remembers me. I haven't spent nearly enough time with her, but I'll make up for that now. I'm so happy to be home! I'm never leaving this place for a man again. Living in the city made me feel lost and weird, and that was before I even found out about Ronan."

"Well, we're just as happy to have you back. Hey, what do you think of your city boy neighbour, anyway? Handsome, don't you reckon?"

Juliet scowled. "Huh. In a pet-tormenting sort of way, I suppose."

"Oh, come on. He thought Roo was a dingo. The poor man was scared. Although how you could mistake something that plump for a dingo is beyond me."

The girls laughed together, looking over at Ruby Roo, who had resumed her 'guard dog' position of being stretched out on the wooden boards, basking in the sun.

"Not plump, if you don't mind," Juliet said, with mock indignation. "Just a bit portly. City life was bad for the two of us. We're both on diets now."

"Roo? Definitely. You? Get out of it! There's nothing of you – unlike me. I'm on my way to impersonating a beached whale again."

"Oh, don't stress. The pounds will drop off once you've had the beautiful babe. I'm on a health kick, really. I need to be cleansed of those city pollutants, so it's all about healthy living and exercise now. I'm starting a regime of early-morning surfing and running as of tomorrow."

"Sounds like hard work. All I want to do at the moment is sleep. This beautiful sunshine is making me drowsy." Isabella stifled a yawn. "Anyway, don't be too hard on city boy. He seems pleasant enough, and he is your neighbour after all."

"I know. I'm starting to feel bad about our encounter. I completely lost it, actually. I was all strung out over Ronan and his threats, I'd hardly slept for two nights, and then the long drive topped everything off and sent me straight to crazy town. The poor guy probably thinks I'm a total nutcase." Juliet shook her head. "What's he like, anyway – have you talked to him a lot? I was too busy ranting at him to take much notice of what he said."

"He keeps to himself, pretty much, but I've managed to have a couple of quick chats. He's polite but doesn't give much away. He's here to write a book, apparently, and wants solitude. There you go, another writer! You two might be kindred spirits." Isabella looked at her sister with a grin.

"Forget it! I've lost faith with the entire male gender over the age of about ten. Apart from Byron, that is."

"And Tom, I hope. I saw him at the store this morning and he said he'd got your message. He's dying to see you."

"Oh, of course, Tom! He gets a good-guy exemption too. And probably there are some more nice ones around, but I can't think of them right now. But . . . are you serious? My neighbour's another writer?" Juliet groaned. "That settles it. He is so *not* a kindred spirit. I suppose he's writing some long-winded tome about law, is he?"

"No, finance. He's an investment banker, apparently, writing a how-to-make-buckets-of-money book. He seems qualified. Did you see that BMW in the carport? It's a luxury sports model, and everyone drools over it when he drives around town."

"That's funny, I thought he said he was a lawyer. Oh well, whatever. I'm curious about why he's way out here with that fancy car, though. It'll rust in the sea air if he's not careful. Has anyone else sussed him out at all?"

"Well, he has been known to have long conversations with Mrs Mac when he goes to the store, but mainly to complain when they're out of quinoa, or kale, or whatever the hell he wants at the time. Mrs Mac calls him Old Grumble Bum."

"That's undignified for someone with a classy car," Juliet laughed.

"Mind you, Fred seems a weird name for someone like him too," Isabella added.

"Oh, is it Fred? I thought he said Finn or something like that. I obviously paid no attention whatsoever, in my wrung-out state. I guess he doesn't realize how far from civilization we are. It's not like Mrs Mac can duck down to the markets every day for fresh supplies. If I ever forgive him for chucking things at Ruby Roo, maybe I should take him a peace offering and explain how we live round here. I could bake a cake, or something."

"Ah, so you do like him," her sister winked.

"Not like that! I feel bad that I yelled at him. Anyway, I told you, I've given up on men. Especially men from the city. If I ever relent and want to look for a decent man someday, he'll have to be a country boy like Tom, or Byron. They're the best guys I know, so that's the standard now."

Juliet was genuinely fond of her brother-in-law. Handsome, gentle Byron, with his love of an alternative lifestyle, was the perfect match for Isabella. The sisters had grown up wearing tie-dyed clothes and breathing the wafting smoke of incense, since their parents were hippies who'd met on a commune in the seventies. The girls' father had been much older than their mother and had died when they were teenagers. Several years later, their mother, Viola, had fallen in love with a nice but eccentric man called Zoot, and the couple had moved further north up the coast. They returned to Mirrabooka regularly, but were so busy starting a modern style of commune on their farm they hadn't visited for a while. They kept in touch through regular FaceTime calls, instead. Even communes need technology.

"Yes, I did find a good man, didn't I?" Isabella said happily. "Don't worry. There's another one waiting for you, when you're ready. Who knows, maybe city boy?"

"Oh, stop it!" chided her sister with a grin. "A cake, I said. Just a cake!"

"First a cake, then a bun in the oven, like me," Isabella giggled, and Juliet couldn't help but join in.

"And what are you two lovely ladies laughing about?" said a deep voice. It belonged to a tall man who had stepped onto the deck and was walking towards them, making Ruby Roo's tail thump on the boards with pleasure. His hair was long and tied in a ponytail and he wore jeans, a faded t-shirt and Blundstone boots. In his arms was a little dark-haired girl who, when she saw Juliet, gasped with surprise and twisted with impatience.

"Down, Daddy. Me down!" She wriggled until he lowered her to the decking, and she launched herself at her aunt with a gleeful yell. "Joo-joo!"

"I think she remembers you," Isabella laughed.

"That was a good surprise." Byron smiled as he watched his ecstatic daughter being lifted high in the air until she squealed with delight and was then hugged ferociously by her aunt.

"It's good to see you, Byron," Juliet said, meeting his eyes over the top of the little girl's tousled hair, and reaching out her hand to grasp his. "Such a relief to be home."

Chapter 4 – Beach solitude

Only a short distance away, Finn was also enjoying the sun at the back of his cottage. As with its twin, the back of the house faced the ocean, but it sat at an angle to the other dwelling, ensuring privacy for occupants on their respective decks.

Juliet had bought the big bush block with a small inheritance from her father and had decided to build two dwellings – despite the bigger mortgage – so she could let one out as holiday accommodation. Mirrabooka had a lively tourist trade in the summer months, with thousands of people enjoying the beaches, national parks, and unspoiled beauty of the area. Juliet had filled the rental cottage with homey touches and comfortable, tasteful furniture, and it was always kept spotlessly clean, so it was very popular with the tourists.

When Finn had enquired about accommodation in the town, he'd been recommended the cottage by the local agent and told he was lucky it was available, even in the quiet season. He'd never stayed in a country town in his life and had been convinced he would hate being so far from civilization. He'd assumed his accommodation would be primitive and uncomfortable, but he'd had to admit when he first arrived that the place was well set up, attractive and had a lovely feel to it. With colourful cushions, framed landscape photographs and tasteful ornaments making each room unique and relaxing, it was very different to his shiny, minimalist apartment. Whoever owned the cottage had a talent for making a place feel like a home, he'd concluded.

Finn stared out to sea and drank his coffee, also making the most of the warm weather. He'd been impressed when he found a top-of-the-range coffee machine in the well-equipped kitchen too. However, even though his lodgings were pleasant, Finn found living so far from the comforts of the city to be a challenge. At home, being a busy professional with little time or inclination to cook, he was always dashing out for Thai food, sushi, or Turkish bread and fresh dips, or taking Sophia to one of the many top-quality restaurants nearby. If one of them wanted to cook, the enormous supermarket up the road sold just about everything.

In contrast, in Mirrabooka during the quiet time of the year, you could eat out at the pub, the golf club or the Indian restaurant, which had the rather grand name of Sashi's Curry House and Coffee Emporium. If those options didn't appeal, you could get takeaway pizza or fish and chips. But Finn had never been a pot 'n parma kind of guy, and he was pretty sure he was going to get sick of the restaurant's offerings, even though the curries he'd already sampled had been excellent. He was trying to learn to cook out of necessity, but it was proving difficult. He'd started by attempting to replicate the sort of dishes he would order in a restaurant, and either he couldn't get the right ingredients, or he would ruin the meal with his lack of expertise. Then he changed tactics; he'd buy whatever fresh ingredients the store actually did have and then try to figure out what to do with them, but that was time-consuming for someone who'd never learned the basics of home cooking.

Mind you, the goat's cheese he'd bought the previous day was delicious – the best he'd ever tasted – and he cut another piece of it now to put on a slice of fresh, crusty bread while admiring the broad expanse of ocean shimmering across the horizon before him. He'd have to try harder to adapt to country life, he realized with a sigh. Perhaps living on good cheese, barbequed steaks and basic salads for a few months wouldn't kill him? If the electricity could stay on longer than three days in a row, and the internet connection would stop dropping out every time he tried to access the news online, then maybe – just maybe – he could start to appreciate the place more.

His surroundings had certainly brightened with the arrival of his attractive neighbour – not that he was thinking romantic thoughts by any stretch of the imagination, he reminded himself sternly. The woman was, quite frankly, a bit of a fruitcake. Although he felt bad about chucking things at her dog, she had completely over-reacted and been almost hysterical. Finn had had enough of highly strung, temperamental women. He was still trying to process everything that had happened between him and Sophia three weeks ago, and that – on top of his work worries – gave him plenty of things to contemplate while he was stuck in the back of beyond. While he stared out to sea, Finn went over in his head for the umpteenth time the events that had led to him being in Mirrabooka.

He was indeed a lawyer – a criminal defence barrister – and he'd been forging a name for himself as a new star on the scene since he'd got a job with a top law firm a year before. His father, Murray McLaren, was one of the country's best barristers, and it had always been expected that Finn would follow in his footsteps. He loved the law and was glad it was his field, but being a barrister was beginning to cause problems. He was good at it, so there was no problem there, but the most recent case he'd handled – and won – was providing a concrete example of everything that made him uneasy about the role of barrister.

He'd defended a man accused of murder. It was a gangland killing, involving two infamous crime families who had been feuding for years. One of the Zanetti family's two sons was found with a bullet hole in his head, and the oldest son of the Kovac family was accused of the murder. Finn put forward a brilliant defence and the Kovac boy was found not guilty, after which he celebrated for three days straight and then went out and shot the younger brother of the first victim, killing him as well.

Finn refused to handle the second case, despite the pleadings – followed by angry tirades – of the Kovac family. Then the police and a few of his 'clients' who had close underworld connections warned him that the Zanettis were not happy with him either. They blamed him for the loss of their second son.

Finn had already spent many sleepless nights wondering if being a barrister was right for him. When he'd first studied law, he'd imagined he would be able to help people – make a difference – by using his skills and the opportunities he'd been lucky enough to be given. He hadn't pictured back then that he'd be helping hardened criminals knock each other off.

After the second murder, threats arrived at his office by email and phone. Word on the street was that the Zanettis, in their grief and fury, had hired someone to go after the barrister who'd got their son's killer set free. It was all talk, Finn was almost certain, but it was upsetting for the receptionist who'd taken threatening phone calls, and the police had recommended he get away from the city and lay low for a while. This advice, and the appeal of having some time out to consider his future, had seen him head out of town. He felt silly using a different name and pretending he was in finance, but the police had recommended an alias as an extra precaution, and he'd thought it wise to take their suggestions on board.

So, there he was, in a small town in the middle of nowhere, and feeling right out of his comfort zone. On the plus side, he was sleeping better in Mirrabooka; country life was good for that, at least. And the scenery was nice. The view of the sea, that is, Finn reminded himself. He pushed the image of a slim, blonde-haired woman out of his mind.

*

The next morning, Finn went for his customary early morning expedition to the beach, walking through the tea-tree scrub along the narrow dirt track that wound its way down to the sand. Emerging from the gloom of the bush, he saw the wide expanse of ocean and, as always, it lifted his spirits. The surf boomed and surged on fine golden sand and seagulls soared in the cool, clean breeze. He picked his way across the layer of coloured rocks and shells at the edge of the tree line to the fine, soft sand that lay beyond, and kicked off his battered old sneakers so he could walk along the edge of the water. When the first wave swirled around his ankles it was sharply cold.

Finn could see other beach walkers to the left, so he veered right, climbing around a rocky headland to a more secluded stretch of beach he often visited. Usually, it was his alone at that time of the morning but, today, there was another inhabitant – a red-coloured dog who was busily nosing around some piles of kelp. It rolled happily on top of its seaweed selection, showing the mottled red and white fur on its belly and neck, then stood up to shake its thick, wet coat. Noticing Finn, the dog loped towards him.

"Hello, Ruby Roo," Finn said cautiously, remembering the intense stare and curled lip of their previous meeting. "And . . . sorry about the other day."

Fortunately, it didn't look like the dog was holding a grudge; she stopped in front of him and wagged her tail, looking up expectantly.

"Good dog." Finn reached down to tentatively pat the damp fur, and the dog rewarded him for his friendliness with another shake of her shaggy coat, covering his legs with a spray of sand and water droplets.

"You've had a swim, I see. You're a brave dog – the water's extra-cold today. But where's your beautiful owner?" He sat down on the sand next to the dog and gave her another pat.

He wasn't sure if he wanted to meet Juliet again or not. His early morning walks served a purpose – solitude. With everything that Finn had on his mind, walking on the beach and hearing only the sounds of the waves and the birds each morning helped ease his worries and make his reluctant stay in the country more bearable. Besides, he felt mortified when he remembered the circumstances of their meeting.

But Juliet had seemed so lovely, even in her slightly unhinged state, that he couldn't help but want to find out more about her. He wanted to sit beside her on the beach while the clouds scudded across the sky and the breakers crashed and swirled, so he could gaze at her perfect profile and say something to make her smile. He had no doubt that when she smiled, her beautiful face would light up—

"Okay, stop it right there! You haven't come here to fall for another woman." He scolded himself out loud. "You really are brainless sometimes."

The dog thought that was harsh, and she nudged his elbow with her nose to tell him so.

"It's true, Ruby Roo. I'm clever at some things but stupid about women. I thought I loved Sophia, and we had something together, but then it all crashed and burned. It turns out that there was no real substance, and our relationship was just a glittery but hollow sham. Wow, that sounds melodramatic, doesn't it? It's true though."

Ruby Roo cocked her head to one side. She was a very good listener.

"On top of all that, I'm trying to decide what I'm going to do with the rest of my life," Finn continued. "I don't know if I'm going to stay on as a barrister, or whether I'll chuck it all in and work at the local coffee shop, or something. I can see it all now – barrister to barista – one man's progression through life, going backwards. What do you think about that?"

The red dog regarded him solemnly, then snapped at a fly and shook her head, flapping her ears.

"Okay, maybe not the barista idea then. I'll try for supermarket checkout boy instead. But the main thing is, Ruby Roo, that I am not – repeat not – going to get interested in another woman in the foreseeable future. Especially not in this one-horse town, and *most* especially not your gorgeous owner. Got it?"

Ruby Roo seemed to get it. She panted doggy breath in his face and thumped her tail on the sand with pleasure as Finn rubbed the small white patch on the top of her head. She really was a very friendly dog, and he could have sworn she was smiling at him, but dogs didn't really smile, did they?

Throughout his heart-to-heart chat with Ruby Roo, Finn had been vaguely aware of the presence of a surfer out past the breakers. Now the figure was wading through the shallows with a surfboard under one arm.

The dog leapt to her feet and showered him with sand once more, bolting towards the water. Finn realized the surfer was Juliet, in a black wetsuit, which stopped halfway down her thighs – very toned thighs they were too, he couldn't help but notice. He watched her laugh at the dog, who was leaping around her feet and splashing in the waves, and then walk straight towards him.

Okay, it looks like we're meeting again, Finn thought with a gulp. Perhaps he could try and seem vaguely sensible when he talked to her this time.

Chapter 5 – A talented goddess

Ruby Roo dashed back to Finn as though they were old friends. Juliet followed, looking hesitant, but then stopped in front of him and propped the surfboard up beside her.

"Hello again. I wondered if that was you sitting with my dog."

"Hello, Juliet. Yes, it's me – the city guy who knows nothing about either dogs or dingoes," he said with a wry smile. "I've been having quite a chat with your dog. I apologized for chucking a clod of dirt at her, and I'm hoping she's forgiven me."

"It looks like she has. She's very good-natured, you know. May I join the two of you?"

"Of course. Pull up a piece of sand."

Juliet put the surfboard down and lowered herself gracefully onto the dry sand beside him, then leaned back and stretched out her legs. The wetsuit was unzipped enough to show honey-coloured cleavage, dotted with beads of water, rising and falling in a gentle rhythm with each breath.

Finn forced himself to look at her face. Her blue eyes had lost their flinty edge of the other day, he was happy to see. The glorious golden hair was dripping wet and tied back in a ponytail, but tendrils of it had escaped and were framing her heart-shaped face, with just a few freckles on her nose and cheeks.

"Ruby Roo's a good name. Does the Roo bit mean kangaroo?" he asked.

"Yes. She's very agile and she's always bouncing around. You should see how high she jumps – she can look me right in the face when she wants attention."

"She's a nice dog. I like her a lot, even though I've never had much to do with animals."

"No pets when you were a kid?"

"No. My father said he didn't have time for pets. All he did was work, really, although I suppose he did his best for me. My mother died when I was young, and it must have been hard for him looking after a kid on his own."

Juliet was looking at him intently as he spoke and Finn felt suddenly nervous, as though he was a schoolboy again. The boys' school he attended used to have occasional collaborations with a nearby girls' school. He and the other boys would be struck dumb by the poised and beautiful young women who would appear from time to time in the assembly hall for the debating competition, or whatever the occasion was. No wonder they always lost the debates. But a lot had happened since then, and he had stopped feeling self-conscious in front of women many years ago. Hadn't he? Then why did this one make him feel so awkward?

"Anyway, I never had a dog as a child and, as an adult, I've never considered getting one. It doesn't fit with inner-city life too well," he continued.

He realized that Juliet was looking out to sea and mentally chastised himself.

What are you doing? She makes you lose the power of rational speech and there you are rambling on about your childhood. She's obviously bored to death.

She turned to face him again. "City life's not great for a dog. We've just come back from two years in the big smoke. Roo hated it. She's much happier now that we're back where we belong. We both are."

"Did you go to the city for work?" Finn asked, with some relief. If he stopped babbling and asked about her life, maybe she wouldn't keel over with boredom.

"Pretty much. I had a book published, and to my surprise people wanted to read it, so I had to do publicity-type things."

"Really?" He thought hard. He'd heard about an author called Juliet recently. "Hey, you're not Juliet Cooper, are you?"

"That's me." She gave a brief nod.

"I've got your book! My fiancée, Sophia, read it and loved it. Then she gave it to me and told me I had to read it too. I haven't yet though, sorry."

"That's okay. I'm glad your fiancée liked it." Her face turned to watch Ruby Roo as she darted across the sand in pursuit of seagulls.

Finn watched the dog too, wishing he'd remembered to say 'ex-fiancée', but it was too late to say that now without seeming weird.

"I was lucky," Juliet continued with a shrug. "The publishers took the story on and their editors polished it up, and I was amazed that lots of people liked it. There's a big following for crime fiction, it seems. I've come back here to finish the next one. It stars the same fearless crime-solving heroine, Anastasia." She gave a little smile. "She's a good girl. I like her."

Finn enjoyed seeing her begin to relax. "And is she like you? Tough and fearless and able to withstand extremely cold water in the surf?" he teased.

"Oh no! We're completely different. Anastasia is tall and graceful, not short and clumsy like me. She is confident and sophisticated and can hold her own with all sorts of clever city people. I'm just a small-town hick. I grew up here in Mirrabooka, you know, and I'm no good in the city. It was okay when I was at university, because I made lots of friends and we had heaps of fun, and I had regular holidays to spend at home. But the last two years were pretty awful – I felt like a fish out of water, just flopping around feeling uncomfortable and out of place."

"I don't believe that for a second," Finn said. "You'd be a breath of fresh sea air in the city, and I bet everybody loved you. You'll be back for another stint there, surely, when the next book is launched."

"I'll visit, when I must, but I'm done with living in cities," Juliet said firmly. "They scare me. Besides, the next book's probably going to be hopeless. It's just a big mess at the moment."

"But your first one's a huge success, and it won awards too, didn't it?"

"Well, yes. Beginner's luck, probably."

"I think you're downplaying your skill, just a bit. And what about your fans in the rest of the country? They deserve to see you too. You can't seriously keep your talents confined to one small town," Finn said.

As he spoke, he wondered how a woman as smart and beautiful as this one could be so unaware of it. "I mean, here you sit, looking like a goddess – like Venus from out of the water – and you're a best-selling author to boot."

"A goddess? In a wetsuit? Ha! You city boys sure can turn on the charm."

She threw her head back and laughed a little, and he saw the water droplets glisten on her throat.

"And hey, you haven't even read the book. You might think it's a load of old rubbish. It's just popular fiction, you know – it's not *Hamlet*."

Her modesty astounded him. If Sophia had ever achieved half as much as this girl had, she would have told the whole world about it. Twice.

"A goddess," he insisted. "And a talented one too." With those tendrils of golden hair curled around her lovely face, she really did look divine. Albeit in a slightly sandy way.

"City people are nothing special, believe me," he continued. "They may have a veneer of sophistication and good manners, but if you look beneath to where the real substance should be, there's only a void, sometimes."

The goddess was looking at him intently. "Well, you may be deluded, but I have to say I'm enjoying the compliments. I'm not used to being told about my apparent brilliance. My boyfriend told me the other day that I was naïve, and I had a boring, small-town mentality." She looked down to the sand and sifted some between her fingers.

Finn could sense the pain from the tightening of her shoulders. "Your boyfriend is an idiot and I hope you've told him so," he said darkly. "I'm sorry, I know that's not a clever response, but that was clearly a stupid and nasty thing to say."

"Thank you, that's exactly what I needed to hear. You may be a charmer, but I'm glad of it right now." She turned back to look directly at him, as her face lit up with the first big smile she had unleashed in his presence.

He was glad he was sitting down, or the sheer radiance of it would have bowled him over. Her eyes glittered and sparkled like the sea, and, in that moment, she seemed to radiate energy and joy. Finn's thoughts leapt into overdrive. He imagined winding a strand of that golden hair around one finger and staring closer at her glorious face. He could see them lying down on the sand so he could kiss the nape of her neck where the water droplets still glistened . . .

Fortunately, while he tried hard to rein in his imagination, Ruby Roo bounded up and dropped something at Juliet's feet. Pleased with herself, she sat down, waiting to be praised.

"There, you see?" Finn quickly collected his thoughts. "You *are* a goddess – and your minions drop precious gifts at your feet."

It was a dead fish.

"Ewww, that's gross," Juliet screwed up her nose. "It stinks, Roo, and so do you! You rolled on it before you picked it up, didn't you? You're a stinky girl!"

The dog thumped her tail on the sand with happiness. It was so good to be on the beach again, with seagulls to chase and delectably smelly things to discover.

"Well, it looks like I have dog-washing duties when I get home," Juliet sighed. "It's time I got going." She climbed to her feet.

"Would you like me to carry the surfboard back for you?"

"Thank you, but no. Carrying the board is part of my exercise regime. Ruby Roo and I have to run across the sand now. She needs to lose weight and I need to get fitter." She gave a brief smile. "See you later, Finn."

"It's Fred, actually. At least, that's a nickname, but that's what I'm usually called." Finn inwardly cursed himself at his lack of ability to stay undercover. Now he was sounding like a complete nutjob.

"Right. Okay . . . Fred. It's been nice chatting to you. Oh, while I think of it – I thought you said you were a lawyer the other day, but my sister says you're in finance. I was wondering which of us is right." She looked at him steadily.

He hesitated only a fraction of a second. "Isabella's right. Finance is my game."

"And you're writing a book?"

"Well, trying to." He glanced away, feeling even more awkward. "It's hard work, as you would know."

"It certainly is," Juliet said. "Maybe we should compare notes someday." She hoisted the board under her arm. "Anyway, I'll see you around, I'm sure."

She headed off over the dry sand, breaking into a run with the dog bounding beside her, and Finn tried not to think about how the wetsuit showed off her trim legs and buttocks.

"You look pretty fit already," he said, to no one in particular. Phew! He had to sit for a while and recover before he could muster the strength to complete his morning walk. He had let slip the other day that he was a lawyer? What an idiot! But he hated having to lie and he was already getting tired of the cloak-and-dagger stuff. And the last thing he wanted to do was discuss writing with her – a woman as smart as Juliet would see through him in two seconds.

He reviewed what he knew about her. She was talented, modest, and beautiful, and she had a drop-kick boyfriend who must be insane. Who was this moron and how could he be so unkind to such a gorgeous woman? Wait . . . now that he thought about it, Sophia had been talking one day about how Juliet Cooper was living with another writer – Ronan Wittington. Sophia said he was quite high up in literary circles. They must be having some type of long-distance relationship, unless he was going to move here too. He hoped not, because the guy was obviously a jerk, and Finn had been surprised at the surge of protective anger he'd felt when she confided the insult and he had seen her pain. If that Ronan guy turned up, he'd be sorely tempted to lecture him about treating Juliet with more respect.

He hadn't liked the way his heart had twinged when she said the word 'boyfriend', either. What was going on? He hardly knew this girl, and in a few months' time, he would never see her again. Once more, he needed to repeat his refrain: *You are not here to get involved with a woman. Even a kind, modest and intelligent one. Even a creative, beautiful one with toned thighs and an alluring cleavage.*

He climbed to his feet and sighed. He had too much time on his hands here – he really needed to take up a hobby.

Chapter 6 – Contemplations

Juliet headed back across the beach and began climbing the bush track with Ruby at her heels, all the while going over the conversation in her head. When she'd walked out of the surf and realized the figure sitting on the beach was her new neighbour, she'd felt a bit anxious, wondering what sort of reception she would get after shouting at him the other day. But he had been perfectly friendly and, when he'd mentioned dingoes, it had been in a self-deprecating way. Perhaps it was his humility that compelled her to stay there and talk to him, rather than just saying a brief hello and walking past, as she'd intended.

She'd enjoyed their chat on the sand and, from what she'd heard about the taciturn stranger from the city, he'd been unusually talkative. She wondered why he'd opened up to her like that. Maybe he felt guilty about piffing things at her dog and had decided to be super-friendly to compensate. But then she remembered how she'd opened up to him too, even confiding in him about one of Ronan's insults. He'd been good to talk to, and now that she thought back to that particular insult, the words had lost their sting. He'd called

Ronan an idiot, and Juliet smiled when she remembered how indignant he'd looked on her behalf.

She'd surreptitiously studied him as he'd sprawled alongside her, talking about his childhood. His long fingers were drawing lines in the sand as he spoke, and his hands looked strong and capable. He was wearing old khaki shorts and a faded plum-coloured sweatshirt. His legs were long, and he looked fit and lean, with the sort of skin that tans easily. Some of his black hair had flopped forward on his forehead, where it was poised above an earnest face with dark eyes and a strong, straight nose. He had an appealing smile and a nice-shaped mouth. His lower lip was quite plump – sensuous, actually. At that moment, Juliet couldn't help but wonder what it would be like to kiss him.

Oh, that was distracting! Embarrassed at the direction her thoughts were taking, she'd felt herself blushing and looked away, then tried hard to focus on what he was saying. Something about dogs? As Juliet walked up the hill, she inwardly cringed as she remembered how flustered she'd felt.

She really needed to get herself together and stop being attracted to random strangers like that. Luckily, she didn't think he'd noticed anything at the time. And anyway, that stranger was taken. In the back of her brain, she recalled the stab of disappointment she'd felt as he said the word 'fiancée'. Sophia – that was an exotic name. No doubt she was poised and beautiful, with that self-assured manner city girls had. Then Juliet recalled how she'd mentioned Ronan, referring to him as her 'boyfriend' – not 'ex-boyfriend'. It was funny how she still automatically labelled him that way. *Oh well, this too shall pass,* she shrugged. It hardly mattered whether Fred – or Finn, or whoever the hell he was – thought she was attached or not. Did it? An image of his face with those dark eyes and very kissable lower lip appeared in her mind again. Oh no – he was infiltrating her brain!

Honestly, Juliet, you're hopeless. You've crawled back home with your heart in pieces, and here you are going all fuzzy-headed over the first nice-looking new bloke you meet. The one you despised until about ten minutes ago. You're crazy!

In annoyance, she forced herself to walk even faster up the last part of the hill, where the steepness of the climb forced her to focus on breathing. Ruby Roo dropped back a bit, probably wondering what the rush was when they'd already done plenty of exercise, but Juliet knew how to hurry her up.

"Come on, Roo – time for breakfast. Food!" The dog pricked up her ears and then galloped past in a burst of sudden enthusiasm. She understood a lot of words, and 'food' was one of her favourites.

Juliet resolved she would get busy with breakfast and cleaning up the wet, smelly dog, and then tackle some household chores. She would file the memory of this interlude away as merely a pleasant chat on the sand. That was all!

*

As always, Finn had plenty to ponder as he continued his walk along the beach after saying goodbye to Juliet and Ruby Roo. But today, there was one new thing to reflect on, and that was the world of difference between Juliet and his ex-fiancée. Sophia would never have plonked herself down on the sand to talk to a man she barely knew. She always liked to be presented at her best in public, with her hair and make-up beautifully done and her outfit carefully selected to show off her considerable assets. There was no way she would have sat down with sand on her nose and wet hair escaping its ponytail, and droplets of water running down her body . . . Forcing his thoughts away from Juliet's smooth skin, and back to his relationship with Sophia, Finn recalled once more the events that had brought about the beginning of the end of their relationship.

The Kovac family had been ecstatic the day their son was found not guilty of murder. They showered Finn with praise and insisted he should attend a lavish celebration with them at the Crown

Casino – and bring his woman too. He had politely declined, pleading fatigue and the need to prepare for his next case. In reality, he had no desire to socialise with criminals; he had a pretty good idea where their money came from, and it didn't sit well with him.

It was true he was tired but, further to that, something was bothering him. When the 'not guilty' finding had been announced, he'd seen a smirk on the Kovac boy's face. Finn knew at that moment that the case he'd put forward was based on a lot of lies, and probably several bribed witnesses.

He knew he shouldn't be dwelling on it. He passionately believed that every person had the right to have legal representation and to be considered not guilty until found otherwise in a court of law, with proper legal processes. That was one of the fundamental basics of a free and just society. All barristers sometimes thought their clients were lying to them, but it was not their job to speculate. Their job was to take the facts as they were presented and work professionally towards the best outcome for the client. It was up to the judge and the jury to consider guilt or innocence.

But, as he had driven home that day, he couldn't stop thinking about the look on his client's face.

"Kovac lied," he told Sophia when they discussed the day's events. "He had a sly, triumphant look on his face that told me so, without a doubt. I've helped a guilty man stay free – a violent man who thinks nothing of gunning someone down in cold blood because his father tells him to."

Sophia had dismissed his concerns with a laugh. "Darling, you don't know that he's guilty. You can't work from a look on a face. You deal with facts and evidence; that's what you're always telling me. You're not the judge or jury – you're the barrister who had a job to do and you did it brilliantly. We need to celebrate! I can't believe you won't take me to the Kovac function at Crown. That's very selfish, but if you take me to dinner at Louie's I might forgive you. We'll tell the maître d' what we're celebrating. He'll have it all around town in five minutes."

Louie's was the hippest, most expensive restaurant in the city, with staff who loved to gossip, and it wasn't much more appealing to Finn than the Kovacs' function.

"I'm sorry, but not this time," he'd replied wearily. "I need a quiet night at home."

He knew Sophia was right, strictly speaking, about his professional role, but why wouldn't she even listen to his concerns? He felt sick about what the next chapter in the feud might be, but all Sophia could think about was being seen at glitzy functions or the right restaurants.

"Let's get some takeaway." He rubbed his forehead, where a lurking headache was threatening to escalate.

"God, you're boring sometimes, Finn!" Sophia had exploded. "If you're not taking me somewhere to celebrate, I'll go out with the girls. You can stay home and vegetate all on your own."

When he refused to be swayed, she'd stormed out the door and slammed it so hard a vase fell off a shelf and shattered on the tiled floor.

Sophia was a high-maintenance girl. She could be good company sometimes – vivacious and generous – but only when it suited her, he was fast coming to realize. When Sophia was happy, everyone could be happy. When Sophia was *not* happy the whole world had to know about it. Finn was glad they hadn't set a wedding date yet.

A few days later, the next gangland execution was carried out, and Sophia approved of his decision to refuse the case.

"I can see why you don't want to take that one on. There's no way you'll win, and it might be bad for your career."

"I'm not taking it on because I don't want to represent a cold-blooded killer. Not this time!" he snapped.

"Who cares? It's not your problem," she retorted. "Your job is to win the case. That's why they pay you the big bucks."

"Do you ever think beyond money?" he asked her. "What about conscience? The victim had a young family, you know."

"The victim was another gangster! Conscience doesn't make you succeed, or pay for your luxury vehicle," she shouted. "Grow up, Finn. If you can't stand the heat, maybe you should get out of the kitchen!"

"Yeah, maybe I should," he said quietly. "This has really thrown me. I don't even know if my heart's still in this job, so I'm thinking of taking some time out. There have been more death threats – poor Gail at work is completely stressed out. The cops are telling me to get out of town and lay low for a while."

"I hope you're not refusing the case because you're scared. I hadn't thought you were a coward." Sophia rolled her eyes.

"I've told you why I'm not taking the case. And no one thinks the threats are serious but, just in case, I've been told to take three months' leave and do some off-site consulting. Much as I hate the thought of country life, I'm going to find a quiet little town out in the sticks somewhere. By the sea, perhaps. I know you won't be happy about it, Sophia, but I'm doing this for the benefit of both of us. I need to get my head straight if I'm going to continue with this career."

"What is this '*if* I'm going to continue' crap? You won't *have* a career if you run away from it. You'll come home to find there's a new barrister who's flavour of the month. You know how ruthless the industry is."

"I'm not sure I'd care," he replied. "Do I want to spend my life helping criminals commit more offences? Isn't there something better I can do? I might start looking into legal aid."

"Legal aid? I don't believe what I'm hearing! One little setback and you're too scared to handle the big time. Well, don't expect me to wait for you." She tossed back her thick, glossy hair. "I agreed to marry Finn the red-hot barrister, not Finn the do-gooder legal aid worker. The second guy doesn't do it for me. If you take this time off, our engagement will be over!"

"I expect nothing from you," he said quietly. "We need some time apart, whatever I decide to do."

"Time apart? You've got it. Permanently!" She slapped her hands on the table for emphasis.

"Fine. I think that's for the best, for both of us. You can keep the ring," he added, noticing the shimmer of the enormous solitaire diamond she'd chosen.

"You bet I will." Her heels echoed across the room and she slammed the door behind her yet again.

After a long talk the next day, involving hours of Sophia's tears, recriminations and protests, they had reached the end. Finn would not back down on his decision to take time out, and Sophia refused to exhibit any understanding whatsoever.

"Good luck to her. We just wanted different things in life," he'd said when word about the break-up got around and friends commiserated. He did his best to be dignified and move on calmly, without blaming Sophia. In private, he wondered how he could have been blinded by her looks and the part she played so well, and why it had taken him so long to see through to the shallowness of her soul. He'd really thought they would have a life together. Now all those dreams of a loving partner, two or three babies, and a home filled with love and laughter – all the things he'd missed out on as a child – had turned to dust.

By the time Finn had finished thinking all this through again – for about the fiftieth time – he had returned to the stretch of beach where he'd left his shoes. He couldn't help looking around to see if the red dog and her owner might have come back. They hadn't, so he brushed the worst of the sand off his feet and dragged on the sneakers, ready for the trek up the hill to the cottage. He'd have a quick shower and then see if the internet would play nicely today and let him check the stock market, and then he'd catch up on the news. Unless, that is, he would be distracted from all of those things by thoughts of a girl with sparkling eyes and honey-coloured hair.

Chapter 7 – Onwards and upwards

Juliet drove around the side of the inlet admiring the forest of tall eucalypts to her left and the dark-blue sheen of the inlet to her right. It was another sunny day, and she was heading for Tom's house for their long-awaited catch-up, so her spirits were buoyant.

She slowed down at the sharp corner in the gully, where she knew kangaroos and wallabies would often choose to hop across the road – she'd had enough of kangaroo encounters for the time being. Sometimes a goanna or even a koala would decide to amble across there too. The koalas always looked incredibly awkward as they clambered over the ground, but as soon as they found a tree to climb, they would scamper up it, strong and efficient.

Tom's place was on the other side of town and further away from the surf beaches than Juliet's, but it sat in a lovely spot overlooking a sheltered arm of the inlet. From Tom's deck, you could admire tiny wrens flitting from tree to tree of the bushy block, and then look down at the water to pelicans and cormorants fishing in the quiet cove, where Tom's boat was moored at his own jetty. His house was small and old-fashioned – "just like me", he would say with a grin – but it was a peaceful, serene place where everyone felt welcome.

As soon as Juliet drove down the tree-lined driveway, she felt its tranquillity wrap around her once again, and then there was Tom, striding out the kitchen door and up the path of crooked flagstones. Seeing a big, boyish grin light up his face, she noticed he still didn't look anywhere near old enough to have done years of medical training and now be the main doctor in a remote, rural town. Tom had sandy hair and a fit, slightly stocky build, and the sort of presence that immediately put people at ease. He was not a tall man, being medium height or "just right", as Juliet had always reassured him. As a general practitioner of medicine, he was perfect. He had the knack of being able to make people relax and confide in him and the sort of brain that remembered enormous amounts of medical knowledge, as well as personal details about his patients, because he genuinely cared about their welfare and was interested in their lives.

In short, he was a lovely, brilliant man, and Juliet often considered the fact that he'd make a fantastic partner. Tom had been living with a girl for a while, but she had returned to the city a few months ago, so he was single again now too. It would have been so convenient at this point in their lives if they'd been able to fall in love with each other. However, having met at school at the age of five and spent a considerable portion of the next twenty-two years being inseparable and confiding just about everything to each other, they seemed to have permanently bypassed romance. The two of them had discussed this fact at length and had determined it was for the best. Girlfriends and boyfriends could come and go, but best friends were around forever.

Tom's two dogs – one a black-and-tan kelpie and the other a golden Labrador-cross – milled around his feet excitedly; as soon as Juliet stopped the car, she let Ruby Roo out to dash over and greet them, smiling at the flurry of jumping, sniffing and tail wagging.

Tom held his arms out wide as she walked towards him. "If I had a tail, I'd be wagging it too. It's been far too long between visits, Jules."

"I've missed you, Tom. It's so good to be back." They grabbed each other in a big hug and then looked at each other's faces.

"Not a day older," Juliet remarked at the same time as Tom said, "You haven't changed a bit." Then they both said, "Liar!" at the same time and laughed.

"Let's go inside." He put his arm round her shoulders. "I've got cookies – homemade Anzac biscuits – and I've fired up the coffee machine. Come on, you hounds, get in there and trash the house." The dogs raced in ahead of their owners and launched into a happy mock-wrestling and chasing game around the living room.

"Roo, slow down!"

"Oh, leave them. My two are so happy to see her again," Tom said. "They'll settle down in a minute. Come into the kitchen while I make the coffee. We need a thorough catch-up."

"We do! You have to tell me all about Amelia's adventures too! Where is she now?" Tom's sister was another one of Juliet's favourite people.

"She's in Prague at the moment, I think. She's backpacking all over the place, so it's hard to keep up with her."

Juliet climbed onto a stool alongside the breakfast bar as Tom moved around the kitchen with ease, getting the coffees underway and setting out the promised biscuits while he chatted about his sister and her exploits overseas. Juliet watched him happily. She admired a man who was competent in the kitchen and didn't assume an air of convenient helplessness as some men did – like Ronan, come to think of it.

"I'm impressed about the biscuit baking. Was it in my honour?"

"Sorry. I'd love to take the credit, but they're a gift from a patient. The ladies in town think I need to be sustained with baked goods, these days. I think they assume that since Anne-Marie has gone I'm not getting any home-cooked meals. Little do they know; I was usually the one doing the cooking."

Juliet pulled a face. Anne-Marie was the female version of Ronan as far as convenient helplessness went. Tom had looked after the girl – who had turned up at Mirrabooka with no home, no apparent family or friends, and very little money – in all sorts of ways. He'd fallen for her as soon as they met and had soon provided a roof over her head as well as lots of emotional and financial support. Juliet had never liked her very much; from what she saw and heard, Anne-Marie did a lot of taking of Tom's generosity and goodwill and not a lot of giving. But, she realized, she was probably always a bit jealous of the girls who took Tom's attention away from her and their friendship. It could be complicated having a guy as a best friend.

"I see there's less furniture here than there used to be. But it's still nice and homey." Juliet looked around the open-plan living area with satisfaction. Was it wrong of her to be enjoying the fact that Tom's house was back to being just that – and not Tom and Anne-Marie's house?

"Yeah. Most of it was mine, as you know, but I let her take a few things. I felt sorry for her leaving here with hardly any possessions."

"Tom, you're far too nice! Didn't she head back to the city to her well-off family, after letting you support her for over a year because she'd said she had no money and *no* family."

"Yep. It turned out to be 'no family' in a temporary emotional sense. They'd had a falling out, as families sometimes do."

"And didn't you tell me that she woke up one day and decided – after you'd made her feel so much better about herself – that Mirrabooka was boring, she'd outgrown you, and she couldn't stand country life for one more second?"

"Yep, that's pretty much it. Look, she arrived here in a fragile state, and you know I'm a sucker for people who need help."

Juliet nodded, sipping her coffee.

"So, I helped her, and she got better and stronger, and then she didn't need me anymore. She'd said she wanted to settle here, that's true – but it's no crime to change your mind. Sure, I felt lost when she'd gone, and angry and hurt and all that stuff, but I've had time to reflect on it now. We weren't right for each other – that's the bottom line. She would never have been happy here, not long-term."

"You're being very generous, I think."

"She's not a bad person. Just damaged."

"Damaged and selfish, it seems to me. Took what she could get from you and then said, 'Rightio, I'm out of here'."

"I can see how you might have that perspective. I'm looking at it more as a learning experience that has enhanced my personal growth."

"How very philosophical of you. Have you been spending lots of time talking to my hippy-dippy family members, by chance?" Juliet grinned.

"How'd you guess? I thought I'd hidden the crystals and the Tarot cards," he smiled back. "Look, to be serious for a moment, your sister and brother-in-law helped me through some dark times over the last few months. They are special people, and I love them dearly. That organic home-brewed beer of Byron's though . . . Jeez! Does that pack a punch, or what?"

"They are special, aren't they? It means so much to me to be back here with them, and with you, Tommo. But we're a couple of wounded souls right now."

"Yes, it's funny how we're both single at the same time. I don't suppose you want to fall in love with me yet, do you?"

"No, sorry. How about you getting all mushy over me?"

"Nope. I wish I could. How good would that be? We wouldn't have to put up with unsuitable partners anymore who don't understand our deep connection to Mirrabooka."

"I know! It would be perfect, dammit!" They laughed together for a moment, and the three dogs came trotting into the room, having a rest from racing around. Ruby Roo gave Juliet's hand a nudge with her nose, as if saying she was glad to see her laughing, then flopped down on the floor beside her.

"How are you feeling now, anyway?" Tom asked.

"Oh, much like I was telling you on the phone the other day – still angry at myself for not being able to see what Ronan was really like. Although, being back here helps, so the self-recrimination is easing off a bit."

"You need to be kind to yourself. Ronan had good points, right?"

"Yes, lots. When things were going his way, he was a great person to be around. He just had that flip side, and he was selfish to the core."

"He kept that hidden from you for quite a while."

"You could see it, I suppose? His selfishness?"

"Well, yes. But love can make us blind. You never liked Anne-Marie much either, did you?"

"No. I didn't. But I thought perhaps I was jealous of her, because of our friendship. I knew you'd never warmed to Ronan, but I figured it might be the same reason."

"Well, I think you didn't like her because you could see she wasn't right for me. And that's why I didn't like Ronan. As well as the fact that he was an arrogant egomaniac who thought he was better than everyone else – including you."

"Okay," Juliet laughed. "I see we're not holding back now!"

"No – and please don't get back with him. I can never pretend to like him now, can I?"

"Don't worry. I can't see that happening."

"Good. I think the truth is that when either of us meets the *right* person, the other one of us will see it and will really, truly be able to like them. I don't think it's a jealousy thing at all; it's a protective thing. We don't want to see each other get hurt, so when you know that's inevitable, it's hard. If I imagine you with someone fantastic, I don't feel jealous at all. I see a great friendship developing that includes all of us. Can you imagine me with a great girl and see that same thing?"

Juliet considered the scenario for a moment. "Yes. I can picture you with someone really lovely, and there I am with my wonderful partner too, and we are all best friends who will raise our children and grow old together right here in this town."

"Well then, that's our quest. We just need to have faith. When you find the right one, I'll know it – and vice versa."

"It's not looking very likely right now though, is it?" she said with a sigh, her shoulders drooping.

"We'll be right, Jules. Onwards and upwards, hey?"

She gave him a fond smile. "That's what you used to say when we were kids. Remember how you'd talk me into climbing the cliff with you after school, the really steep one around the point, and I'd get stuck halfway and start to cry?"

"You did not cry! You were as brave as a lion, from what I remember. You'd stop for a rest and complain a bit, and I'd tell you to stop whinging, and then you'd scramble all the way to the top. Then we'd perch up there together and look across the ocean and talk about how much fun we'd had."

"I'd cry on the inside, but I wanted you to think I was brave."

"Well, it worked. Hey – that's a metaphor you know. We're both halfway up the cliff right now, and a bit stuck."

"Yes! And you're telling me to keep going."

"Exactly. So, don't worry. One day we'll both be up the top, admiring the view, and it will all be worthwhile. I know it, okay?"

At Tom's kind words, Juliet's eyes filled with tears, and he held his arms out to her again.

"Hey, come here, you."

She climbed off the stool to be enveloped in his strong, comforting hug.

"Thank you, Tommo. You always know what to say. I just feel so strung out at the moment. Every little thing makes me either yell or cry. Or both." She rested her head on his broad shoulders and gave way to the tears properly, but this time they were healing ones.

"Brave as a lion, you are. Remember that." He stroked her hair for a moment. "Now, when you've finished getting my shoulder all soggy, let's take these dogs for a walk around the inlet. I want to show you a big tree where I spotted a nest the other day. I think they're either eagles or hawks up there, but I need you to help me decide."

Juliet grabbed some tissues and blew her nose. Tom was right – they had to go onwards and upwards. Being back in this town with the people she loved was exactly what she needed.

"Well, you're not much of a bird classifier," she said, wiping the last of the tears away. "They're probably pelicans."

"That's more like the girl I've missed for too long – the one who gives me a hard time," he grinned.

He whistled for the dogs and they jumped to their feet, all shining eyes and wagging tails, and they all set off for their walk, while the blue waters of the inlet shimmered under the sun.

Chapter 8 – The simple things in life

After visiting Tom, Juliet woke up next morning feeling far more optimistic; their conversation having soothed the rawness of her wounds and given her back some determination. She'd been giving in to her feelings of sadness and regret too much, she decided, and – while it was necessary to have time to grieve – it was important to look to the future too. She also needed to stop berating herself over Ronan. She remembered how Tom had summed up his relationship – a learning experience to enhance personal growth. While he'd said it partly in jest, deep down, he meant it. She felt better knowing that he'd got things wrong as well. Not that she wanted him to be hurt, of course, but it was comforting to know she wasn't the only one who'd made a poor choice of partner.

Well, she wasn't going to do that anymore! If she ever wanted to consider romance again, it would have to be with someone truly compatible. Maybe she'd enlist help and get her friends and family to vote on any future candidate's suitability. And if she got it wrong again, she'd let them stage an intervention. She smiled at an image of Tom, Byron and Isabella carrying some man out the door.

Ridiculous, but potentially useful! In any case, she wasn't going to be looking for love again for a long, long time.

Juliet leapt out of bed, ready to greet the day. She had been sticking to her early-morning fitness campaign easily, as it was second nature for her to get up early and head for the beach. Mornings were usually glorious in Mirrabooka, and the interplay of light, water and clouds as the new day awoke was nearly always worth marvelling over. It had to be very inclement weather for Juliet to have a sleep-in.

After sitting on the point and watching a low-key sunrise spread pastel colours over calm seas, Juliet and Ruby Roo enjoyed their usual outing to the beach, where small but nicely formed waves gave Juliet some fun in the surf. She occasionally looked across from her surfboard to see if there might be a tall dark-haired man walking along the sand, but there was no sign of him this time. She tried hard to not feel disappointed. Returning home, she realized with satisfaction that both she and Ruby Roo were getting fitter already, as the climb up the hill had been easier and faster. After completing the morning chores and having a blissfully hot shower, she sat down at her workstation in the corner of the living room, ready to get to work.

Her new enthusiasm for life wasn't yet enveloping her manuscript, unfortunately. She wasn't finding the first draft easy; in fact, it was proving stressful. It was all very well to say things like "onwards and upwards", but harder to put them into practice. Whenever she felt tired and fragile, or unsure of herself in any way, her writer's demons would come and sit on her shoulder. "Who's going to want to read this rubbish?" they'd say. Or "This is terrible. Really boring stuff! You think you're a writer – what a joke!"

She'd had success with the first book, that was true, but that was a kind of mixed blessing. While it enabled her to defend herself to the demons and tell them she was indeed a writer, and had respectable sales figures and reviews to prove it, the pressure was now well and truly on. The second book needed to be as good – or better – than the first, and that expectation was adding to her keyboard paralysis.

"Ha! That one was a fluke!" the demons liked to jeer.

She'd been struggling with the new book for weeks. Her anxiety about Ronan had made it hard to focus back in the city and, since the confrontation with him and her return home, those struggles had magnified into full-on writer's block. Now she was beginning to wonder if she'd ever be able to finish the draft. Maybe she'd go down in history as a one-hit wonder. Maybe it would be better to give up now, rather than publish something that was terrible. Maybe she should look for another job in town to pay the bills, and forget all about this writing lark . . .

An image of Tom's kind face jumped into her mind. "Brave as a lion, you are," the face said. She smiled, thinking of his recollection of her stopping halfway up the cliff to complain. Well, she was certainly doing that now!

She sighed and stared at the document on the screen. The thought of writing the next chapter seemed like torture, so she decided to re-read what she'd done the previous day and jot down some notes about the next section. She was heartened to find that the new material wasn't too bad after all. Her imagination – fuelled by those nasty demons – had led her to believe it was all jumbled-up garbage, but that wasn't the case, even to her critical eyes. As soon as she re-read the new chapter, some interesting ideas for a crucial next scene popped into her head and she jotted them down into her 'ideas' notebook, then typed a couple of pages of dialogue. It would need fleshing out, but it was a start.

Realizing she had stiffened up from sitting at the desk for hours, she did a few exercises to loosen her tight shoulders and neck muscles and decided to have a break for a while. She needed to be kinder to herself, like Tom said. She'd be back into a regular routine with this book soon enough. Just not quite yet. She may be still stuck on the cliff, but at least she was starting to plan the next part of the climb.

Anyway, the book wasn't the only part of her life, and she could spend a few hours making progress with something else. It was still nagging at her that she'd been way out of line when she'd flipped out and yelled at her neighbour. He was not only a neighbour – he was a guest, too, since he'd rented her cottage, and she always went out of her way to be friendly to the people who came to stay. Sometimes the visitors could be exasperating, and they often didn't understand country life, but she was always polite to them – even when she had to explain to their children that they shouldn't chase the wallabies or the lizards or any of the other creatures who lived on the bushy blocks.

She smiled as she remembered one occasion when the lizard had chased the children. It was a particularly large goanna, or lace monitor lizard – about five feet long from nose to tail – that one day got sick of being taunted by children when it was trying to sunbathe at the base of a tree. It was never a good idea to make a goanna angry, as they could move quickly when they wanted to. The two boys, who had been particularly tiresome guests because they wouldn't take 'no' for an answer about anything, had come racing around the corner of the cottage, screaming about a giant lizard that was trying to kill them.

"Well, I told you yesterday to leave the goanna alone," Juliet told them, with absolutely zero sympathy. "Did it bite or scratch either of you?"

"No." The boys shook their heads.

"We were too fast for it." The older boy tried to resurrect his wounded pride.

"Just as well," Juliet said. "Did you know that goannas are usually placid and harmless, but if they get a fright – like being poked at with a stick, for instance – they can mistake a person for a tree and try to climb up them? And they have extremely sharp claws and teeth, so that wouldn't be much fun, would it?"

"No," the boys had agreed, looking pale, as they quickly dropped their sticks behind their backs. She was glad to remember they'd been a lot more respectful of the native creatures after that, and she'd overheard them telling the goanna people-climbing fact to their pale and insipid-looking father, who had developed a habit of peering anxiously around the undergrowth on the rare occasions he left the house.

At least she'd managed to remain civil to those guests. Even though the two boys could have tried the patience of a saint, she hadn't ranted and shouted at them. There was no denying it – she had been unfair and inhospitable to Fred, and she should make amends. She would make him a cake and apologize, as she'd mentioned to Isabella.

Juliet loved to cook, especially if she was feeling out of sorts, and baking banana or carrot cakes was her specialty. She liked to kid herself they were healthy, because of the fruit or vegetable components, even as she mixed the sugar, flour and butter together. She'd made a banana cake recently for her sister's visit, so this time she would make a carrot cake topped with a thick layer of cream-cheese frosting.

She whistled for Ruby Roo and they jumped in the car, heading for the general store to buy a couple of things she needed. Ruby insisted on getting out of the car and trotting across to the shops with Juliet; even though she had to stay out the front of the store, she knew she'd get lots of attention from passers-by. The store owner, Mrs Mac, a sturdy middle-aged woman who nearly always wore baggy overalls, was rearranging the front window display as they walked across. While her surname was really McNamara, she was called Mrs Mac by everyone in town.

"Hello, love!" Her face lit up when she saw Juliet, and she opened her arms wide for a big hug. "It's beaut to have you back in town. The girls told me you came in the other day when I was out playing bowls. I was sorry I missed you, but I figured you and Roo would turn up again soon."

Ruby Roo gazed up at her adoringly, and the woman bent down to pat the dog's head with gusto, then straightened up and gestured to Juliet again. "Ah, come back here, darls, I need another hug!"

"Me too! It's great to be back, that's for sure."

Mrs Mac could be gruff sometimes, but she'd bend over backwards to help someone if she thought they needed it. In the dark days after Juliet's father had died, she'd been there to help the grieving girls and their mother in countless ways and had always brushed off their thanks. She was an unofficial favourite auntie for Juliet.

"So, how's tricks? I hear you dropped that fella you'd been seeing. Didn't like him, truth be known. Always thought his eyes were too close together."

"Is that right?" Juliet laughed. "I'm better off without him, that's for sure. He ended up being not too nice at all. So, now it's the peaceful single life for me."

"You'll meet someone else, love, soon enough. Good lookin' girl like you isn't going to fly solo for too long. Hey, how about the bloke with the shiny sportscar who's rented your cottage? The girls and I reckon he'd be perfect for you."

"Oh really?"

"Yeah. Handsome, eh? He could leave his boots at my bedroom door anytime, but he's more your age than mine." Her burst of raspy laughter turned into a coughing fit. "Damn smokes! Gotta give 'em up."

"Yes! I thought you'd quit smoking already!" Juliet had her hands on her hips and a stern look on her face.

"I have! About ten times. I'll win the wretched battle someday. But by jingo, it's great to have you back, darls."

"Thanks, Auntie Mac. I'm glad to be here. And being single is fine, honestly." Juliet smiled at the thought of Mrs Mac checking out the new man in town. "My neighbour seems very nice, but I'm surprised you're endorsing him. Isabella says he's always complaining about the store, and that you've given him some undignified nickname."

"Yeah. Old Grumble Bum, I call him," she grinned. "At first, he seemed to have this chip on his shoulder about being out here in woop woop. Dunno why – since he's chosen to lob up here. He kept coming in and asking for all these fancy-shmancy city things like mutcha or matcha or what have you, but he's given up on that now. We had it out the other day when I told him I was sick of his whinging, and we just have real food here. Plain, ordinary food that you don't have to travel to the Himalayan highlands to get or sell your first-born to afford. I said if he didn't like what I stocked he could go and get stuffed – and grow his own hipster-bloody-vegetables."

"Really! How did he take that?"

"Very well, as it happens. He thought about it for a second, then said, 'Okay, fair enough'. Now he thinks up something ridiculous to ask for every time he comes in here, so we can have a joke around. He's alright, actually – makes a good sparring partner. You could do worse, you know."

Juliet narrowed her eyes and stared at her, trying hard to repress a smile.

"Alright, alright! I'll give it a rest," the older woman laughed. "Now, leave that mutt of yours out here and come on in. What can I get you today?"

"I'd like some white Russian kale and pickled pufferfish, please," Juliet said with a grin, and was rewarded with a snap of the tea towel Mrs Mac always had hanging from the pocket of her overalls.

Yep, it was good to be home.

Being back in her own kitchen to bake another cake was great fun, and Juliet played favourite old CDs as she prepared the ingredients and mixed them together. Soon the delightful aroma of baking carrot cake was wafting through the cottage and, when one of her favourite Motown tracks came on, she turned it up loud, sang along, and danced around the living area, enjoying the lightness of heart that had returned after being absent for too long. Her world was looking better, and it was the simple things in life that were soothing her psyche, Juliet realized, as she twirled and shimmied to the classic track: a good dog, fresh air and saltwater, great music, old friends who loved her . . . a delicious man next door . . .

Oh! That's not right – damn subconscious!

It was supposed to be a delicious cake that was next on the list. "Oh no!" She stopped twirling and threw up her hands. "The cake!"

She raced to the kitchen to hear the oven alarm still bleeping. She and Aretha Franklin in full voice had been drowning it out. Fortunately, she got there in time and, after testing the cake with a skewer, judged it as perfect. She let it cool, tidied the kitchen, and added the frosting, before getting changed into more presentable clothes and putting on a touch of lip-gloss.

She glanced at her reflection in the mirror. The face that looked back at her appeared to be happy. Most of the shadows under her eyes had gone, and her cheeks had a healthy glow.

I am not dressing up for him. I'd do this before visiting anybody, right?

Her reflection stared back at her knowingly.

Chapter 9 – A peace offering

Finn had been working hard all morning. He'd had a long online meeting with some colleagues, as he was working as a consultant when any of the other lawyers wanted his input, which was turning out to be quite often. This morning's call had involved a complex situation and long discussion, so he'd got up early to prepare and had bypassed his customary beach walk.

After finishing the call, he went for a run along the track around the inlet to clear his head, then showered and dragged on old track pants and a faded sweatshirt. He followed up a few things on his laptop, then compiled and emailed the detailed information to his colleague, satisfied he'd done a thorough job. He liked it when the office needed his help, as he was used to being busy all day and found it strange to have so much free time. He made a coffee and decided to quickly read the news headlines and then get to work on a new project he'd thought of.

He'd resolved to do something useful with his time in Mirrabooka to stop him dwelling on Sophia and their breakup, and to try and prevent any pleasant but inappropriate daydreams about his attractive neighbour. Mind you, it hadn't helped that morning to be able to hear the music she was playing. Motown tracks – he loved them too. He wondered if she was dancing to the irresistible rhythms of The Temptations, and the image that popped into his mind of Juliet swaying to the music had been truly distracting.

He stopped browsing the news and opened up a Word document. Time to get to work and make the most of the fact that the internet connection was behaving itself today.

He'd decided he really would start writing a book, so at least that part of his alias wouldn't be a lie. It wasn't a book that would ever get published, but he'd print off a few copies himself and see if the Mirrabooka History Group might be interested in it. He'd started researching the shipwrecks in the area, as there'd been many over the years, dating back to the early 1800s. Although there were bits of information here and there in the tourist booklets and the one history of the town that he'd been able to find, it wasn't very comprehensive. He would research as much as he could, and then collate and write it up so at least the information would all be together.

He liked history and often tried to imagine what life was like in days gone by. Sometimes, since he'd started reading about shipwrecks, would stand on one of the rocky headlands and stare out to sea, trying to envisage what it must have been like in the old days. He would imagine being in a small ship caught in stormy weather and think about how it would feel to be at the mercy of the ocean. Watching the immense power of the waves smashing onto the rocks made him shiver. They were brave folk who went to sea in those days.

He found some information on Trove, the national library database, and was engrossed in a survivor's account of a wreck further up the coast when someone tapped on the front door of the cottage. That was surprising. It wasn't likely you'd get Mormons or electricity salespeople all the way out here.

Glancing out the front window, he saw the red coat of Ruby Roo nosing around near the carport and immediately wished he'd chosen more respectable clothes that day. He looked at his work area and moved a pile of legal books onto a chair, then shut the laptop screen down, hoping there was nothing else that Juliet might notice. Trying to stick to this ridiculous story about writing a book on finance was a complete pain in the behind. If she asked him anything about it today, he'd have to change the subject.

Opening the door, he felt suddenly nervous again. "Hello, Juliet, this is a nice surprise. Would you like to come in? And Ruby Roo of course."

She was wearing baggy cotton pants and a turquoise top. The colour suited her, emphasising her blue eyes.

"Thank you, that would be nice," Juliet replied. Ruby Roo didn't need any more encouragement; she dashed past their legs and trotted around the house, seeming to approve of his presence in it, if her wagging tail was any indication.

"I brought you something. A cake." Juliet held up a plate with a plastic cover on top. Her face was looking sun-kissed, with a few more freckles already, and her hair tumbled around her face, looking glorious, as always.

"That's very nice of you," Finn said. "Let's go to the kitchen."

She walked ahead of him, and for a moment, he wondered how she knew where the kitchen was, before he mentally slapped himself.

Wake up, dopey! It is her house, after all.

He followed her, admiring her shape through the soft cotton fabric. She had a simply gorgeous body, no doubt about it; trim and fit in a strong and healthy way, but still with that oh-so-feminine appeal.

Okay. Better stop ogling my guest now.

In the kitchen, Juliet lifted the cover off the plate and Finn could smell the delicious odour of still-warm cake, with a heap of frosting on top.

"I'm in a baking phase," she said. "It must be something to do with getting home and wanting to enjoy my own kitchen. I thought you might like to have this carrot cake."

"I certainly would, as it looks delicious, but only if you'll share it with me. Why don't we sit out on the deck? Hopefully, it'll be warm enough now the sun's out. I can make tea, or coffee if you'd prefer."

"A cup of tea would be lovely, thank you. Black, no sugar, please."

"Same as I have it," Finn said. He boiled the kettle and made tea as Juliet sliced the cake, and they chatted about the unseasonably warm weather before taking their supplies out the back. Ruby Roo followed closely, eyeing off the plates.

"No cake for you, Miss Plumpy." Juliet reached down to pat her. "Go and lie down. Off you go!" The dog did as she was told, knowing it was forbidden to hang around the humans and beg for food, even though she would have dearly loved to.

"There's another reason for the cake," she said, once they were settled at the outdoor table. "It's an apology cake, really." She tapped her fingertips lightly on the side of her mug. "Now that I've had time to reflect on our . . . umm . . . meeting, I realize I went a bit overboard."

She looked directly at him and once more he was assailed by some weird sense of connection. "That's fine, honestly. I don't blame you. I feel bad about hurting poor Ruby Roo."

"Well, you just gave her a fright. There was no harm done. Look . . . I won't go into the details, but I'd had a couple of very stressful days, and I was pretty strung out by the time I got here. I'm sorry that I took it out on you. I'm not usually so hysterical, honestly." She gave a wry smile.

He already knew enough about Juliet to assume her outburst had been out of character, and he wondered what could have caused her to be so on edge. Well, it wasn't his business if she didn't want to discuss it. And the 'don't go there' look she had on her face said she clearly didn't.

"Apology well and truly accepted. Thank you for the cake. It looks delicious, and I think it's time we ate it."

Juliet smiled, and again he noticed how her presence seemed to light up her surroundings.

"So, how is the book going?" she asked. "Is it your first one, or are you already an old hand at such things?"

Finn groaned inwardly. This was awkward. When he'd arrived here, he'd imagined he would keep mainly to himself, so he didn't think it would matter if he made vague claims to people that he would never get to know. He hadn't dreamed he would be sitting down for afternoon tea with a woman he really liked – and that he liked not only because she was gorgeous, but because she was so damned genuine and nice. He hated having to tell lies to her and the thought of discussing writing with an actual best-selling author made it even worse. He should have pretended to be a brain surgeon with sprained fingers or something.

"No, I'm not an old hand at all," he muttered. "It's hard, and I'm not making much progress. Writer's block, you know?"

"Tell me about it!" Juliet pulled a face. "That's another reason why I've been baking, truth be known. It's one of my advanced procrastination techniques."

"Let's not talk about such tedious things. Tell me about what it was like growing up here in Mirrabooka," Finn said, and her face brightened as she started to describe the joys of being a child in a small coastal town, or "living in paradise", as she called it.

They sat and talked for about an hour, getting through half the cake and another pot of tea, before Juliet said she'd better go home to do some more work. Finn was relieved they'd chatted about other things rather than writing. He'd enjoyed the conversation with her very much but afterwards felt even guiltier about the deception.

He watched through the window as she walked between the trees to her own home, the dog trotting around in the bush and sniffing at various things. His head was full of the stories Juliet had related to him about when she and Isabella were young. They'd had all sorts of exploits with the gang of kids they used to run around with, which included Tom, the very likeable town doctor Finn had met a few times, and his sister. Juliet had described how they used to picnic on the sand dunes and swim in the surf and the inlet waters. They would walk the edges of the lake to net fish and other sea creatures and then let them go again; intrigued by the varieties of sea life they found. She talked about how they used to dare each other to climb up cliffs, or over rocky headlands with the surf pounding at their feet, or to swim across channels with the tide ripping out to sea. It was a wonder those kids all made it through to adulthood unscathed!

Finn had been captivated by her stories, not just because he was becoming more enthralled by her beauty and vivaciousness with every word she spoke, but also because he was fascinated about what it must have been like to have all those experiences as a child. He was envious of Juliet and her 'gang', and the freedom and adventures they'd had.

Far too polite to monopolise the conversation, she had asked him about his own childhood, but he'd not been able to match her anecdotes. He'd talked a little about the school he went to, the organised sports and swimming training he'd done, and the occasional holiday with his father in coastal areas close to the city. He hadn't gone into detail about the loneliness he'd felt as an only child, with a parent who was usually working – even on a holiday. His father would send his son out on his own to go for a walk or book him into an organised tour. He'd never had a gang of kids to run around with during the holidays.

Still looking out the window, he noticed that Juliet had stopped to peer up into the big stringybark gum on the fence line, and then began walking slowly around it. No doubt there was an interesting creature of some sort up there to see. A goanna perhaps, or maybe a koala, curled up in a fork of the tree. He had a sudden vision of what it would be like if he and Juliet were involved with each other. She would dash back inside to get him. "Finn! Come and have a look at this!" she'd say, her eyes shining with enthusiasm, and she'd take his hand and drag him out the door to share her excitement. How nice that would be. He wished she'd come back now to tell him what she'd seen.

He sighed, and shook his head, deciding he really must banish these fanciful thoughts and stop staring at his neighbour. It was ridiculous, possibly verging on creepy – he was really starting to lose the plot in this town. The conversation with Juliet had led him to realize that her childhood was exactly what he would wish for his own children, were he ever to have any, and he couldn't stop thinking about her and imagining things, dammit. He pictured three little fair-haired children leaving her side to run towards him with buckets and fishing nets.

"Dad! Look what we caught!"

Their mother would smile at him as he would kneel beside the children and exclaim with wonder, and then he would help them gently return their catches to the water.

If he did ever become a father, there was no way his kids would be dismissed and sent off somewhere out of the way. He was not a slave to his career, like his father had been, and indeed still was. Finn liked his work, but there was something far more important than a successful career that he longed for, and that was a full and rich family life, with all the chaos and upheaval that would bring. How that would include kids running wild with fishing nets when he lived in the city, he couldn't quite reconcile, but – hey – they were just silly daydreams, after all.

Juliet had gone inside now. He'd go and have a look at the tree himself later on and see if it was a koala up there. There were several around, and he'd heard one just last night.

He smiled to himself when he recalled the first time that he'd heard a koala in one of the trees. It had sounded like a wild creature that was half angry pig and half lion was about to jump onto his head – absolutely terrifying! He'd walked inside very quickly, locked the door and immediately googled 'Australia, tree, roaring, grunting'. The search results had told him he'd probably heard the territorial warning calls of a frisky koala. So much for thinking that these creatures were cute, cuddly and placid – this one had sounded like it could rip your head off.

He'd mentioned the encounter to Mrs Mac at the store the next day, just to check that the koala theory was correct, and she'd laughed so hard she'd doubled over and knocked down a whole display of melons. Finn had helped round them up as they rolled around the floor, and had to reassemble the display for her since she was still debilitated by hysteria.

"Oh dear, Fred-me-lad," she'd said weakly, wiping the tears from her eyes. "I'm sorry to laugh so much, but that's a very funny story. A big, tall man like you dashing back to the sanctuary of your electronic devices and searching for information about tree-dwelling native lions, when it's really a randy koala. Priceless!"

"Yes, well, I can see the funny side today," he said. "At the time, I was deeply traumatised and ready to drag heavy furniture in front of the doors."

He'd always been good about taking a joke, and he didn't mind embellishing the story to entertain her. He liked Mrs Mac, who didn't put up with any "city bullshit" as she called it and wouldn't hesitate to launch into an argument with him, or to tease him. She had a good brain, a good heart, and a fearless demeanour – all things he admired.

"Well, it's unusual this time of the year," she said, settling down enough to rearrange several of the melons he hadn't stacked to her liking. "They usually get vocal like that in spring, which is breeding time. Your bloke must have been getting into some argy-bargy to warn off an intruding male. They're very territorial creatures."

"Well, I probably won't be here in spring but, if I am, at least I'll be prepared. It's no fun thinking you're about to be torn limb from limb by marauding creatures of the night. Now, might you have any shiitake mushrooms, by chance?"

"No!" She glared at him with hands on hips. "What's wrong with good old ordinary mushrooms? And don't you go giving me the shiitakes about having limited stock here, 'cause I couldn't give a stuff. What the hell are you wanting to cook anyway?"

She'd ended up giving him lots of advice about cooking a much simpler meal that involved plain mushrooms, which turned out to be delicious. It seemed he was gradually managing to make edible meals. He was learning a lot about goannas, koalas, and various types of birds too. There were so many birds flitting around the house and the deck that he'd bought a book about local varieties, so he could learn what some of them were. He'd be able to teach the children about them. Those children he was probably never going to have, that is.

He shook his head again and stopped gazing out the window, beginning to clear up the plates and mugs and half-wishing there was a dog at his feet to talk to as he pottered around the cottage. Country life sure was doing weird things to his brain.

Chapter 10 – Mirrabooka magic

There. That had been easy – and fun. Juliet felt an irrepressible sense of elation when she and Ruby Roo returned to their own cottage with the empty plate. They'd dawdled for a while on the way back, as the dog had stopped at the big stringybark near the fence to sniff the air, and Juliet had peered up through the branches to see what creature she'd noticed. Sure enough, there was a koala perched there, probably the big male she'd heard making a racket the previous night.

"Yes, I heard you, pal," she'd said, walking around the tree for a better view from the other side. "I bet half the town heard all that kerfuffle! I suppose you scared off the intruder, did you? Well, that's okay, there are plenty of trees around here."

She'd stood and studied the sleepy marsupial for some time. He was a fine big specimen. Then she spotted another one higher up the tree, and that one had a little joey clinging to its back. The baby looked so cute! She'd fleetingly thought of dashing back to get Fred to come and look too, then dismissed the idea as silly. He was probably working on clever financial-type things by now and wouldn't want to be interrupted for a koala family. She'd taken up lots of his time, anyway, going on about her childhood. Had she talked too much?

Reviewing the conversation while she cleaned up the kitchen, she didn't think so. Her companion had seemed genuinely interested in her Mirrabooka childhood, asked lots of questions, and laughed in all the right places when she'd told him some of the funny things she remembered. His favourite had been the story about Tom who, when they were all aged about ten, had been at the front of the group one time when they'd been racing along one of the bush tracks. He'd only seen the big red-bellied black snake stretched out in front of him at the last second. Having no time to stop, he'd leapt over it with a yell, jumping so high and then sprinting away so fast that all the rest of them thought it was hilarious. Not that anyone else wanted to get too close to a sun-bathing venomous reptile either – they'd all given it a wide berth as they detoured around. They'd teased Tom about his mighty leap for years and invented all sorts of nicknames for him. The most popular had been 'Rocket-bum', since he'd leapt so high in the air. Tom had been known as Rocket-bum for a very long time.

When Juliet had been halfway through relating that story, she'd wondered if Fred would think it was silly and crass; after all, he'd had a privileged upbringing by the sound of it, attending an exclusive private school. But he'd shouted with laughter when she'd described Tom's reaction and the nickname and had said he'd be sure to use it the next time he saw Tom at the pub. He mentioned he'd had a few beers with both Tom and Byron a few nights ago and, for some reason, Juliet had been glad to hear he'd been socialising with her favourite people. He wasn't stuck up at all, not like other men she'd met who had been to that type of school, who thought they were superior to everybody else.

Yes you, Ronan, as a matter of fact.

Fred was different, and she liked him.

Putting away the baking dishes, Juliet tried to examine what it was about him that she was drawn to. He was attractive, of course, although he wasn't some big, buff, alpha male, and she didn't go for that type anyway. No, he was handsome in an understated way. He was tall and lean, rather than buff, although he did have nice broad shoulders under the tatty old sweatshirt he'd been wearing. She'd noticed his thighs too, as he'd leaned back in his chair and stretched out his legs. Despite the baggy track pants, she could tell he was in good shape.

She'd tried not to stare at him too much as they'd sat out the back sharing the cake. She liked his angled face and the way he smiled, when his dark eyes would crinkle at the corners. Usually, he had a slow, gentle smile that suited the considered way he listened and paid attention to things, but occasionally he would put his head back and shout with laughter, and his face would relax with unconstrained joy, as though he had reverted to being a kid for just that moment. But then he would switch gears and click back into his polite and restrained adult persona again. She'd liked making him loosen up and laugh a couple of times. He'd been a lonely child; she'd realized as they chatted. He hadn't said so, but it had become clear as he mentioned a few things about his childhood.

How fortunate she'd been, to grow up in Mirrabooka, and how true it was that money couldn't buy happiness. Sure, it could help, but – although her family hadn't been well off – they'd been comfortable enough. She'd never cared about new toys, or make-up or fashion when she got older, and most of the time she still didn't. She was incredibly lucky because she'd grown up surrounded by all the important things, like love and affection from parents who really cared about her.

She'd led a charmed life, up until the day her gentle father had decided to stay home for a rest when they went to the beach. It was their mother who'd had found him on the bed when they returned; taken by a sudden heart attack. Juliet vividly recalled the stricken look on her mother's face when she told them what had happened, but the rest of that afternoon was a blur. She had flashes of memories of the doctor – Tom's father – arriving in a rush, people tramping through the house, her mother sitting at the kitchen table with her head in her hands, and Tom – who didn't know what to say, but handed her a special shell he'd found on the beach that morning. Well, that had been a long time ago. The town had gathered around them and they had got through it. She still missed her father all the time, but she felt his presence around her in Mirrabooka when she gazed at the land and seascapes he'd adored. When she was home, she always felt he wasn't far away.

Fred had dealt with grief too, having lost his mother at a young age. He'd had professional help, he'd said, but it sounded like there'd been little, if any, emotional support from his father. He hadn't had the close family, the community, or the gang of friends that had helped Juliet cope with her loss. She was the lucky one, but he didn't seem to have become hardened or bitter from his loneliness. He just had a kind of wistfulness about him as she'd talked about her childhood, her friends and their adventures. It was odd how comfortable she'd felt, sitting with him all that time. And he was *definitely* attractive. That was now official. God help her, what did all that mean? She reminded herself that he was engaged.

Nothing. It meant nothing.

Ruby Roo nudged her leg, and Juliet snapped out of her contemplations with a start. She'd rinsed the same plate about twenty times. What a waste of water! And Roo needed her afternoon walk. They headed out the back door and down the track to the beach, where Juliet was determined to think about the plot twists for her book and not whatever plot twists seemed to be wriggling their way into her own life.

*

The next day, Isabella, Byron and Clementine dropped into Juliet's for a visit. The sisters launched into baby discussions and Clemmie fell asleep on the spare bed after playing a vigorous game of hide and seek with Ruby Roo. Really, it had been Clemmie doing all the seeking, and the good-natured dog doing all the hiding. Fortunately, Roo didn't mind being interrupted every time she thought she'd found a new snoozing spot. At least this young human didn't squeal or pull her tail like some of them did, and she didn't seem to mind being licked sometimes. Ruby Roo was always gentle with little people, and she knew Juliet was very fond of this one, so she gave her extra attention. Even so, she and the humans were relieved when Clemmie crashed out on the bed and the cottage was suddenly bathed in serenity.

Byron, though, was restless, pacing from room to room.

"He's got too much energy – he's the opposite of me." Isabella was propped on the couch with her feet up. "Why don't you go to the club for a game of golf?"

"Tom's working," Byron sighed. "So's my mate Eddie. And I know I could play with some of the other guys that hang out at the club but, quite frankly, they drive me nuts sometimes with the same conversations. If I have to hear one more time from Wally about how his missus won't let him clean his fish in the laundry, I'm going to tell him the truth – which is that I'm on her side. There's a perfectly good fish-cleaning bench at the boat ramp; no need to stink your house out with fish guts."

"Best not to say that, or you'll be shunned at the nineteenth hole, right?" Isabella said.

"Yep, I'll be the one drinking in the corner, with no mates."

"Ask Fred, next door. He might play," Juliet suggested. "And he'll be more interesting company than Wally and his gang."

Isabella raised her eyebrows. "You're sounding a lot friendlier, all of a sudden. Been for a visit?"

"Just a cake and an apology, as we'd talked about it. And that's it!" She noticed the grin on her sister's face and couldn't help but follow suit.

Byron began to look hopeful. "Good idea! But . . . no. Won't he be working? Isn't he writing a book or something?"

"He says he has writer's block, like me. He might be glad of an excuse to get out of the house. I'm pretty sure he's home; I haven't seen the car go out."

"And you're not tracking his movements at all, are you?" Isabella said. "They call that stalking, I believe."

Juliet poked her tongue out at her sister. "If you weren't almost ready to pop, we'd be having a massive cushion fight right now." She threw a small one at Isabella's head, and her sister grabbed it with a neat catch and popped it under the small of her back.

"Perfect. Thanks!"

It was enough encouragement for Byron, who disappeared next door for a few minutes, then ducked back in looking much more cheerful, saying that he and Fred were going to walk to the club, play nine holes and have a beer or two.

"Good! That'll take care of those restless legs of yours," Isabella said. "And there's no rush. I might have a nap too, if you don't mind me parking myself here for a while, Jules." She settled further on the couch.

"Of course not! You have a nice snooze, and I'll watch Clemmie," Juliet volunteered. "You can move to my bed, if you like."

"Nope. Not moving. Comfy right here." Isabella closed her eyes.

Byron waved farewell and Juliet peeked in at Clementine, who was still sound asleep in the second bedroom, while Isabella was already dozing on the couch. Juliet was happy to be able to help now that her sister was in the final months of the pregnancy.

She tidied the kitchen and watched Fred heading out along the track with Byron, the two men deep in conversation. She liked the way he walked, and the long-sleeved t-shirt and jeans he was wearing definitely showed off his appealing physique. She dragged her attention away from the window. "Stalking", Isabella had said, Juliet remembered with a sheepish smile.

*

Finn had again been surprised at the knock on the door. This phenomenon of people 'popping in' didn't happen in the city. There, everything revolved around smart phones and comparing hectic schedules through online calendars, but life in Mirrabooka was a lot more laidback. He was happy to see Byron and interested in the golf idea – he'd been feeling bored and restless too – but he had to confess he wasn't much of a golfer.

"Mate!" Byron replied. "That's no excuse around here – most of us are pretty useless. Playing golf is an excuse to stretch your legs, admire the view, whack a few balls, and then go for a beer. Come on, it's a great day for a stroll. Help me out, would you? I need to escape from all the talk of bootees, bibs, and bunny rugs!"

His cajoling worked, and Finn had gone with him and thoroughly enjoyed himself. Byron hadn't seemed to care that Finn lived up to his claim of being an average golfer, even though he'd downplayed his own abilities.

The barmaid at the golf club wanted to close up early so she could watch her son's soccer game, so they decided to have their beers at the pub in town.

"Righto, Freddie-boy," Byron had said. "Let's go. I'm sure my girls will be happy at Juliet's for ages yet. I felt like I was just getting in the way there. And Izzy will ring if she wants me." He patted the back pocket holding his phone.

That was an advantage of a small town like this, Finn mused, as they headed off together – nothing was very far away. And everyone was so relaxed. There was no way the bar staff in the city golf clubs could decide to close early and send patrons elsewhere. Those people had paid for their memberships and they were going to get full value! Here, the blokes in the bar just said, "No worries, love. Hope your boy does well. Go the Sharks!"

The two men strolled on the coastal track along the clifftop above the ocean, and Finn noticed a couple of boys pop up over the edge of the cliff. No doubt they'd been carrying on what he now knew was the old Mirrabooka tradition of daring each other to climb up from the beach below. His mind flashed momentarily to the little fair-haired girl with grubby knees that Juliet would once have been.

"I take it the Sharks are the school soccer team?" he said, remembering the comments in the golf club bar.

"Yes, and there was a lot of discussion about that name, let me tell you," Byron laughed. "Lots of people wanted to call them the Mirrabooka Dolphins. A special parents' meeting was called, and a couple of the mums spoke passionately about negative energy and how dolphins were much nicer creatures than sharks. They said that the boys and girls in the soccer club would subconsciously take on dolphin characteristics, which would be much better than shark characteristics, and so on."

"Seriously?"

"Yes, there's a strong hippy vibe in this town, you might have realized."

"Nah, hadn't noticed a thing. I just thought you liked wearing your wife's gear and you keep forgetting to get a haircut," Finn teased, referring to his companion's multi-coloured cheesecloth shirt and long, tied-back hair.

"Cheeky buggers, you city blokes," Byron grinned. "Anyway, you'd have also noticed there's quite a non-hippy component, who get sick of being preached at by the tree-huggers, as they call us. That lot were insisting on the Sharks as the name, with the rationale being that they wanted the kids to be determined and ruthless and win the games, and not waft around being nice and dolphin-like to everybody."

"So, the rednecks triumphed over the tree-huggers, I see."

"Yes, it went to a confidential vote and the Sharks proved to be much more popular. Izzy and I voted Sharks, actually, and I think a few of the other hippy dads jumped ship too. It must have caused upset auras in a few households that night, with all the negative ions zinging around."

"You're full of surprises, Byron." Finn shook his head with a grin. "You and Isabella are hippies too, yet you poke fun at your own lifestyle sometimes."

"Look, you've got to have a laugh, mate. Lots of people come to this town and plunge right into the alternative lifestyle to re-invent themselves. They take it so seriously, and they start preaching to all-and-sundry, driving everybody nuts. But there's five hundred people of all types in this town, and we need to get along. That means respecting each other and finding your own style, for your own reasons. Izzy and I are passionate environmentalists, we do yoga and we meditate and, yes, we even hold little ceremonies to celebrate the full moon. We believe in the power of the mind, but we also believe in science and modern medicine, that's for sure. There's lots about the alternative lifestyle that's great, but it's not sacred. On the other hand, I may poke fun at something, but that doesn't mean I dismiss it. Who knows how this world works? What are the secrets of this planet, the sky, or that awesome ocean out there?" He gestured towards the horizon as he walked. "Or death? What happens next? I've got no freaking idea. But . . . look at that, mate. Doesn't it make you grateful to be alive?"

They had rounded a corner of the track, and a gap in the trees revealed a wide expanse of ocean, with a lighthouse on an island in the far distance and a line of golden sand dunes separating the churning surf from the silky-smooth waters of the inlet. The sky was a vivid expanse of blue, wide and cloudless, and the water of the ocean was layered in hues of blue and green. The two men stood together and gazed at the panorama before them.

Finn took deep breaths of the clean ocean air. "It sure does. That's absolutely stunning. I'm beginning to see why you people want to live all the way out here. If this place was anywhere near the city, it would be full of mansions and restaurants, and you'd have cars and crowds swarming all over the place. But here we are, a billion-dollar view in front of us, and all we can hear is waves and bellbirds. And an eastern whipbird," he added, as the distinctive 'whip' sound echoed through the bush behind them.

"Hey, you're starting to know your birds of south-east Australia. I'm impressed!" Byron grinned.

"Well, I bought a book in the store, and I've been browsing through it. I never knew so many birds existed, until I came here. I even saw a lyrebird the other day. They're weird-looking things, aren't they?"

"They are, but – uh oh – look out! It's happening!" Byron raised his hands in mock horror.

"Oh yeah? What's that?" Finn said, amused.

"Mirrabooka is working its magic on you. It starts with a pretty scene and a lyrebird, and then you realize you're leaving windows open at night – even in winter – so you can hear the surf. After that, you start to get up early, so you can watch the sun rise over the sea. Am I right?"

"Well . . . yes," Finn admitted. "I have done all those things."

"I thought so. You're doomed, mate. You'll be hooked on this place soon, and once the Mirrabooka magic gets to you, it never lets you go. When that happens, you don't ever feel right anywhere else. If you leave, you yearn for the look and the sound and the smell of this place, craving it like a lover you can't get out of your mind. I'm serious, man – if this place gets to you, you're a goner!"

"Well, it's a nice theory," Finn laughed. "I can almost imagine how it could happen, but there's no chance of that with me. I'm a city dweller through and through. When Mirrabooka gets reliable internet and proper phone coverage, and the power stops dropping out at regular intervals, I may be more of a convert, but that could take a while!"

"You may doubt me now, my friend, but some day you'll see that I'm right." Byron looked at him sagely. "But, come on, we need that beer. I'm as dry as the proverbial dead dingo."

They walked on, as Byron launched into a discussion of which brand of beer was best for after-golf thirst quenching.

Finn took one final glance at the ocean before the track took them back into the scrub.

Get hooked on this place? Hardly!

The boys who'd been climbing the cliff raced past them, calling out a greeting to Byron, since everybody knew everybody in Mirrabooka, of course. They ran ahead and out of sight, and the three little fair-haired kids that Finn kept imagining were there in his mind again too, until they also ran around a corner and disappeared.

Chapter 11 – The gatecrasher

It took Juliet a month to feel that her jangled nerves were settling down and the stress over Ronan was ebbing away. Isabella, Byron and Clementine were frequent companions, drawing her back into town life and inviting her to visit their farm on the other side of the inlet, where she helped them tend to the goats, chickens, and vegetable gardens.

The little farm produced organic eggs and vegetables for the farmers' markets in the area, but goat's cheese was its specialty. The Daisy-Belle brand was becoming more and more well-known, and the business was getting as much demand as the herd of goats could produce. Isabella and Byron loved their goats; each one had a name and they never got rid of any of the herd. Once their milk-producing days were over, the older 'girls' enjoyed a comfortable retirement in the paddocks overlooking the inlet, with cosy barns to keep them warm at night and safe from predators. Isabella would joke about the goat retirement village they were creating, but she loved the animals as much as Byron did, and they were both grateful for the living they provided. Clemmie treated them all as her special pets; which, in a way, they were.

There were always plenty of jobs to do on the farm and, whenever Juliet visited, she rolled up her sleeves and worked hard, whether it was mucking out the barns, carting hay, helping build new chicken runs, or turning the soil over in the garden beds. Isabella and Byron kept saying how grateful they were for the help, but Juliet knew she was the one receiving the favour. There was nothing like good, honest work in the clean country air to make you sleep well at night.

When she wasn't busy on the farm, working on her book, or pondering the fine line between interest and stalking, Juliet spent a lot of time with Tom, who regularly offered his company in between shifts at the medical centre. They often went fishing in Tom's big, comfortable boat and then would stand side-by-side at the bench cleaning their catches, with Tom teasing her about her fish-cleaning skills being so out of practice.

"Well, hey! At least I can still catch them!" Juliet would retort. She was a skilled and patient fisherwoman, and she nearly always ended up with a better catch than Tom did.

She took her own boat out of storage and enjoyed seeing it slide off the trailer and into the water again. Her boat, known as the *S.S. Minnow*, was a much smaller vessel than Tom's, but the little aluminium dinghy was just the thing for zooming around the islands, sandbars and channels of the inlet. It could go in much shallower water than Tom's boat and, when they took both boats out, Juliet would laugh and wave as she and the *Minnow* took a speedy shortcut between a couple of islands. The hours out on the water made her cheeks glow, and Tom was glad to see the signs of stress disappear from her face.

After a few weeks, Juliet realized she'd stopped recycling the same old thoughts and, to her surprise, she wasn't missing Ronan much at all. She missed the feeling of being one of a couple, as she was naturally geared to want to share her life, but the man himself – no. In all honesty, she'd realized how much more pleasant and relaxed her life was without him in it.

She was feeling so relaxed, in fact, that she'd had some quite sensual dreams during the restoring nights' sleep she'd been enjoying in her cosy cottage. Juliet was a little embarrassed that her tall, dark-haired neighbour had starred in some of them. Okay, all of them, to be totally honest. She debated with herself about whether that meant anything.

So, he's attractive – that's a fact. No big deal.

And she kept seeing him everywhere, so that probably explained it too. His sporty BMW stood out in Mirrabooka; you couldn't help but notice whenever it cruised around town.

Worried that she was becoming obsessed with the man, she'd started surfing at different beaches, so she'd be less likely to see him, but then he'd sometimes turn up there too. Even from her boat, she would spot him; he liked to jog along the inlet track that ran beside the main boating channel. Oh well, she couldn't control her dreams, and his running shorts showed off a fine pair of legs. Eventually, Juliet decided to stop worrying and just enjoy the view.

*

Finn, too, had noticed that he saw Juliet almost everywhere he went. Was that life in a small town, where you saw the same people all the time, or was fate taking a hand and throwing them together? He decided it was the latter. The universe had decided to taunt him by putting this gorgeous woman – who was off-limits anyway – right under his nose at the most inconvenient of times.

He tried walking on different beaches in the morning, but often he'd see her – in the surf or on the track or walking with Ruby Roo along the shoreline. When he went to the store, he'd glimpse her in the main street, chatting and laughing with the local teenagers or some of the town's senior citizens, who all seemed to adore her. If he went for a run around the shore of the inlet, there she'd be, chugging along the channel in her little boat, or walking Ruby Roo with Tom and his dogs. Yep, fate was teasing him, but Finn was determined to withstand the challenge and soldier on.

One night, bored with his limited cooking skills, he decided to have dinner at the pub, but of course fate decreed that was the night Juliet, Tom, Isabella and Byron would be there too. As soon as Finn walked in the door, he saw Tom and Byron at the bar and hesitated, not sure what to do, but by then Byron had noticed and walked towards him, his hand held out in greeting.

"Gidday, Fred. Good to see you. You here for dinner too?"

"Um, I think so." He returned the handshake, realizing it would be awkward to pretend he wasn't, since he was standing in the middle of the restaurant. If he'd just gone for a drink, he'd be in the front bar. "I thought I'd pop in and see what was going on. I haven't eaten here before."

"Well, the food's not bad. Beats doing your own cooking sometimes."

"Especially if you cook like me," he agreed.

"Izzy and I are here for a last night of freedom before she gets too tired, so Mrs Mac is looking after Clemmie. We're having a catch-up with Juliet and Tom. Come and join us!"

"Oh, well, I don't want to be a gatecrasher . . ."

"Don't be silly, mate! We'll enjoy your company. I'll get some free financial advice from you over dinner if that'll help. But first, come to the bar, where me and Tom are solving the world's problems over a beer. The girls are getting Clemmie settled in with Mrs Mac, but they'll be back any minute."

Having flinched at the comment about financial advice, Finn felt even worse about the stupid alias thing, but realized he would have to go with it for now. He followed Byron to the bar and was greeted with a slap on the shoulder by Tom, who immediately ordered him a beer.

*

Juliet and Isabella strolled towards the hotel, having left Clementine dictating to Mrs Mac about which of her favourite bedtime stories must be read and in what order.

"I'm really looking forward to an uninterrupted dinner," Isabella said. "They're about to become even more of a rare thing." She rubbed her rounded belly with a smile.

"Yes, I'm ordering you to sit and completely relax tonight, Izzy."

"I will. I'm planning to not move at all – except for the 15 or so trips to the bathroom," she laughed.

"Only 10, surely!" her sister replied. "Oh, by the way, guess who I got an email from today."

"Well, if you're anything like me, it would be a Middle Eastern Prince saying he wants to give you millions of dollars. Or perhaps a Viagra salesman, or a Russian lady who wants to fall in love with you."

"Oh yes, I get all those people too. But no, this time it was from Ronan."

"Ronan!" Isabella stopped abruptly and looked sideways at her sister. "Is that good?"

"I think so."

"So, tell all. I'm dying to know what the slimy little rat has to say."

"Wouldn't that be a slimy toad, rather than a rat?"

"You writers are so pedantic. Tell me, Jules, before my waters break with suspense."

"Okay, okay . . . Please stay calm! You've still got weeks to go!"

"I know, and that seems like forever, right now," Isabella said wearily. "But I beg of you, please tell me what he said."

"Well, mainly he was asking about some furniture I'd left behind, but then he also happened to mention that his injured leg – which Ruby Roo had 'savaged' – had healed up well. He told me he'd put his plans of reporting her to the council on hold, for now."

"Oooh, what a manipulative creep! He wanted to remind you about it and stress you out some more, while pretending he was being nice!"

"Yep." Juliet looked smug.

"Did you respond?"

"Oh yes, very politely. I told him that Ruby Roo and I were also improving after the extensive bruising and trauma he'd caused us. I said that the statement about the assault I'd provided to Victoria Police was also on hold. For now!" Juliet burst out laughing. "I felt so good sending that email. I could picture him reading it on his iPhone as he sat at his favourite trendy café. I hope he choked on his skinny soy decaf latte when he read it!"

"Me too!" Isabella laughed so hard she had to clutch her belly. "You go, girl! High five!"

The girls continued their stroll to the hotel, still laughing and talking non-stop. Walking across the room to their reserved table, Juliet noticed the extra man standing at the bar, then felt embarrassed about the jolt of attraction that surged through her.

"It looks like we might have another person joining us for dinner," she said, once they'd settled themselves at the table.

"Really? Who?" Isabella's back was to the bar, and she was the wrong shape to be able to twist around with ease.

"My neighbour. He just bought beers for Tom and Byron, and it looks like they're having a good old chat."

"Oooh, that's interesting! We'll be able to get to know him a bit better."

"I guess. But why do we want to? I was hoping to have a good catch-up with you three, actually."

Juliet had been trying so hard to not think about that man, and there he was again, stirring up these restless feelings in her that she didn't know how to banish.

"Hey, stop being such a boring old stick-in-the-mud. I thought you said you liked the guy. He seems nice – and he's easy on the eye, that's for sure."

"I'm telling Byron you said that."

"He won't care. You can look, but you don't touch, that's our rule," Isabella said with a cheeky smile.

"You two lovebirds make me sick! As if either of you seriously look at another person!"

"Yeah, alright. I'll admit it. From the moment I first saw Byron, I've never wanted any other man. He looked into my eyes, and I was gone. It was that simple!"

Juliet smiled at her sister. "You're so lucky. If there's such a thing as soul mates, you two are it, without a doubt. I hope someday I'll find what you have. I just love being around you as a couple. I mean, you're great to be around on your own, Izzy – of course – but there's something about the vibe between you and Byron that is extra special. It creates joy, for everybody, because you two are so good together. Do you know what I mean? Or am I talking rubbish?"

"I know exactly what you mean because I've thought about it too. It's the synergy. What we have together is bigger and better than the two of us as separate beings – a greater force, or something."

"It's love, in perfect harmony."

Isabella nodded. "Doesn't mean I don't bawl him out on occasion. He drives me crazy sometimes. I mean, yesterday, he was supposed to be in charge of Clemmie while I had a nap, and she was sitting about ten feet away from him making goat dung and mud pies. He said he hadn't noticed. How can you not notice your daughter has started making her own range of manure-flavoured delicacies and is *eating* them, for heaven's sake?"

Juliet burst out laughing at the horrified look on her sister's face. "Maybe it's true that men can't multi-task! She didn't munch on too many, surely?"

"Hopefully not, but she was covered in mud and manure. She'd had a lovely time, though, and couldn't see what all the fuss was about. Neither could Byron! He said he was concentrating on fixing the fence, and she was quiet, so he figured everything was fine." Isabella snorted. "He wasn't the one who had to get goat poo out of her tiny little ears!"

"Good effort, Clemmie!" Juliet laughed. "Hey, remember when Mum once went ballistic because you and I had a mud fight with those kids who owned the horses? The Patterson kids, remember?"

"Oh yes, we'd helped them clean out the horse trough, and then we started playing in the mud. It was hilarious! Half of that was probably horse manure. No wonder Mum said we stank when we got home."

"See? It runs in the family!"

They were still laughing about that episode when the three men left the bar and walked to the table.

"We thought we'd come over and join all this hilarity," Tom said.

"I was just hearing all about Clemmie's venture into mud-pie making," Juliet said with a grin on her face.

"Oh no, don't remind me!" Byron pulled a face and shuddered. "I was only allowed out of the doghouse tonight because it's my turn to drive the boat home."

"And because you might have to carry me down to the jetty," Isabella added. "I think it's quite likely I'll be too tired to walk."

"That too. I know . . . I owe you!" Byron grinned. "Now, ladies, as you can see, we've managed to recruit an extra person for our table this evening, so that should improve the quality of conversation no end."

"I hope you don't mind me butting in on your dinner." The extra person, who'd been standing back a little, looked apologetic.

"Of course not!" Isabella gave him a big, genuine smile.

She looked far happier to see Fred than she'd ever been to see Ronan, Juliet realized. She made herself glance at the man in question and noticed he was still looking a bit uneasy. Was he waiting for her approval too?

"It's nice to see you again," she said. "Have a seat."

"Thanks." His eyes met hers, and Juliet felt her cheeks warm.

The men sat down and Sharon their waitress handed out the menus. They knew Sharon well; she often helped out in the pub and had started up a new coffee shop in the main street.

While Byron, Isabella and Tom were busy chatting to Sharon and asking about the new business, Juliet took a few steady breaths and tried to get herself together. The real reason she felt a bit weird about Fred joining them for dinner was because she'd had a particularly erotic dream that morning, just before she got up, and it had been in her thoughts all day. And now, here he was sitting right across the table – the star of the show! It was hard to look him in the eye without turning bright red. She tried to think about mundane things, like whether to order the 'fish of the day' or a steak but kept being distracted by the presence of her neighbour, who looked particularly appealing in his blue linen shirt and faded jeans.

Managing to place an order of some sort, she focused on the group's conversation, which was about running businesses in Mirrabooka and the difficulties of obtaining fresh food supplies. They were laughing about the title of 'Old Grumble Bum' that Mrs Mac had awarded the town's newcomer, and he looked abashed. He admitted he had well and truly deserved that nickname when he first arrived, but he'd stopped expecting the store to have gourmet products and was learning to appreciate simpler fare.

"Mind you," he said, "I've learned that there are some really excellent products available here that I've never found in the city. There's a range of goat's cheese, Daisy-Belle, which I think I'm addicted to—"

The rest of his sentence was drowned out by his companions' delighted laughter.

"What? What did I say?"

"That's us!" Isabella explained. "Byron and I own Daisy-Belle Farm and make the cheese. We sell eggs and vegetables too, but the goat's cheese is our pride and joy. You'll have to come over and have a tour of our place. It's on the other side of the inlet."

"Seriously?" He looked from one to the other.

Byron's face shone with pride. "Yep. Izzy and me do something with our days here, you know, besides making babies and meditating. Man, that's cool! A fussy city slicker likes our cheese!"

"The Belle part of the name is me," Isabella continued. "But I play second fiddle to a goat. Daisy was the founder of our herd and Byron's favourite. We were all very sad when she died of old age."

"Bereft," Byron nodded. "She's buried in our front garden and I planted a daisy bush there. I normally insist on native plants, but I made an exception for Daisy. And let's not talk any more about her passing, or I'll cry. She was such a gentle, forgiving goat—"

"Yes, yes, we know. You've told us once or twice or thirty times," Tom said. Noticing the indignant look on Byron's face, he quickly added, "I'm not being disrespectful of her, you know. She was a fine animal. RIP, Daisy." He raised his beer and they all followed suit.

"Daisy-Belle is truly excellent cheese," the city slicker continued. "I think I'm probably your best customer in this town. I could introduce you to some people who run a chain of gourmet delis, if you want. I reckon they'd love your cheese."

"Maybe next year," Byron replied. "We're only just keeping up with demand at the moment. I've got plans for expansion, and we're working on some new variations and techniques, but that's all going on hold for a while." He leaned over and put his hand gently on Isabella's rounded tummy. "This one's going to be taking lots of our attention soon enough."

"A farm and a dairy must be a lot of work. How do you manage it all?"

"We have help," Byron explained. "There's an old guy called Archie, who's a bit of a hermit, really, who does most of the feeding and milking, and heaps of other things. He loves the farm and the goats, and he lives in a little cottage on our land. He has all the fresh produce he wants, and we pay him a modest salary. He reckons he doesn't need the money, but I keep telling him he's not slave labour, and he has to be paid for his work!"

"He likes a quiet life, Archie does," Isabella said. "He loves to read, go fishing, and work on the farm. That's about it! He reckons Mirrabooka is too busy for his liking. He's being a great help teaching a new boy we've got helping out, as well."

"Who's the boy?" Juliet asked.

"Jayden. He's related to Eddie from the golf club," Byron said. "The parents are no-hopers, and the kid was getting in strife in the city, so Eddie and Bev brought him here to live with them. They didn't know what to do with him, at first. He didn't want to go to school, but the teachers coaxed him into attending a part-time program they run for troubled kids. Then I suggested he come and work on the farm a bit. He's a very quiet kid, so I wasn't sure if he liked the place, at first. But Archie taught him how to milk the goats and gave him some responsibility, and the kid's starting to come out of his shell now."

"Oh, I know who you mean," Juliet said. "Some of the teenagers in town were talking about him the other day. They said he'd been in trouble with the police. Little gossips, they are!"

"I think that's true, but I don't know any details," Byron said. "Some kids have a bad time of it, don't they? They don't have the luck that we all had, of being born into good families. Jayden needs a new start, so I'm putting my faith in him. The goats like him, and they're good judges of character. So far – so good!"

"That's a great thing to do," Tom said, and the others nodded.

"It sure is," Fred agreed. "Now, I don't know anything about goats, so please pardon my ignorance . . . but how do you know whether or not a goat likes somebody?"

"Well," Byron said. "That depends on the goat. They all have different personalities, you see." He launched into an explanation about the various members of the goat herd, which – due to Byron's sense of humour, along with his genuine affection for the animals – made it hugely entertaining. The table of five talked and laughed their way through their meal with ease.

Chapter 12 – The new recruit

Once Juliet was able to relax in her neighbour's presence, the whole evening became a lot of fun. Having an extra person in the group changed the dynamics, but in a good way, as he was so interested in everybody and asked exactly the right questions. Fred could laugh at himself too – when he told them his koala story and described the terrifying pig-lion he'd thought he'd been about to encounter; it had caused so much hilarity that Sharon had come over to listen in as well.

Then Tom told the account of why he'd christened Juliet's boat the *S.S. Minnow*, an outing that had involved it running out of fuel and being marooned on an island, until Tom had come looking for Juliet and ended up towing her boat home with his – once he'd stopped laughing at her, that is. He never tired of telling that tale, Juliet thought with affection, and Isabella and Byron always loved to hear it. Fred seemed to find it entertaining too and had thrown his head back and laughed out loud when Tom teased her again by singing the *Gilligan's Island* theme song.

After dessert, when the five of them had reluctantly called it a night, Juliet went back to Tom's place with him, as she'd left Ruby

Roo there for the evening. Tom offered Fred a lift, but he said he was happy to walk, and Juliet couldn't help but think it was a shame she wasn't going to walk home with him. Still, it was nice to jump in the car with Tom and head around the inlet together, just like they'd done so many times before.

Tom made tea and got out the latest batch of home-made cookies, and the two of them rugged up and sat on the deck with the dogs at their feet. It was a crisp clear night, and the moon and stars were out.

"Look, there's the Southern Cross," Tom said. "Mirrabooka is the Aboriginal word for the Southern Cross, did you know that?"

"How could I not know it, Tom? You first told me that fact when I was six, and you began your astronomy phase. And you've been re-telling me at regular intervals ever since." Juliet smiled into her mug of tea.

"Just checking that you've remembered all the essential things I've taught you."

"Absolutely. I am still well aware that you are the font of incredible wisdom and vast knowledge."

"Correct response. Good girl. Have another cookie." He slid a plate closer to her and reached down to pat the dogs that were sprawled under his chair.

"Oh, please – no more! They're really nice, but I ate far too much at dinner."

"Me too. We were crazy to have dessert as well." He leaned back in his chair and stretched. "That was a good night, I reckon. Heaps of fun. Do you like him?"

"I assume you mean my neighbour," Juliet said with a sigh. "Don't you start, as well. I'm beginning to realize that at least half the town thinks I should fall for him, since I'm now a single woman. Sharon drew me aside when I went to the bar tonight to tell me he's a great catch, and I happen to know that Mrs Mac and all the girls in the store agree. A woman can't be happy on her own for two seconds, right? Don't tell me you're in that club too, Tom."

"You haven't answered my question. Do you like him?"

"Of course. What's not to like? He's good company, nice looking and smart."

"I still don't think you've answered properly." Tom drummed his fingers on the table.

"Well, that's all you're getting! Maybe I could elaborate, but what's the point? He lives in the city, and he has a fiancée there, anyway."

"No, he doesn't."

"He said something to me about a fiancée, I'm sure of it."

"He had one, that's true. Her name's Sophia. But they broke up just before he came here."

Juliet tried to ignore her heart's sudden little dance. "Did he tell you this?"

"He told Byron when he was playing golf, and Byron told me."

"What a pair of gossips you two are! You're worse than the teenagers. And why were you discussing his partnership status, anyway? You hardly know the guy."

"Well, umm . . ."

"Come on, why?"

"We both thought he might be a possibility for you."

"You *are* in that club! Can't I manage on my own? Do women always need a bloke by their side, to help them cope with life? Wow, Tom! You surprise me. I can change a tyre, reverse a trailer and catch a fish as well or *better* than the blokes in this town. I can even change light globes too, all on my little own. It's incredible!"

"Oh, stop ranting, Juliet! You *are* incredibly capable, and you know I know it. You're trying to change the topic, but I'm aware of your cunning plans. I'm not talking about *needing* anyone."

"Well, what are you talking about?"

"You both seem good together. That's all. Like there's a connection. And it's a special one."

"We didn't even talk much tonight. He was chatting to all of us, not just me."

"Exactly. You don't even *have* to talk much. I could see how you looked at each other, and it's obvious you're good together. It's a feeling – a vibe or something. Like you get from Izzy and By. I can't explain it."

"Now you've really flipped, Tom. Have you been dipping into your medical drugs cabinet? Or overdosing on chick flicks since Anne-Marie left? You're talking like a crazy guy. Seriously."

"Well, I'm not the only one. Isabella and Byron are in the crazy club too. Tonight's dinner confirmed what the three of us already suspected. You make a good pair."

"And when did you three decide that?"

"You went to the bathroom, and he went to the bar for more drinks, and we had a very quick discussion. It was unanimous!" Tom grinned. "But hey, no biggie. If you can't see what's right in front of your face, that's fine."

"Oh my gosh! You *are* all crazy." She glared at Tom. "Look – I like the guy, sure, but I hardly know him. And I probably won't ever *get* to know him. He's only here for a little while, and then he'll be doing important things back in the city."

"Okay."

"What does 'okay' mean?"

"It means, 'Pfft, to your mere practical aspects. Love works in mysterious ways'. But I know if I say that, you'll throw something at me."

"You're incorrigible, you really are. I'm not throwing these cookies at you, because they're too good to waste. But count yourself lucky, and lay off the drugs, okay?"

"Yes, ma'am," Tom said and then yawned, reaching his arms up to the sky. "Hey, look at those stars. There's the Saucepan, nice and bright."

They studied the night sky for a while, and then Juliet decided to head for home. Driving back around the shore, she pondered Tom's words about the connection he'd noticed. He didn't normally say such things without a reason. And, if she was totally honest, she had noticed there was something between herself and her neighbour too. Something that didn't make any real sense, but meant he was always popping up in her thoughts, in all sorts of ways. But, as she'd said to Tom, what was the point of thinking along those lines? Their lives were too different.

"It was still a great night, though," she said to Ruby Roo, who was nearly asleep on the back seat, but wagged her tail anyway.

*

"How on earth did Tom talk Fred into playing football?" Juliet was standing at the sports ground a couple of days later with Isabella and Byron, watching the Mirrabooka Mullets warm up before the Saturday afternoon game. The footballers were practising running backwards and then forwards, lifting their knees up high, which made them look like overgrown, hairy and not-very-elegant ballerinas.

"Typical Tom – he used great charm and persuasiveness," Byron said.

Isabella raised an eyebrow at him. "Really?"

"No, actually, he begged. He said – correctly – that last time our team played the Gipps Beach Goannas we were absolutely slaughtered, and he was practically in tears as he described how, without their star forward, the team was really going to struggle."

"The star forward being you, right?" Juliet said.

"Yes. Sadly, I'm not allowed to play at the moment, in case I aggravate my knee injury and put the rest of the season in jeopardy."

"Ahem!" Isabella looked at him through narrowed eyes. "You mean in case you aggravate your knee injury and put your *life* in jeopardy, since your wife will kill you if you're useless around the house when the new baby's here."

"Well, yes, that too. Then Fred said he hadn't played football for years, not since he was at school. And Tom said, 'If you're telling me you used to play football for one of those posh private schools in the city, you're in this team. End of story.' So, look – there he is." Byron grinned.

"Nice legs," Isabella nodded with approval and gave Juliet a nudge, which she chose to ignore.

"He cracked up laughing when he heard the team was called the Mullets," Byron continued. "Reckoned he'd have to grow his hair, until we pointed out we're named after the fish – not the 1970s hairstyle. He told us we should all grow mullets anyway, as a team bonding thing. He's a funny guy when he lets loose."

"Well, go, the mighty Mullets! Hopefully, they'll avoid a complete thrashing this time." Juliet picked her bag up from the ground.

"The game's about to start – don't tell me you're not going to stay and cheer them on!" Byron was appalled.

"I might pop back later, but I promised to take Clementine to the playground, so that's where we're heading, isn't it darling?" she said to her niece.

The little girl was sitting at their feet, busily picking bits of grass and putting them on Ruby Roo's head, then clapping her hands with glee every time the good-natured dog shook them off. She stood up and took Juliet's hand. "Swing?" she said hopefully.

"Of course, the swing. And the slide too, if you like." Clementine jumped up and down with excitement, and Ruby Roo pulled at the leash, eager to be on the move. "Are you coming with us, Izzy, or staying to cheer on the Mullets?"

"Neither. I'm heading to Shazza's. I want to put my feet up and relax." Mirrabooka's newest coffee shop was the one owned by Sharon from the pub – Chez Shazza's.

"Sounds good. Clemmie and I will hang out at the playground for a while, then we'll come and find you."

They walked away as the siren sounded to start the game, and Byron settled down to the serious Australian pastime of barracking for a football team.

*

The Mirrabooka Mullets put up a very respectable show. They lost the game, but only by a couple of goals and, since the Goannas were the strongest team in the league, it wasn't a bad effort. Tom and his new recruit combined beautifully, and their efforts led to several Mirrabooka goals. Tom loved to be in the thick of it, using his strength and agility to get the ball out of a scrum, while Finn had the knack of being able to read what he was going to do with it next, so was nearly always in the right place to field the handball and run. Once he was on the move, none of the opposition could catch him.

Tom wanted their new recruit to stay and celebrate after the game, but he pleaded fatigue, preferring instead to stretch out his tired legs by walking home along the clifftop track, while looking forward to a hot shower. He knew he would have lots of sore muscles the next day from the rough and tumble of the game. He set off for home, enjoying the still-mild weather. It was late afternoon, and the light was clear and mellow as the sun sank low in the sky. Finn was feeling good about the game and enjoying the walk and, when he turned a corner to see Juliet ahead of him, was extra glad he'd chosen to head straight home.

She was at the lookout, with Ruby Roo at her feet, and she turned to glance at him as he approached.

"Hello, Juliet." He walked onto the boards and stood beside her. "And good evening to you, Ruby Roo." He leaned down and stroked the dog's head.

"Hi," Juliet said with a smile. "I'll ask how the football went in a minute. But first – look at that! Have you ever seen anything more beautiful?"

They stood together and gazed at the scene before them. White and grey clouds dotted the sky, and the tops of them were beginning to take on an orange hue from the sun sinking behind the ranges. The water of the inlet was almost completely still, spread out like a sheet of satin and reflecting the shapes and colours of the clouds. Further across, the line of sand dunes shone gold in the evening light and the white foam of breaking waves seemed to shimmer with all sorts of subtle colours. A trio of pelicans soared overhead, majestic wings spread wide as they tilted their wings and prepared to land on the smooth inland waters.

"That," said Finn, "is absolutely superb."

"I was just thinking it looks like an Impressionist painting. I went to the Impressionist gallery in Paris once, and I loved it. Those artists could really capture the essence of nature."

"You've been to the Musée d'Orsay?"

"Yes. I'm not a complete hick, you know. I have travelled."

"I wasn't suggesting that for a moment! It's just that the Musée d'Orsay happens to be my absolute favourite museum. I much prefer it to the Louvre, which I found too overwhelming."

"Same here! In the Louvre, you go around a corner and there's yet another massive, ornate room full of priceless art. There's so much to take in – it's exhausting. I do love Paris though, despite my general aversion to cities. Paris is special."

"Agreed! Did you learn French at school?"

"Yes, but only in the lower forms. I couldn't do it in the senior school here, so, I can't pronounce the names of the museums as beautifully as you do."

"That was one good thing about the big school I went to; you could study anything. Even so, I couldn't stand the place – it was full of boys growing up with a massive sense of entitlement. But we did have a fantastic teacher in our final year who taught French conversation. She was the real deal – a Parisian – and she was smart, gorgeous looking, and didn't take any crap from us boys. If anyone started to misbehave, she'd unleash a tirade in French and then threaten, in English, to complain to the principal and tell him what disrespectful oafs we were. Strong women, those Parisians. She had wavy golden hair, just like you, and that innate style French women have."

"So *not* like me!" she laughed.

"Don't sell yourself short," Finn said, thinking how much more beautiful she was than the French woman.

"How did the footy go?" Juliet asked. "Let's keep walking and you can tell me all about it." They strolled side-by-side through the tea-tree scrub, their feet scrunching on the stony path.

"We lost, but it was a good game."

"Does that mean you didn't get completely walloped?"

"Two goals. A respectable loss, in my book. Gipps Beach are a strong team, but they're not unbeatable by the Mullets."

"That's not bad at all! You must have been a real asset to the team, Fred."

"I think I did okay. Tom was happy."

He had winced once again when she called him Fred. Surely, it was time to drop this stupid secrecy now. He would phone the police officer who'd been advising him and get an update on Monday. He'd had enough of the deception.

"I bet he was!" Juliet smiled. "Tom was thinking you'd be thrashed. Next time could be interesting, especially if Byron is playing, and a couple of the other guys who are either away or injured. Go, the Mullets!" She jumped up and down, punching the air. "The pub will be lively tonight."

Finn laughed at her enthusiasm. "I'm sure it will! I've never been in a place where the same football game is important to everybody. It's nice."

"I guess we're light on for serious issues here, but I like it that way. I'm so glad to be back home again."

"Is your boyfriend coming to visit soon? He must miss you," Finn said, and then immediately wondered why he had asked such a personal question.

Uh oh. I'm starting to think aloud, and that could be dangerous!

"Boyfriend?" She looked at him quizzically. "Oh yes, I told you about Ronan insulting me, didn't I? *Ex*-boyfriend, I should have said. We'd broken up by then, but I think I said 'boyfriend' out of habit."

"I'm sorry," said Finn, who certainly wasn't. That was the sort of lie he didn't mind telling at all. In fact, he was delighted to hear she wasn't with her idiot partner any more. Whether that was for her benefit, or his, he didn't want to examine too closely.

"Don't be sorry. It was well and truly time for that chapter to end. I'm much happier without him."

"Good. Life's too short to be with someone who makes you unhappy."

She nodded and they continued their stroll, not saying much, but it felt relaxed and comfortable with the two of them just walking together, Finn realized.

Around the next corner, they stopped abruptly when the bush in front of them shook and seemed to explode with noise and colour. A flock of lorikeets burst out of it and flew away with loud squawks.

"Oh, look! They're so pretty!" Juliet exclaimed.

Ruby Roo gave a few woofs and bounded after them, then gave up the chase. It was so unfair that those feathery things could fly.

Finn laughed at the dog's dejected state. "What would Roo do if she caught one?"

"Spit it out with surprise, I think. I hope so anyway!"

He realized they were nearly home. "I really enjoyed dinner at the pub the other night," he said. "Thanks for not minding me gatecrashing."

"It was fun. Lots of fun, actually." She met his glance for a moment, and this simple gesture gave him a jolt of longing for something that he couldn't even define.

"Well, here's my turn-off." Juliet looked half over her shoulder at him as she turned to veer along the track to her house, and he saw a flash of blue from her gorgeous eyes. She was wearing a floaty floral top that made her look a bit like a gypsy. A gust of wind made it cling to her curves, and she grabbed at her hair that was beginning to dance around her face.

"Wait! I was wondering . . . Would you like to have dinner again some night? Just with me?" Again, he surprised himself with the words that came out of his mouth.

God, Finn, what are you saying?

She looked at him steadily.

She thinks you've gone mad.

"I'd like that."

She'd like that!

"Oh good. Let's do it then. Maybe at the golf club, for variety. Tomorrow, seven o'clock?"

Is this a date? Have I just asked her out on a date?

"That would be lovely, thank you . . . Oh, stop that, Roo. Be patient!" Ruby Roo was jumping up and down in front of her, giving little snaps at the air. "Well, it's probably time I fed this hyperactive dog. I'll see you tomorrow then, Fred. Well done with the football."

"Thanks. I'm hoping I'll still be able to walk later on. I'm a bit out of shape."

"Doesn't look that way to me." With a grin and another flash of her blue eyes, she turned away and was soon out of sight behind the trees.

"And that," Finn said to himself, "is the very last time anyone around here calls me 'Fred'." He'd just decided to not even bother talking to the police. He'd had enough, and tomorrow he would explain to Juliet, and then everybody else, what his real name was and why he had turned up in their town.

Chapter 13 – A revelation

Juliet shut the cottage door with an emphatic click. She stood still, glued to the spot, as Ruby Roo raced up and down the hallway, trying to make her human realize it was past her dinnertime.

"Whoa! What just happened, Roo? Did he ask me out on a date?"

The dog jumped up and down in front of her.

"And did I say 'yes'?"

Ruby Roo leapt so high she was at eye-level with Juliet for a moment.

"I did say yes. Well, maybe it wasn't a date, as such," she said, ignoring the dog's next bout of attention-seeking antics, which was a series of kangaroo hops around the lounge room. "Maybe it's a 'let's get together as friends' thing."

Ruby Roo leapt onto the sofa, then launched herself off it, snapping her teeth at the air a few times.

"You're going to agree with everything I say, aren't you? Because all you're thinking about is food."

At the word 'food', Ruby pricked up her ears and bolted towards the kitchen, her feet scrabbling on the floorboards.

"Alright then, let's get your dinner. I know, I know . . . it's late and you're hungry."

Juliet fed the dog, then made a salad and cooked some fish for herself, still pondering what the invitation may or not mean, but deciding it should of course be treated as a 'just friends' thing. It was ridiculous to think otherwise. Wasn't it? Still, she couldn't repress the feelings of happy anticipation that bubbled up inside her when she thought about going out, just the two of them, and being able to have a proper conversation across the dinner table.

She slept soundly and woke up early with her head full of ideas for her book. That was more like it – the old enthusiasm for writing was back. Her brain was buzzing with ideas and the characters were talking to each other in her mind – a sure sign that she needed to sit down and let the words flow. She was so keen to get started, she bypassed the early morning surf and got straight to work instead.

After a few productive hours, she stretched and looked with satisfaction at the word count of the file. That was a good session. Getting the first draft down on the page was always the hardest bit, but these scenes had really flowed and been fun to write. They had included a romantic liaison for the heroine, Anastasia, and Juliet had enjoyed picturing the new love interest in her mind. The fact that he was tall, lean and dark-haired was not significant, surely – lots of romantic heroes had those features.

Ruby Roo had been very patient, lying stretched out on the lounge room floor most of the morning with only a couple of forays outside, but Juliet knew she needed a proper walk. First, though, she wanted to finish off the morning's work with a few minutes of research. The storyline in her novel was heading towards a gangland killing, and she knew there had been some real-life events in the city recently. She'd saved a few links to online newspaper articles that she'd been meaning to read for weeks.

Juliet opened up the first few articles, skimming through the information. They were all about the same case – two victims in the same family – and there'd been quite a public backlash after the second murder, as she recalled. She shook her head after reading about the first cold-blooded killing and then focused on the photo of Kovac standing outside the court. What sort of man could do something like that? He was quite young, too, but he'd grown up in a family of gangsters, of course.

Then she blinked, and stared closely at the screen, a strange, constricted feeling grabbing at her chest. Her interest in the accused was quickly forgotten, and she zoomed in on the man beside him in the photograph. Despite the wig and the gown, he looked familiar. Very familiar.

"Ivan Kovac with his barrister, Finn McLaren, on the steps of the Supreme Court," she read aloud.

His name is Finn, and he's been deceiving us all this time!

She felt dizzy for a second, as though the floor had tilted under her. That first day, she'd thought he said his name was Finn, and that he was a lawyer, but when she asked him about it later, he straight out lied! Juliet rubbed her forehead, as the tight, sick feeling from dealing with Ronan's lies – which she thought she'd put behind her – swept back like the incoming tide. Her body was rigid with stress, and her heart seemed to be rattling around in her chest. Was she so stupid that people *knew* she could be easily fooled? And what sort of a man was this nutcase living next door, who enjoyed inventing alter-egos and telling lies to all these nice, naïve people in the country.

And she'd started to like him. *Really* like him. She'd only just got some equilibrium back in her life, and she knew a good deal of that could be attributed to him and his calm, friendly – and undeniably attractive – presence in her life. She'd been looking forward to this evening, to sharing a meal with him; starting to feel brave enough to explore the feelings that seemed to be developing. But, all this time, she was being deceived. Again!

She grabbed her laptop and stormed out of the house, slamming the door behind her, which made Ruby Roo jump with fright and flee to her basket. Reaching the cottage that sat alongside hers, Juliet banged on the front door with her fist.

*

Finn had heard the door slam and looked out his window to see Juliet charging towards his cottage. The flash of pleasure he always felt at the sight of her turned to anxiety when he saw the look of anguish on her face. She pounded on the door and he opened it immediately.

"Juliet! What's wrong?"

She turned the laptop so he could see the screen.

He glanced at it, silently cursing himself for not having spoken up earlier. "I see. Yes, that's me. I can explain all this. Come inside and I'll tell you the whole story."

"If you think . . ." she said with a shaky voice, then paused and took a deep breath. "If you think I will have *anything* more to do with you, you're crazy!" she exploded. "What sort of a man comes up here and calls himself Fred – a really stupid name, by the way – and tells straight-out lies to the people he's starting to get to know, who actually *like* him? Is this some weird game?"

The look on her face was heartbreaking.

"Juliet, please—" He was desperate to explain.

"No! Don't answer that!" She put her hand up, palm facing him. "Because, on second thoughts, I don't want to know. I don't *care* anymore, Fred, or Finn, or whoever-the-hell you are. I've gone through too much grief lately from men who tell lies. That's enough!"

"Look, I understand you're—"

"You understand nothing about me," she said in a low voice. "You don't know me, and I certainly don't know you. I'm sure you can figure out where to stick that dinner invitation. Please, do *not* try to speak to me."

She shut the laptop with a click and turned and stalked away. As he saw her shoulders hunch over, he realized she was starting to cry, and he felt sick with guilt. "Too much grief from men who tell lies . . ." You didn't have to be Einstein to figure out she was referring to the ex-boyfriend. He'd probably cheated on her, the weasel. It was all so recent for Juliet; her wounds had barely had time to heal. And, even if they'd started to get better, he'd just ripped the bandages right off. He hated seeing her look so hurt and bewildered, and knowing he had caused it made him feel tight with stress. He should have been honest with everybody much sooner than this. He needed to try and repair things between himself and Juliet but had no idea how to go about it. Finn went back inside, cursing himself for his stupidity.

*

Juliet had slow tears rolling down her face as she went back through her front door, shutting it quietly this time. Ruby Roo was curled up in her basket, shivering a little, her brown eyes full of anxiety. She was frightened of loud noises. Juliet had found her at a rescue shelter, and it had taken months for the young dog to trust her new owner and not flinch at sudden noises or shrink back every time she picked up a broom or a rake. No one knew what Ruby Roo had suffered before she'd been found, starving and filthy, on the side of a road and been taken to the shelter, but it was clear she'd been mistreated.

Juliet saw the fear on the dog's face.

"Oh, Roo!" Juliet's heart broke for her, and she sank to her knees beside the basket and let the tears flow in earnest. "I scared you. I'm so sorry!" she sobbed, ruffling the dog's fur. "It's okay, you're such a good girl."

The dog's nose nudged tentatively at her owner's arm.

"You're such a beautiful girl. I'm sorry, Ruby Roo. Come on, let's go to my room."

The dog followed her, trotting at her heels, and jumped up onto the bed, where they curled up together.

Juliet put her face close to Ruby's soft fur. "Everything's gone all wrong, Roo. I'm sorry I slammed the door and scared you. You're such a good girl. Do you forgive me?"

Ruby Roo snuggled close to Juliet and licked her hand. There was nothing to be frightened of, after all. Her human was sad and needed comforting, and Ruby Roo was good at that. She crawled closer still, leaning her warmth against her owner, as Juliet cried and cried – not so much about Finn, but about Ronan, and the feelings of inferiority and humiliation he'd engendered in her for so long. Eventually, exhausted, she slept for a while, with the dog not leaving her side.

After she woke up, she rang Isabella, breaking down again as she tried to explain about the torrent of emotions that had swept over her. Isabella was also surprised about the Fred/Finn revelation, but tried to soothe Juliet, saying there was probably a perfectly good reason and she should let him explain.

"I've over-reacted again. That's what you mean, right?"

"Well, yes, although I can see why. But I really do think he's a good guy and there must be a reason for what he's been telling us."

"I suppose you're right. But . . . I can't get past the fact that he lied. Straight to my face! He lied – and I feel a fool. End of story." She didn't mention the dinner invitation or confess to the feelings that had been sneaking up on her.

"You need to calm down, go for a walk, and get a good night's sleep. Everything will be better tomorrow."

"That's exactly what Dad used to say."

"Yes, and he was always right, wasn't he?'

"Yep. He was."

She took her sister's advice and walked with Ruby Roo along the surf beach. As always, the sound and the rhythm of the waves soothed Juliet and allowed her to put the events of the day into some sort of perspective. She tried to breathe calmly and deeply as she watched her dog – happy now – dash to and fro across the sand.

*

Finn heard a second knock on the door late that afternoon, and it also seemed to be an urgent one. Had Juliet sent in the troops to demand an explanation? Well, he'd be delighted to provide one. He walked quickly to the door and swung it open.

"You're a lawyer, so I hear."

Even normally laid-back Byron looked stressed.

"Yes, I am, and my name is Finn McLaren. Look, I'm sorry I haven't been straight with everybody here. It didn't sit well with me, but I was supposed to be—"

"Mate, it's fine. You had your reasons, I'm sure. Tell me later, if you like, but right now I need your help."

Chapter 14 – Finn steps in

"You've got it! I'll do whatever I can."

Finn was relieved that everything seemed fine between him and Byron. "Come into the kitchen and tell me what's going on."

"Righto." Byron pulled off his elastic-sided boots and followed Finn along the hall. "It's this kid Jayden I was talking about the other day."

"Oh yeah," Finn said. "The one who's doing some work for you."

"Yes. Oh! By the way . . ." Byron gave a quick smile as he sat down at the kitchen table. "I never thought for a moment your name was really Fred, you know. It doesn't suit you at all. But hey, we get all types here in Mirrabooka. Finn is much better, although I may have to use 'Freddie' sometimes as a nickname."

"Fair enough," Finn replied. "I can hardly complain about that. And it's better than 'Fishy' at least."

"Fishy? Oh right, Fishy Finn, I suppose."

"Yep. My schoolmates were not blessed with terribly original wit. But, anyway, what's up with Jayden?"

"The boy's in trouble. As you know, he's living with my mate Eddie, from the golf club, and his wife, Bev. They brought Jayden here a few months ago. He's only fifteen, and he's had a rough time of it. Eddie's nephew went off the rails many years ago, got into drugs and shacked up with another junkie, and Jayden was the result. The nephew overdosed some time back, and the boy's mum has had several new partners, all of them users too, by the sound of it. Eddie and Bev are wishing they'd stepped in earlier, but the mum and Jayden had moved to Western Australia for a while and they couldn't track them down. They came back east last year, and that's when Eddie and Bev stepped in. The mother was glad to offload him, apparently. The kid's been badly neglected; it's no wonder he's been a troublemaker. Eddie said he'd never had clean clothes to wear or regular meals put on the table until he came to live with them." Byron shook his head. "Makes me want to cry, hearing about kids growing up like that. He's skipped a lot of school, and he's got learning problems too."

"No surprises there," Finn said. "Keep talking while I make us some coffee."

"Great. I'll have a double shot, thanks. I need caffeine today. So, it turns out the kid's in trouble with the law. Eddie and Bev knew about some of it, but he hadn't let on about the worst bit until this morning."

"What happened then?" Finn operated the coffee machine on autopilot, his mind already in professional mode as he processed and mentally filed all this information.

"Jayden was supposed to be working in one of the veggie gardens on the farm this morning, but then I realized he'd disappeared. I went to look for him, and he was in the barn with the goats, sitting on the straw with two of the babies on his knees. He was crying his heart out like a little boy. I sat down and patted the goats with him and asked him what was going on. He said he reckoned I'd hate him once I heard what he'd done. He was going to be sent to jail, so he was saying goodbye to the goats. Poor little tacker. I mean, he's nearly as tall as me, but he's still a kid."

"Did he tell you what had happened?" Finn put the mugs on the table.

"Yeah. It's pretty bad. When he was still living in the city, he and some other boys, two brothers, stole a car and went joyriding, then decided to light a fire for some fun. They meant to burn down an old shed at the back of a derelict building at the docks, but the fire took off. The whole building went up, and the worst thing was that there were some homeless guys living there. Two of them were burnt in the fire."

"Oh no! Were they killed?"

"No, they managed to get out, thank goodness. They're recovering okay, I believe, but even so . . . Oh yeah, I need to tell you what set Jayden off today. He's been hiding this for months, even though there's a court date set and all that. But this morning he got some text messages from one of the brothers. They're from a well-off family and their dad has hired a top-notch lawyer. This kid was bragging that they'd be let off, because the lawyer was going to put all the blame on Jayden, and he'd be the one to get locked up."

"Like hell, he will." Finn felt a stab of anger over the arrogance money provided. "Nice 'friends', those brothers, eh? Well, I'm glad you came to me, mate. We've got lots of work to do. I need to meet Jayden, Eddie, and Bev, as soon as possible. And I need to talk to his caseworker, if he has one. Drink your coffee and take it easy for a minute, while I make some notes about what you've just told me."

He opened his laptop and began touch typing.

"Whoa! Hang on," Byron said. "Does this mean you'll be able to help him by giving us legal advice? We're happy to pay you—"

"Of course, I'll help!" Finn butted in. "I'm a barrister, so I'll be advising you all *and* representing Jayden in court. I'm reasonably well known, actually, so this other guy might get a shock when he sees me turn up. I'm looking forward to it, I have to say." Finn sat back with a grin and sipped his coffee. "And don't insult me by mentioning money again. I just want a regular supply of Daisy-Belle cheese. Is that okay?"

"No worries, mate." Byron looked at him in amazement. I'll be willing to give you a few of my best goats if you can sort out this mess and help the kid."

"Just the cheese, that'll do fine." Finn turned his attention back to the laptop.

*

Things moved quickly once Finn had talked to Jayden, Eddie and Bev. They had to, since the court case was scheduled for the following week and that meant a long drive to the city. Byron stayed behind with Isabella, while Finn drove the other three in his luxurious car. They stayed in his apartment, where Eddie and Bev marvelled over the expensive furnishings and shiny appliances, and Jayden gazed at his surroundings as though he was in a dream.

In fact, Jayden seemed too traumatised to function much at all, so Finn tried to get him to relax the second night they were there, inviting him to sit on the balcony and share some junk food from the burger joint downstairs. He hoped they might be able to have a quiet talk together, and maybe he'd be able to get Jayden to open up a bit.

"At Mirrabooka, it's dark at night, isn't it? Pitch black – so different to all this." Finn gestured to the vista of sparkling lights below them.

"Yeah." Jayden opened his can of drink.

"You always hear animal sounds there, especially in the dark," Finn continued. "There are creatures rustling around in the trees, and the birds across on the islands – they make weird noises, even during the night. At first, I found it strange and even scary, sometimes, but I'm used to it now."

"Me too."

They sat in silence, except for the munching of their burgers and fries, with Finn concluding this was probably going to be a short conversation. Oh well, at least he'd tried.

"You can hear the surf," the boy said, his voice low and unsteady. "All the time."

"Yes. It's great, isn't it? When it's stormy, I like to lie in bed and listen to the waves crash on the sand."

"Yeah. It gets real loud at Bev and Eddie's place when it's wild outside. Me and Eddie sit out on the veranda, if it's not too cold, so we can hear it better. I like it when the waves make a big 'boom' sound, and then sometimes it's like a loud crack."

"You're right." Finn smiled in the dark. "It is."

"I like listening to the waves. They help me sleep. Before . . . I used to have bad dreams a lot," the boy confessed. "But in Mirrabooka, it's good. I can sleep there."

Once Jayden started to talk, the words gathered momentum until they began to pour out of him. He described how Eddie and Bev were the first people who'd really cared about him, and how Mirrabooka was the only place where he'd ever felt safe. He said he loved the farm, and all the things he was learning, and especially the goats. It was the way he spoke about the animals – his friends, he said they were – that Finn found particularly heart-wrenching.

"Byron said you're doing really well on the farm."

"Yeah!" Jayden turned to look directly at him for the first time and, in the hazy glow from the city lights, Finn could see the look of amazement and delight on his face.

"He was watching me milk old Muriel the other day. She can be a bit cranky, sometimes, but we get on okay. I talk to her and give her lots of pats, but I don't take any crap from her either. Byron said I milked her better than anyone, even Archie, and that I was good with all the other goats too. Me!" He shook his head. "No one's ever said I'm good at stuff, before."

"Well, they say it now. You're learning a lot from Archie, right? What's he like?"

"He's cool. *Way* cool. He doesn't talk much, but I like that. At first, I thought he was just . . . like . . . real old, but then I saw all the stuff he can do. He knows everything about looking after the animals, and he builds fences and fixes the sheds and the truck too. He's teaching me how engines work and all about fishing. I got a big bream the other day. 'Catch of the day,' Archie said. Then he showed me how to clean it and I took the fillets home, and Bev cooked them for dinner. Eddie said it tasted better than any fish you could ever buy."

The boy smiled again, but then his face fell. "I don't want to leave there. What if they lock me up? I know you said it wouldn't be jail, but there's that juvenile place . . . I want to go back to Mirrabooka. I miss the farm and the goats and everybody." His eyes glistened with unshed tears.

"I want you back at Mirrabooka too, okay? Tomorrow in court, I'll be doing everything I can to help. You just tell the truth, like we've talked about. I know you feel sorry about the men being hurt, and you never meant any of that to happen, and I'll help you tell that to the judge. Eddie will be talking too, and your caseworker, and they'll say how you've settled in really well at Mirrabooka, and you're working and going to school part-time now. Byron and your teachers have made statements about how well you're doing. I'm hoping all four of us will be driving home together on Thursday."

*

As it turned out, only two of them drove home that day.

Eddie and Bev had decided to stay in the city for a long weekend and Finn insisted they use his apartment. They wanted to have a little holiday and see some of the city's attractions – and enjoy the enormous relief they'd felt after hearing the court's decision.

It had been a most satisfying day. The brothers' lawyer had turned wide-eyed with shock when he spotted Finn. He'd quickly whispered something to the boys' parents, who'd suddenly looked agitated as well, no doubt realizing their plans of putting the blame on Jayden were about to unravel.

Jayden received a good behaviour bond, without conviction, for his part in the events. The other two boys were also put on bonds, with one of them being convicted of theft and criminal damage and given a hefty fine. The older brother had admitted, thanks to Finn being able to coax information out of him, that it had been his idea to steal the car and light the fire. He'd even confirmed that Jayden had wanted to go home, but the other two had goaded him into staying. It had been Jayden who'd helped the homeless men out of the building and called an ambulance.

Even so, the boy had been involved in criminal activities, including car theft and arson.

On the long drive home to Mirrabooka, Finn impressed on his young companion the seriousness of what he'd done, the harm and the stress he'd caused other people, and how it could have ended up so much worse for the men who'd been in the building. The result could also have been quite different for Jayden, had the judge been less willing to give him a chance.

"Everybody has put their faith in you to do the right thing now. The judge, Eddie and Bev, Byron and Isabella and Archie – and me too. Don't let us down, Jayden."

"I won't. I promise."

"Good. Because if I find out you're causing grief to any of these people who care about you, you'll have me to deal with. Me and a tribe of angry goannas, or stingrays, or whatever else I can find in Mirrabooka to help me get you back into line."

"Maybe you could throw me in with the giant jellyfish," the boy grinned. "The cove near the farm jetty was full of 'em the other day. They were enormous! I can't wait to get back and see if they're still there."

"Okay, hordes of monster jellyfish too. Good idea! And hey, you know I don't mind joking around a bit, but you made a promise, right? And that's a serious thing."

"I know, Finn. Don't worry. I won't let you down. I want to fix everything now. I'm good at stuff on the farm, and Archie reckons he's got heaps more for me to learn. I want him and Byron and everyone to be proud of me. And the goats too!" he said with a grin.

Finn let the topic rest then, and Jayden plugged in his earphones to listen to his own music as the miles whizzed by under the wheels of the sleek sportscar.

That was when Finn let his thoughts return to Juliet. Of course, he hadn't forgotten about her, even when he'd needed to focus on Jayden and the court proceedings, but he hadn't been able to decide what he should do. In the short time after their confrontation and before he'd left for the city, he hadn't seen her around town, and he'd respected the "don't speak to me" order. He felt confused about how he seemed to really care about her, all of a sudden, and he hated knowing he'd upset her.

He'd confided in Byron, who advised he should let things settle down for a while.

"Juliet has been through heaps of stuff lately, mate," Byron had said. "That creep Ronan has a lot to answer for; it turns out she had an awful time with him. It's not up to me to tell you any details; Juliet will do that one day, if she wants to. But she's still pretty strung out. Just let her think things through."

"Sure, but I want to explain, and apologize again," Finn muttered.

"That's a bit hard to do, Freddie-boy, if the door's slammed in your face," Byron had said, with a sympathetic grin.

Now that Finn was going back to Mirrabooka, somehow, he'd be able to explain what had led to him telling variations on the truth. He couldn't come up with any concrete plans as to how this might happen, so he had to let it go for the time being and concentrate on the long drive. He had a teenage boy sitting next to him who had also been through a lot, and he needed to be safely delivered into Byron and Isabella's care for a few days while Bev and Eddie had their city break. Byron had been ringing Jayden every day and giving him updates about what was happening on the farm, which meant the world to the boy, Finn knew.

He glanced at his passenger and saw he'd fallen asleep, his head resting on a scrunched-up jacket against the window. He was a nice kid. As Byron had pointed out, it was luck that determined what sort of family you were born into. Well, thanks to Eddie and Bev, Jayden was getting a second chance. The couple hadn't had children of their own, but they were doing a great job with this teenage boy who'd practically been a stranger to them. They'd already grown to love him, Finn knew. He'd seen the look of utter relief and joy on Bev's face when the judge announced his verdict, and how Eddie had been too overcome to speak.

Jayden had looked stunned at that moment too, as though he didn't know whether to believe what he'd heard, until Finn put his arm around his shoulders and said, "It's all good, mate. You're going home. Home to Mirrabooka."

The boy had broken down then and put his face in his hands. Finn held him tight for the few seconds it took for Bev to reach him. She'd grabbed him in a big hug and looked over his shoulder to Finn, tears streaming down her face.

"Thank you," was all she'd said at that moment, but it was all that was needed. It reminded Finn of why he'd chosen to study law in the first place – to help people. Winning this modest victory for a teenage boy meant far more to him than all of the high-profile cases he'd worked on.

Driving along the winding roads of the national parks, through mile after mile of tall eucalypts and majestic tree ferns, he allowed himself to enjoy his surroundings and look forward to getting back to Mirrabooka. The funny thing was that returning to his city apartment had meant nothing to him but, now that he was heading back to the little rented cottage in the bush, it felt like going home.

Finn smiled to himself. If Byron was there, he'd be laughing and saying, "See? It's the Mirrabooka magic!"

Finn flexed and stretched his shoulders and drummed his fingertips on the wheel, humming along to Vivaldi's Four Seasons, one of his favourite classical CDs. Apart from the situation with Juliet, everything was perfect. He was happy to be returning to the country town and enormously relieved at the outcome of the case. Surely, he'd be able to work things out with her somehow. He just had to be patient and let things develop naturally.

Chapter 15 – Crazy cormorants

Juliet set off for a walk around the inlet track, hoping that the wide expanse of calm inland waters would help soothe her jangled feelings. She'd left Ruby Roo at home for once, as she'd already had plenty of exercise that day, and she'd be bound to jump into the water and end up soaking wet. It felt strange, though, to be walking the track without Roo's red tail waving like a furry flag ahead of her.

Being late on a cold afternoon, Juliet figured she'd have the track to herself. Sensible folk would surely be tucked up in their homes already, lighting their wood fires and settling in for the evening. She hoped so, anyway. She didn't want to encounter other people and have to stop for polite chats – especially other people called Finn.

She knew from Isabella that he'd come back from the city a couple of days earlier, and she was doing her best to avoid him, with great success so far. The last thing she wanted was to be reminded of how she'd been so attracted to him and then had been sharply disillusioned. It was yet *another* learning experience, she thought with annoyance, as she marched along the track. After everything she had resolved, she'd dropped her guard completely and developed feelings for a man from the city she knew hardly anything about – and the bits she *did* know had turned out to be lies.

It took a long distance for Juliet to work off the worst of her irritation and gloom. She walked all the way to where the walking track ended, and the thick forest of the national park began, and then turned and retraced her steps. As the sun dropped behind the inland hills and the clouds turned delicate shades of pink and orange, the pastel colours were reflected across the water, giving the whole inlet a rosy hue. As always, the beauty of her surroundings charmed her, pushing negative thoughts out of her mind and forcing her to feel grateful for living in such a peaceful and beautiful part of the world.

I am so lucky, I know. I really have to stop with all this self-indulgent stuff.

As she reached a stretch of boardwalk that crossed the entrance to a lagoon, Juliet heard a plaintive cheeping sound. A baby cormorant, all on its own, was paddling in a wide arc a few feet out from shore, and she stopped and looked at it. She loved baby cormorants. They were so cute, especially when they practised their underwater swimming skills in a group and would take turns to disappear under water and then pop up again. She'd only ever seen them in flocks though; never one on its own like this. It would be dark soon – not a good time for a tiny bird to be alone. She frowned and cast her eyes around, looking for other cormorants. The water was looking dark and mysterious now as the colours ebbed away, and all the other creatures seemed to have retired for the night. Then she half-remembered noticing movement in the water back near the fishing jetty, so she took another anxious look at the baby bird and jogged back the other way. There they were! On the far side of the jetty, out of sight of the loner, was a family of two adult cormorants and half a dozen babies paddling together, parallel with the shoreline. A couple of others flew overhead, making a direct line for the island across the channel. Watching the direction of the little family, which was starting to divert from the shoreline and head into deeper water, Juliet realized they were probably going there too. Since the babies couldn't yet fly, it looked like the family was going to paddle across to get to the relative safety of an island free of foxes or feral cats.

Juliet had a sudden feeling of panic. If they kept going in that purposeful way, the lost one would never see where they went, and it would never catch up. She swung around again. The straggler was still going in the wrong direction. Stupid bird! She couldn't bear to think of the baby being left all alone, at the mercy of whatever predator fancied a seabird entrée for supper. There was only one thing for it. She would have to try and herd the family group back around towards shore and delay their departure long enough that the lost one would notice them, or they would notice it. She glanced down at her shoes. Well, they were about to be ruined, but it was for a good cause. There was no way she was going into the water barefoot –there would be all sorts of sharp and revoltingly squishy things underfoot.

She raced further along the walking path then diverted onto a swampy headland, passing the cormorant family, who were luckily still close to shore. With a last look of regret at her favourite trainers, she waded into the water until she was about thigh deep, trying to ignore the shock of cold water on her legs and concentrate on keeping her footing in the mixture of sand, weed and silty mud she could feel oozing into her shoes.

"Stop, birdies! Whoa!" She got in front of them and clapped her hands, making the little ones cheep in fright and the two parents take off with a flurry of indignant flaps, abandoning their offspring.

"Right, you kids go back into shore, that's the way." She gently herded them in the right direction. "Your parents will come back in a minute. I can see they haven't gone far. They're hardly going to win any parenting awards, though, are they? I mean, they've lost one of your siblings! Didn't anybody wonder where little Clancy Cormorant had gone? You're all useless," she lectured.

*

Finn, who'd skipped his morning run because of a day full of Skype meetings, had decided he needed to stretch his legs before it got dark. Jogging around the corner near the fishing jetty, he was more than a bit surprised to see Juliet thigh-deep in water and apparently talking to birds.

Still painfully aware of how upset she'd been at their last meeting, he wondered if he should head back the other way and leave her alone, since she hadn't seen him yet. But she probably wasn't wallowing around in that cold water for fun. What on earth was she doing? He lurked behind a couple of trees and watched as she waded ashore then ran along the track. She set a good pace, despite the wet jeans clinging to her shapely legs, he couldn't help but notice. Near the boardwalk, she went back into the water – and then Finn noticed the small lone bird that seemed to be the object of her attention.

Now he was completely intrigued. He walked briskly towards her and could hear her talking to this bird too.

"Come on, Clancy. You really are a dimwit, aren't you? Your family is over there, stupid. Look! Go that way!" She gave a few gentle claps and waved her arms in the air, but then stopped abruptly, gazing into the distance. "Oh no!" She clenched her fists. "They're going to leave you behind, poor baby!"

Finn could see that the first lot of birds seemed to be heading out across the channel. "Umm, can I help?" he asked.

Still intently focused on the birds, Juliet jumped with fright, lost her footing, and fell forward into the water with a big splash. "Ahh! Dammit, that's cold!"

Finn was horrified he'd caused her to fall. *You idiot!* he chastised himself, as Juliet wallowed around in the water.

Way to fix things up. Not!

She clambered to her feet.

"I'm so sorry I gave you a fright!" he said.

"Oh, it's you." She stood dripping in knee-deep water, flicking mud off her hands.

"Are you okay?"

"I'm terrific. Just a bit damp, as you can see."

And still beautiful, even when freezing cold, soaking wet, and splattered with mud.

"I'm sorry—" he repeated.

"Don't be," she cut him off. "My fault for being a klutz." She turned away and looked across the water again.

That's a cold shoulder, literally.

Then she turned back. "Oh, that's good!" All of a sudden, the hostility was gone from her voice and her face had brightened. "My big splash gave that lost bird a hurry-up. He's heading in the right direction, at last!"

"He belongs with those other birds over there, right?"

"Yes, I'm sure that's his cormorant family, but his stupid parents are heading off to the island without him. I'm worried he'll be abandoned, poor thing."

"What can I do to help?"

"Nothing. You'd have to get wet, and your expensive Nikes would be ruined, so don't bother."

"That's easy fixed." He started to take off his shoes. He would have stripped off everything to help her, if necessary, but figured that would probably be counterproductive right now.

"Don't do that, you'll cut your feet to bits – it's all sharp bits of shell and mud from the lagoon around here," she said, with her hands on her hips. "But maybe you could keep an eye on this one for me," she relented. "I'll try to head the others off again. Surely, they'll spot each other soon."

She waded ashore and squelched past him, racing back to the dysfunctional parents and their offspring and walking back into the water. She went in even deeper this time and was able to turn them back to shore with the water lapping at her waist.

Sick of watching Juliet do all the work, Finn began to wade in too. His trainers could be sacrificed. God, that water really was freezing!

"Go on, birdie," he said. "Paddle your little heart out, would you? It's freaking cold in here."

He flapped his arms gently and the tiny bird headed towards Juliet and the family group. "Shoo, shoo, little fella, that's the way. Good job! Keep it going . . ." Working as a team, they should be able to do this, he realized. Juliet was still managing to keep the flock of chicks away from the deeper water.

The parent birds had flown a short distance away and were perched on a jetty. Then one of them gave a squawk and flew right over its missing offspring, landing on the water only a few yards away.

"I think they've seen it!" he called out.

"At last! I'll come in and we'll see what happens," Juliet replied. She waded slowly out of the water and he did the same, meeting her in the middle of the boardwalk.

"Let's just be quiet and watch what they do," she said in a low voice. "Well done, by the way."

His heart gave a little jump. "Thanks. I often round up waterbirds, you know. It's one of my favourite hobbies."

Thank you, crazy cormorants, you've given me another chance.

Juliet's eyes were focused on the lone baby. She and Finn stood completely still, and finally the parent bird paddled straight to it, while the other flew across to the siblings and started to turn them back around.

"Look at that! Hooray!" she whispered, and they stood together, shivering in the gloom for the few minutes it took for the group to be reunited and set out once more for the island.

"We did it! High five!" She turned to him, a big smile across her face, and they slapped hands, jubilant.

"I'm so glad – poor little guy. And I'm even more glad we don't have to go back in that water. Where's your car?" Finn asked.

"Back at the main wharf. Looks like I'm in for a soggy walk."

"No, you're not. Mine's just over here. Come on, I'll drive you back." He was already striding towards the BMW parked near the fishing jetty.

*

Juliet hesitated. She'd been dodging Finn for days. Did she want to get into the car with him? On the other hand, a twenty-minute walk in wet clothes was not an attractive proposition. Besides, a lot of her hurt and anger had evaporated when she'd seen him wade into the lake. How could you stay angry at a man who would volunteer to get soaking wet in very cold water, ruin his shoes and look ridiculous, all to help a baby bird?

"I'll get your seat all wet," she called out to him.

"Doesn't matter. Come on – my car has a really good heater," he replied over his shoulder.

The thought of getting warm was way too enticing, so she followed to where he was waiting, holding the car door open for her.

She looked at the plush interior and leather seats. "Are you sure? Do you have a towel?"

"Yes and no. Don't worry about it." He strode around the car and got into the driver's seat. "And please stop being so nice to me. I'm not quite sure how to take it after our last conversation," he said, exasperated.

"Ah, yes. Look, Finn, about that . . ." she began, as she climbed into the car, knowing in her heart that she'd been unfair to him – again.

He had already started the engine, but he let it idle and switched the heating on as he turned to face her.

"Wait. Can I say something first? I really need to explain, and I'm worried that if I don't say it now the moment will pass, and everything will go wrong again."

She nodded, clasping her cold hands in her lap.

"I'm sorry, Juliet. I did lie to you, and I hated doing it. I feel like a fool now. I should have known it was a ridiculous idea to try to keep up a pretence with someone who . . . someone that . . . Well, with you," he said.

Juliet sat in silence. Was he on the verge of saying something more personal? And did she want him to? God, this was all so confusing.

"Can I interrupt at this point?"

"I still need to explain."

"Okay, but can you turn the heater up more? I'm starting to feel warmth and it's divine!"

"Of course," he grinned, turning both the temperature and the fan up higher. "Okay, I'll be quick, because you must be freezing. Basically, I'd handled a case involving a gangland murder. The one you read about, right?"

She nodded, rubbing her numb hands under the blast of hot air.

"I started getting death threats, and word on the street was that the Zanetti family had hired a hit man. They blamed me for keeping their son's killer out of prison, and then he murdered their other son. The police told me to lay low for a while, preferably a long way from town and using a different name. So here I am. I made up an alias and I feel like an idiot. I've given up the charade now – it was ridiculous. I'm sorry, Juliet. Please believe me."

"That's pretty full-on." She could feel some sensation returning to her fingers and warmed them some more. "Are you worried about the threats?"

"Not anymore. I was at first, mainly because Gail, our receptionist, was really upset. She was the one dealing with the emails and phone calls, and she was reading and hearing some very nasty things. I thought it would be better all-round if I wasn't there, and the firm encouraged me to take leave and do consulting work off-site. The other reason I decided to get away was because I'm doing a lot of soul-searching about the job. I won't bore you with the details, except to say I was happy to have a break and reassess things. All that part was good – it's just the deception that wasn't. I *am* an honest person. But that's what all the crooks and liars say, as I know from professional experience." He gave a wry smile.

"That's quite a story."

"Yes, but I'll be glad to put it behind me. Please accept my apology. I feel terrible that I lied to you."

Juliet had a panicky feeling that she might cry if she looked for much longer at his earnest, troubled face.

"Okay," she muttered, pretending she was looking out the window.

"Thank you." He gave a sigh and relaxed back into his seat. "And now, it's time to head for home." He put the car in gear and drove slowly back around the inlet.

Juliet felt strange being driven around Mirrabooka in such an expensive car. It was a stark reminder of their differences. She'd been out of her mind to think there could be anything between them, but she was glad to have heard his explanation and for her hurt feelings to be ebbing away. She really liked this man, above and beyond the physical attraction she felt for him. She knew what he'd done for Jayden, too, as the town was abuzz with the news, and she couldn't help but be impressed – and grateful.

In a few minutes, they were back at the main wharf, and Finn pulled his car up beside hers. "Did your car keys get wet?"

She pulled them out of her pocket. "Hmm, yes, they are a bit damp."

"I'll wait to see if the remote's still working, and whether your car starts okay."

"Thanks, but first . . . Finn, now I need to apologize. I went completely over the top the other day – again. I should have realized you would have a reason for the things you told us, and you do. I just . . . well . . . I was deceived by someone else recently, and I'm still getting over that. And when I realized you'd lied too – I felt sick and hurt all over again. It wasn't your fault, and I can see now I was completely irrational. I'm sorry."

Realizing that she was again close to tears, Juliet jumped out of the passenger seat and fled to her own car. "Thanks for the lift!" she called out over her shoulder, as the remote control bleeped into life, and she climbed into the driver's seat, thankful that her car started straight away.

"Juliet! Wait a second . . ." Finn said.

"See you round. Thanks again." She gave him a wave, then slammed the door shut and drove out of the carpark, her heart thudding in her chest and tears cascading down her cheeks.

Juliet, you really are a basket-case, she lectured herself. *Thank goodness you were able to escape before you embarrassed yourself completely. Now get home, have a nice hot shower and try to act like a grown-up!*

*

Finn watched the vehicle's tail-lights recede into the distance. He wished he'd had an excuse to drive her home, so they could have talked some more. She was definitely the most exasperating, appealing, unpredictable, and beautiful woman he'd ever met. He was totally confused about how things stood between them now. She'd accepted his apology, and seemed more relaxed, and then had started to explain why she'd become so upset the other day – but then, all of a sudden, she just bolted. What did that mean? Did she like him or hate him?

Finn gave a heavy sigh. If he ever got to understand the ways of women, he really would write a book, and that would surely be a best-seller.

Oh well, it was time to get back to the house and warm up a bit. Smiling to himself as he remembered how he'd jogged around the corner to find her standing in the water and lecturing a flock of birds, he slowly headed for home.

*

Any hopes Finn had of things being improved between himself and Juliet were soon dashed. In contrast to only a couple of weeks earlier, he hardly ever saw her, and he became convinced she was avoiding him.

When he finally spotted her on the main street one day, heading into the store, he decided he too was in urgent need of groceries and followed her inside. She was standing in the tinned vegetables aisle, reaching for canned tomatoes and putting them into the basket she was carrying. Excellent. He'd stocked up on that very item the day before, but she wasn't to know.

She glanced at him walking towards her. "Hi, Finn." She gave him a nod and a tight smile.

"Hello." He reached for a can of tomatoes. "Looks like you're making a casserole too. It's certainly the weather for it. Pasta bake?"

"Sorry?" She looked up from studying her shopping list.

"I was wondering if you're cooking a pasta bake. That's what I'm making. With tomatoes in it." He found himself waving a can of tomatoes in front of her face, as though she might not know what it was.

"Oh. I'm not sure. Possibly a stew." She walked away from him briskly.

Well, that was awkward. He'd been hoping he might have the chance to reissue the dinner invitation but, from her curt response, that idea was off the cards.

"More tinned tomatoes?" Mrs Mac walked towards him. "You gone through all yesterday's ones already?" He flinched at her loud voice.

"No. I forgot about those." He put the can back on the shelf. "Just a brain snap," he sighed.

Mrs Mac looked from him to the retreating figure of Juliet. "Don't worry. This too shall pass," she said. "Now, can I interest you in some hot roast pork? We just took some out of the oven."

"With crackling?"

"Of course. I'll give you extra. Might cheer you up."

"Sold. Thanks, Mrs Mac." At least somebody was on his side, Finn mused, as he followed her to the counter.

Chapter 16 – Isolation

Finn walked along the main street of Mirrabooka on a Saturday night. This was what he couldn't get used to. It was seven o'clock in the evening and the place was almost deserted. Sure, there were a few cars at the pub and a couple more outside the takeaway food place, but where were all the people? In the city, he and Sophia were always out and about at restaurants, galleries, wine bars, or the theatre, and the city streets were vibrant and busy at all times of the day or night. Here, you could just about watch the tumbleweeds roll along the street as soon as the sun went down.

Apparently, the town got very busy over summer. He'd been told how, when the schools closed for the long end-of-year holiday at Christmastime, the place was transformed as thousands of tourists swarmed into the area, pitched their tents, and parked their caravans in the enormous waterfront camping reserve. They filled up the holiday houses and units in town and tied up their expensive boats at all the moorings and jetties. The bakery and cafés were so busy they often had lines of people extending out their shop doors.

Finn thought it would be a much better time to be in Mirrabooka, but the locals he chatted to said that, although they were grateful for the tourist trade, they couldn't wait for the holidays to end so the town could return to its natural, peaceful state. He couldn't understand that. After the hustle and bustle of the city, the empty main street seemed lonely and forlorn to him.

He ordered grilled fish and chips from the takeaway and opted to take a stroll outside for the ten-minute wait, since he was feeling too restless to sit still. He walked past the main bar of the hotel and looked through the big front windows, mainly to be reassured that there were, in fact, other people around. Half a dozen men and a couple of women were clustered around some tables, with a few hardy souls sitting out in the beer garden smoking cigarettes. They all seemed to be enjoying themselves. Was this enough for some people? A chat with friends at the hotel and maybe a meal, then back home? No theatre, no galleries, and no choice of whatever international cuisine you wanted to try, unless it happened to be Indian.

Finn stopped at the end of the street, where he could see right across the inlet to the ranges. The evening was still and calm, like the whole world was sleeping. A big, round moon hovered above a bank of clouds, its silvery path shimmering on the water. The moon looked so clear, and so close, it seemed to Finn that he could just about reach out and touch it. He could hear the mutter of the surf in the distance but, other than that, and the occasional shouts of laughter from the group in the beer garden, everything was quiet. He stared at the moon again. In the city, he'd never noticed what an incredible sight was. There, that was an advantage of living here – the moon and the bright stars and the lack of traffic and noise. If only it wasn't so damn lonely.

He headed back towards the shops, knowing his order would soon be ready, and watched a couple walk out of the pub and across the road to their SUV. They probably hadn't noticed him walking in the shadows, so he felt almost voyeuristic when he realized they'd stopped to embrace before they got in the car. He waited in the darkness under a tree, not wanting to disturb them.

"Come on, lover boy, let's get home and get comfy," the woman said when they drew apart.

"Sounds good, darl. I'll get the fire going if you pour the wine. Tough life, hey?"

"Sure is!" The woman reached up to kiss her partner once more.

Soon the couple were on their way, heading for their house and their open fire, ready to share a bottle of wine and – no doubt – the delights of each other.

Finn watched the vehicle glide away. There! That was the answer to living in this town. If you were in a good relationship, maybe – just maybe – this would be a nice place to live. A loving relationship could make anywhere a whole lot more bearable, he thought with a pang, realizing that there was nothing like that in sight for him.

Juliet was still avoiding his company. He'd only encountered her around town a couple of times recently and, while she'd been polite, she clearly hadn't wanted to chat. She had made an excuse and fled whenever he'd tried to make conversation.

A feeling of isolation swept across him. He was completely and utterly alone. It was funny that, until he'd met Juliet, he hadn't minded. Once he'd got over the shock of his relationship with Sophia ending, he'd been happy to be independent and enjoy the freedom that entailed. But, all of a sudden, things were different, and he couldn't get thoughts of Juliet out of his head. Oh well, he thought with a shrug, he'd better stop feeling sorry for himself and head back to the takeaway, or he'd be having a cold fish dinner to add to his woes.

*

Finn tried to keep busy over the next few weeks by focusing on the shipwreck research, which he was becoming more and more absorbed in. He also ramped up his exercise routines, enjoying his improved fitness. Tom had seen him setting a good pace with his daily runs and had coerced him into joining the town's ironman team. Now they ran together regularly and also met early a few mornings a week for swimming training in the quiet waters of the inlet. Tom had been delighted to find Finn was also a strong and fast swimmer – a real asset to the team.

The two men were becoming good friends. They fell into a routine of going back to Tom's place for breakfast after swimming training if Tom had a later shift at work. It was now well and truly into winter, and often cold and rainy for the morning sessions, so they always looked forward to getting back inside, where Tom would cook bacon and eggs for them to eat in front of the fire.

One morning, Finn confided in Tom about the issues he was having with his job. He described how satisfying it had been to help Jayden, compared to the organised crime gangs and other hardened criminals he'd been dealing with in the city.

"Have you ever thought about working in legal aid?" Tom asked. They were sitting in front of a roaring fire, with their feet resting on the brick surrounds of the fireplace, and the two dogs stretched out on the floor beside them. "There's a job going in the Gipps Beach centre, a bit further up the coast."

"I have thought of legal aid, quite seriously," Finn replied. "So seriously that my ex-fiancée told me I was turning into a boring do-gooder – but only because I was too scared to handle the big time."

"Wow! I'm forming an opinion that the two of you may have differed on some fundamental and rather important values."

"Gold star to you, Tommo," Finn nodded. "I guess it's not until you face challenges together that you get to learn the real substance of a person," he mused. "Sophia can be great company, but that's when things are going her way and she can tick them off her wish list. Being involved with a successful barrister was on the list – but a legal aid lawyer most certainly was not."

"Legal aid lawyers aren't paid that well, comparatively speaking, are they?"

"Nope. And nor should they be. Legal aid organisations should use their funds for the benefit of the clients as much as possible, not the lawyers. I don't have a problem with that. Sophia did, though. She wasn't going to stick around if I went in that direction."

"She dumped you over a potential career change?"

"I'm sure she would have, but I saved her the trouble. I'd realized by then we had 'irreconcilable differences', as they say. As soon as she'd started sneering about legal aid workers – and particularly their clients – she'd rung the death knell on the relationship as far as I was concerned. She tried to do a lot of back-peddling the next day, but it was too late."

"You're well shot of that one, mate." Tom threw a couple more logs on the fire, making sparks leap into the air.

"You can say that again," Finn said, and thought of Juliet, as he seemed to be doing a thousand times each day. Now *there* was a woman who would be compassionate and understanding, he was sure of it. She wouldn't look down on legal aid jobs or the people who needed help. He sighed. He'd given up on his resolve to not think about women for a while, being forced to accept that Juliet had a hold over him he could not ignore. What a pity he'd managed to ruin whatever had been starting to develop between them. He wasn't sure about most of the things in his life at that time – like where he wanted to live, or what sort of job he wanted to do – the only certainty was that he was desperate to spend more time with the woman he couldn't get out of his mind.

"So, tell me what you know about this job in Gipps Beach," he said to Tom.

*

Juliet was managing to stick to her plan to avoid Finn as much as possible and to keep any interactions to a minimum whenever she did see him around town, but it wasn't making her any happier. She woke up every morning feeling sluggish and gloomy and kept making excuses to skip going for a surf when the day was new and bright. She was still walking every morning – she had to, for Ruby's sake – but she felt she was operating on autopilot, and nothing was bringing her joy. The last time she'd felt light-hearted and enthused about life had been the morning she'd woken up full of ideas about her new book – the day she'd thought she was going to have dinner with 'Fred'.

She'd stopped feeling hurt and angry with him and understood now why he'd fudged the truth, but the episode had made her slam the brakes on any thoughts of spending more time with him. What was the point? It would only end in tears. See? It already had. It was much better to be practical about it. Sensible and rational – that was the way to go. But . . . why did she feel so terrible?

Juliet pondered that question one morning as she took off in her little boat, deciding to go for a ride around the inlet and get some fresh air and true solitude. There was no chance she would encounter Finn when she was in the middle of the lake so, even though there was a bank of grey clouds gathering strength over the ranges and a cold breeze stirring up whitecaps, she dropped Ruby Roo off at Tom's place for doggie playtime, untied the *Minnow* from the jetty and took off, enjoying the blast of cold air on her cheeks. While she rode around in the boat, enjoying the isolation, she was able to examine the reasons why she was feeling so low.

Firstly, she didn't like the way she was behaving towards Finn. She was being rude when she brushed off his attempts at conversation, and she could see he was hurt by it. Although he was unfailingly polite and tried to seem nonchalant, she would always notice a look of disappointment rest fleetingly on his face before she turned and walked away. She was being abrupt and hurtful, and those things weren't in her nature at all.

Secondly, truth be known, she wanted to talk to him. *Really* wanted to talk to him, for no other reason than she liked being with him. She liked his voice, his smile, the things he said, the way he looked – but what was the point of spending time with him and growing to care about him even more? It would just be even worse when he left.

Oh, it's all impossible!

After going around and around the topic in her head umpteen times, and finding no solution, Juliet decided it was pointless dwelling on it anymore, so she turned the boat around and headed for home.

When the breeze suddenly swirled into a roaring gale and rain was swept almost horizontally into her face, Juliet realized it would have been prudent to check the forecast before she'd set out. The weather had turned nasty, very nasty, and going for a joyride wasn't the best idea she'd ever had. She turned the collar of her jacket up, preparing for rough water in the middle of the channel, and the first wave that slapped across the bow of the dinghy and splashed into her face made the rain feel warm by comparison. Oh well, she'd been out in rough water plenty of times before, and she had her mobile phone in her pocket. If it got too dangerous, she could pull into one of the inlet's sheltered coves for a while and ring Tom to let him know where she was.

*

Finn stood on the main wharf, staring out across the water. He'd been shopping in town when rain started pelting down; drumming on the roof of the supermarket and forming instant rivulets across the footpaths and carpark. When it eased off, he'd decided to drive down to the water's edge and look across the water before he went home. The day had changed quickly, becoming dark and volatile, with black clouds sweeping across from the south and bringing an oppressive feeling with them.

The weather matched Finn's mood. It wasn't in his nature to feel gloomy or down, at least not for very long but, with Juliet rebuffing any attempts at friendship, his spirits were at rock bottom. He missed her smile and the way his day would brighten every time he saw her, and the feeling he had when he was near her that everything was right with the world.

The weather was wild now, with strong gusts whipping across the water. A big bank of storm clouds threatened another downpour, although at the moment they were wrapped around the shoulders of the ranges like a heavy woollen blanket. The wharf was deserted, and he couldn't see any boats anchored around the islands, but that was no surprise. With the inlet covered in whitecaps, you'd have to be extremely keen on fishing to be out in this weather.

Then Finn noticed something moving over to the left of his field of vision, and when he focused on it, he could see a small boat making its way along the main channel at high speed. The way it was bouncing over the whitecaps must have been giving its occupant a rough ride. It looked like Juliet's dinghy, but why on earth would she be out in a storm? Well, he was about to find out because, as the boat rounded the turn, he could see it was heading straight for him.

She was still driving fast. Even he knew that there were speed restrictions there, but they were being ignored today. It wasn't like Juliet to break rules, but it was definitely her driving the boat. He could see blonde hair streaming behind her in the wind and swirling around her face.

The *Minnow* reached the channel near the boat ramps and Juliet eased back on the throttle, letting the vessel sink back into the water. She drew into the wharf with the engine idling, but the little boat was being tossed around by the waves. Reaching the jetty, its aluminium hull banged hard against the wooden posts.

"Finn, I need your help," Juliet shouted up at him. "Get in, quick!" She gripped hard onto the edge of the wharf and was nearly pulled over as the boat pitched and swayed. "Please! Will you come with me?"

Chapter 17 – A Southerly Buster

Finn felt tension grip at his gut. Something was very wrong. Juliet's normally calm demeanour had deserted her, and she looked close to panic as she struggled to hold onto the jetty.

"Of course, I'll help. What's wrong?"

He knelt down and grabbed the edge of the boat, helping to hold it steady and getting ready to climb into it.

"Isabella rang me. She's worried she might be in labour and she's all alone. She can't get Byron or Tom on the phone, the medical clinic's shut, and she's scared. The baby isn't due for four weeks yet. I told her I'd be right over, and that I was already in the boat, but then I thought I'd better find someone to take with me. I'm so glad you're here! Please get in – we need to get to her fast and keep trying the others on the phone."

Finn swung his long legs over the edge of the wharf and lowered himself into the boat, steadying it from the sudden rocking his weight caused, and then sitting on the seat beside Juliet.

"Put this on." She handed him an inflatable life jacket like the one she was wearing.

He hung it around his neck. "Okay. Let's go. I sure you hope you know how to drive this oversized tin can of yours," he said with a grin, hoping to ease her tension.

"Don't be cheeky." She looked sideways at him with the hint of a smile on her face as she pushed the boat off from the wharf and the wind grabbed it and swung it around. "You know I was born and raised driving boats here, and the *Minnow* is as sturdy as anything. You're going to get wet, but you're perfectly safe."

She slipped the outboard engine into gear and they were off, thumping over the choppy waves. In shouted conversation, Finn heard that Isabella was supposed to have been heading to a more civilized location tomorrow.

"She and Clemmie were going to go and stay with our aunt in Newtown – much closer to where our mother lives and also to the hospital – just in case the baby turned up early. They'd intended to go a week ago, but Clemmie had a cold, so they delayed it, not thinking there would be a problem."

"Could it be a false labour?" Finn was wracking his brain for anything he knew about childbirth.

"Yes, very possibly. That's what she's hoping, but she's worried in case it's the main event. Byron took Clementine out for the afternoon and she can't get hold of him. The phone signal's a bit spasmodic around here."

"You're not wrong!" Finn grabbed onto the side of the boat as they passed an island and met the full brunt of the wind, and the small vessel started to pitch and bounce across the whitecaps.

"This is called the Southerly Buster," Juliet shouted. "It can get pretty rough with the wind coming this way."

"Southerly Buster? I can see why. A regular boat buster, this is." The dinghy slapped down hard in a trough and slewed sideways, and Finn held on tight.

After that, the conversation ceased. The centre of the lake was heaving with swells and whitecaps. Finn marvelled at Juliet's skill in handling the boat. She skirted the larger waves and slowed down for the ones she couldn't dodge, then sped up slightly when there was a lull, keeping the small boat hopping and skipping across the grey-green water. Even so, and despite the rain holding off, they were both dripping wet. Every time the bow dipped into a trough, a curtain of water would douse the small boat and its occupants. It was exhilarating, and in better circumstances, Finn would have found it enormous fun. He couldn't help but grin with excitement every time the boat soared over a crest and fell into a trough with a mighty whoosh. He looked at Juliet. She was concentrating hard on reading the water ahead with one hand on the wheel and the other on the throttle. She wiped water from her eyes and caught his glance, giving him a quick smile. He could see the exhilaration on her face too.

"Here we go again – woo hoo!" she shouted, as the boat soared over another big swell, and they braced for the drop, ducking their heads in preparation for the next wall of water to come over.

"You're an expert at this," he said, as they got closer to the shore and the waves calmed down enough for them to talk.

"I've had lots of practice, that's for sure. I usually love it when it's rough like this. But now . . . Finn . . . I'm worried about Isabella and the baby. What if she's in labour? What if something goes wrong?"

"We don't know if it's labour, yet," he said. "It might be a false alarm – but in any case, we'll find out soon." He could see the jetty in a sheltered cove, straight ahead. "We'll be with her in a minute and we'll get hold of Tom and Byron. She'll be okay, Juliet."

"I'm so glad you were there on that wharf. I was wondering who on earth I could find to go with me, and there you were like a gift from the gods."

"That's me, a divine gift alright."

They drew into the small jetty, and again Finn admired her skill at steadying the boat and taking it in slowly, judging the distance and the forces of the wind and waves perfectly.

He grabbed the wooden edge of the jetty and Juliet picked up the rope attached to the front of the boat and gave quick instructions to Finn; soon they had dropped their life jackets on the seats and tied the boat up securely, and were racing up the slope to the house.

The front door was open. Juliet went in first, calling for her sister, as Finn caught his breath from the run, feeling suddenly apprehensive.

A voice replied from further inside and he followed Juliet into a bedroom, where they found Isabella on her knees on the floor, leaning against the bed and surrounded by towels.

"Hello, you two. You look a little bit damp," she said weakly, managing a smile. "Thank you for coming to my rescue. This baby is on its way, no doubt about it. It's got much more intense in the last ten minutes . . . Ohhh!" Gripped by a powerful force, she shut her eyes and clutched the quilt with both hands. "These contractions are getting close together and strong," she said, when it had passed. "And my waters broke. I haven't done a great job of cleaning up, but luckily, we have floorboards. I think this is going to be a home birth . . . and soon!"

Juliet was on her knees beside her sister, with an arm across her shoulders. "Oh Izzy, don't worry. We'll look after you now and we'll get Tom and Byron too. You'll be okay."

"I'm so glad. I was getting frightened on my own," Isabella clutched Juliet's hand.

"I'll call the boys again." Finn took out his phone.

"No can do." Isabella shook her head. "There's no mobile signal here at the moment – it's always terrible in a storm – and now the landline's out as well. There's probably a tree down somewhere, blocking the road. Archie went to town in the truck to get stock feed and supplies, and he's not back yet. He would have been home hours ago if the road was open. When the pain got stronger, I tried to call an ambulance to come down from Newtown, but there's no dial tone. I'm lucky I'd already got hold of you, Jules, before the storm set in, and I left messages for Byron and Tom earlier." She grimaced as another contraction gathered force.

When it was over, and Isabella was able to breathe freely again, Finn knelt beside her too. "Isabella, we'll get you some help really fast, but Juliet and I need to talk for a minute. We'll just be in the hall, is that okay?"

"Sure. I'm not going anywhere." She leaned against the bed, drawing a deep breath of relief in the momentary absence of pain.

Finn gave a quick glance towards Juliet and they walked around the corner together.

"This is serious." She turned to face him. "The real thing."

"It sure is. You stay with her and I'll take your boat and go back, call an ambulance and find Tom. I'm not much use as a midwife, but I'll get help. Hopefully, I'll find Tom straight away and we'll be back by boat much quicker than the ambulance can get here."

Finn knew it was a slow trip by road at the best of times to get to Isabella and Byron's house, and it could take an ambulance several hours if there were fallen trees in the way. But, with luck, he might have Tom and Byron back here in forty minutes or so. Surely nothing much would happen in that time. Would it?

They heard Isabella stifle a moan and looked at each other with concern.

"Okay, that's a good plan," Juliet agreed. "I'll get her comfortable while you're gone. Have you driven a boat much?"

"Umm, no . . . never," Finn admitted. "But I wondered if it might come to this, so I watched what you were doing pretty carefully."

Juliet screwed up her face but then took a deep breath. "Okay, here's what you need to know. You won't capsize. Probably. Not unless you do something stupid. Just pick your way through the waves like I did, don't go too fast and stick to the channels. No heroic short cuts, because if you run aground and get the outboard motor choked up with sand, we'll really be in strife."

"Got it. Will you be okay?"

"I hope so," she whispered and rubbed her forehead. "I'm praying you'll find Tom. What if the baby arrives and there's only me here? What do I do if there are complications?"

He could see fear etched on her face.

"It's going to be fine. I know it. If anyone can stay calm and clear-headed, and make Isabella feel safe, you can. You are so smart and capable, Juliet . . . Just stay positive and let nature take its course. You've got this, okay?"

He reached out and lightly touched the side of her face with his fingertips and she met and held his gaze. The force that passed between them at that moment seemed to be an almost tangible thing, a warm, vibrant current reaching from his body to hers. She stared at him. Had she felt the strength of their connection too? He didn't want to take his eyes off her, but then Isabella gave another soft moan from the next room. He had to go – fast.

"I'll let Isabella know what we're doing," he said, and she nodded.

He walked briskly to the other room and knelt beside Isabella on the floor. "Juliet's staying here, but I'm going back to get Tom and Byron," he said. "Everything's going to be okay."

"Is it? I'm scared, Finn . . ."

"Don't worry. You're doing really well, and I'll be back with the boys in no time. Juliet's going to look after you and you can just focus on what you need to do. Believe in yourself, okay? You're strong. You can do this, and you and the baby are going to be fine."

"Okay. Thank you," she whispered, and then concentrated hard on the next wave of pain.

*

Juliet watched Finn race out the door and down the hill. He managed to untie the boat and get it going, then speed away from the jetty easily – a quick learner. She prayed he would manage to get across the rough water out in the centre with no problems. It was a big ask for a rookie.

Her mind was still reeling from the power of what had passed between them. He had looked at her with such tenderness and, when their eyes had met, something truly powerful had happened. It had felt like some sort of force had flowed between them, filling her with strength and confidence – as though the two of them, together, could do anything. Her fingertips went to her cheek where he had stroked it; her skin seemed to be tingling from his touch.

She had no time to think about what any of that might mean, but somewhere inside her, a warm well of joy and self-assurance lifted her spirits. She could do this – just like Finn said. She tore herself away from the window and returned to her sister's side, rubbing her back soothingly.

"It's okay, Izzy. We'll get through this. The fearless Cooper sisters – remember all the escapades we had together?"

"How could I forget?" Isabella said weakly. "We were always getting tangled up in adventures."

"Well, this is another one, and we're going to talk about it together for a long time. And now I'm going to get you comfortable. Do you want to get on the bed?"

"Floor. Here!" was all Isabella managed to say, as the pain swept back like a tempest, but it was all Juliet needed to know. She immediately put her mind to the practicalities of how she could make Isabella feel comfortable and safe on the floor, and the other things she needed to prepare.

*

While Juliet prepared for an unplanned home birth, Finn steered the boat towards town, trying to remember exactly what Juliet had done, and wondering what her definition of 'stupid' might be that could make the boat capsize. He straightened his lifejacket and clipped the strap securely around his waist, glad that the wind had dropped momentarily so he could get clear of the jetty with no problems. It picked up again – with gusto – once he'd moved out of the cove, and he concentrated on copying Juliet's driving technique in looking ahead and skirting around the biggest waves if he could, and constantly adjusting the boat's speed. Not too fast, or it would bounce too much and risk getting airborne – but not too slow, or it would wallow in the water and have waves slosh over the edge. Letting it fill up with water and sink would probably equal 'stupid'. He held tight to the steering wheel and the throttle as the boat pitched and swayed and spray swept across his body, and he realized how hard it was to see with eyes full of saltwater. It wasn't until he got to the far side of the inlet and reached the shelter of the island that he was able to grab his phone from his pocket and steer the boat at the same time. Being glad of a water-resistant phone, and muttering a short prayer to the communications gods, he tried Tom's number.

To his enormous relief, the call went through and Tom answered immediately. Finn quickly explained the situation and arranged to meet him at the main wharf. Then Tom spoke briefly to someone in the background, and Finn felt even more relieved when he realized it was Byron.

"I'm there already in my boat," Tom said. "It's a lot bigger and faster than the *Minnow*, so we'll all go back in that. By the time you get here, I'll have rung the ambulance and made sure they're on their way, although I've heard some trees are down, so they might take a while. Byron's with me too. I was with him at my place treating Clemmie and we didn't hear the phone. She had a little accident and was having a good old yell, but she's okay now. Izzy's messages suggested a false labour, so I wasn't too worried, but the two of us were heading over anyway. Byron's taken Clementine to Mrs Mac's place, as it's too rough for her to be in the boat, but he'll be back by the time you get here."

"What happened to Clemmie? Is she okay?"

"She fell over and got a cut on the head, and needed a bit of patching up, but she'll be fine. Mrs Mac will look after her. It's all happening today!"

True to his word, Tom was waiting in his boat at the wharf as Finn sped up in the dinghy, and he could see Byron climbing out of his car. Finn went into the wharf too fast, realizing too late that boats don't have brakes, and the *Minnow* hit one of the wooden upright posts with a loud thud. Byron had raced over to the jetty and managed to grab the front of the dinghy before the wind could swing it away, and the two men quickly tied it up and jumped into Tom's reassuringly big boat, which was idling in wait.

With a nod to the two of them, Tom pushed off from the wharf as his passengers sat down and, with a roar from the powerful outboard motor, they were soon speeding across the water.

Chapter 18 – Gratitude

"Finn! What's happening? How's Izzy?" Byron's face was tight with worry.

"She's having strong contractions, but she's doing well," Finn assured him. "She's staying calm and Juliet is looking after her."

"How far apart are the contractions? Any idea?" Tom was also ignoring the speed limit, letting his boat cut through the waves at high speed as they zoomed past the islands. This boat could handle the conditions much better than the *Minnow*, so they were making good time.

"About five minutes, I think. No wait, the last few were closer than that. She said they were speeding up and getting really serious."

"Okay, no worries." Tom gave a reassuring nod, but he pressed the throttle even further down, making the boat leap over the bigger waves.

Finn gripped the side of the boat and felt his stomach drop as they were momentarily in mid-air over one of them. Then they were in the centre already, where even the big boat had to slow down as it bounced across the swells. Finn was thankful that, despite the bumpy ride, at least this time he was not getting doused with walls of water, although he was still dripping wet from the last trip. He squeezed some water out of his sodden jacket.

"Mate, you're soaked! I owe you some of my home-brewed, organic beers," Byron said, giving Finn a quick smile, even though his eyes still glittered with fear. "A whole barrel, in fact. I'm so grateful you and Juliet got to Izzy and she's not alone . . ." His voice cracked a little, and he tightened his lips and stared across the inlet towards his farm, which was coming into view.

"Just remember, Byron, your wife is strong, fit and healthy," Tom said. "She had no problems at all with Clemmie's birth. Everything's going to be fine." Tom sounded calm and reassuring, but Finn could see tense lines around his mouth as well.

The boat trip seemed to have taken no time at all, and soon they slowed down for the approach to the jetty; the big boat sinking back in the water with what seemed like a sigh of relief. Tom took it in with practised efficiency and Byron was up and on the wooden boards in a flash.

"I'll tie up. You two go ahead." Finn was already holding the boat steady and had the mooring rope in his hand.

"Thanks, mate." Tom grabbed his medical bags and followed Byron as they raced across the jetty, their feet pounding on the wooden boards, and then up towards the house.

Finn tied the knots securely, front and back, almost feeling like an old hand at these things now. He followed the other two up the hill but at a slower pace, since there was nothing he could really do now. Reaching the verandah, he was suddenly full of apprehension. What if something *had* gone wrong? So many people would be devastated. He cared about all these people. And Juliet would never forgive herself, even if there was nothing she could have done. She would be so distraught . . .

Shaking his head, Finn did his best to banish the negative thoughts and strode up the stairs to the open front door, his gut still tight with anxiety. He kicked his shoes off and padded along the hallway in wet socks, leaving a trail of damp footprints on the polished floorboards behind him. Hesitating at the end of the hall, he wondered what to do next, but then he didn't need to wonder any longer, because Juliet appeared in the bedroom doorway.

"Finn!" A joyous smile lit up her whole face – her whole *being*, he thought later, when he remembered that glorious moment. She stepped towards him, radiating happiness and love as she smiled straight into his eyes, and again he felt an invisible connection that almost knocked the breath right out of him. She had tears running down her face, but he knew they were tears of happiness. She grabbed his hands.

"The baby's here. Everything's fine!"

"Oh, that's good. That's *so* good. What a relief!" He felt the worry lift off his shoulders like a bird taking flight. "How's Isabella?"

"She's fine – and so happy now that Byron's here. She was amazing. I'll never forget this day and the privilege of being here with her. It was like a miracle, Finn. A wonderful, messy, joyous miracle! And right now, I feel a bit silly, but I can't stop crying!"

She half-laughed, half-cried, as she put one hand to her cheeks to brush some tears away.

Finn thought that he too, would never forget this day, because he had never before seen anything as beautiful as the awestruck, tearful woman with tousled hair who was standing before him, and he had never felt the way she made him feel.

"Come here, Juliet." It was a reflex action to take her in his arms. She buried her face into his chest and held tightly to his back as he wrapped his arms around her.

"You're not silly at all – you're amazing too," he murmured. Their embrace brought them so close together he could feel her heart pounding, or was it his own? It felt like the two of them had become one, and never had anything seemed so right. He held her tight while she pressed her face against his chest and wept with joy and relief.

"I'm sorry." She lifted her head after a few moments and smiled at him, her eyes still shimmering with emotion. "I've cried all over your shirt."

"Well, it seems you haven't noticed I'm still soaking wet – just like you – so you can cry over whatever you like. I'd offer you a handkerchief, but that's soaked too."

"I think I'm okay now. What a day this has been!" She shook her head, still smiling. "Wait here for a second, and I'll see if they're ready for a visitor."

She peeked into the bedroom and then returned to his side, taking his hand again. "Come with me."

He followed her into the bedroom, where they stood together before a tableau – a classic, timeless scene of delight and wonder. Isabella was on the bed with Byron sitting beside her, his arm around her shoulders, and they both gazed in awe at the bundle that Isabella cradled in her arms. The baby sucked one tiny fist as Byron turned his head to kiss the cheek of his tired but triumphant wife. Finn and Juliet stood beside them in silence for a moment.

"Hey, mate." Byron looked up, his face glowing with relief and happiness. "I'd like you to meet our son. This is Arlo. He's a little tacker, but he's fine!"

With the big, proud smile Byron gave him, Finn felt a rush of happiness, but also a pang of envy. What a lucky man! He had everything Finn wanted from life – love and family. Then he felt the warm hand of Juliet in his, and the envy was replaced with gratitude at being able to be part of such a joyous event. He leaned over to look at the serene face of a brand-new human being.

"He's beautiful," he said. "Congratulations!"

Isabella looked up at him, with tears in her eyes. "Thank you so much, Finn, for everything you did."

"I did nothing. You and Juliet had it all under control, and Tom and Byron were already on the way."

"It was a team effort," Isabella insisted. "I was here all on my own, starting to panic, and then you and Juliet appeared to save me. You were so calm and reassuring, Finn. You made me feel everything would be fine and I could focus on what I had to do. And look at you – you're soaked! Juliet said you'd never even driven a boat before, and you took that little dinghy right across the lake in a Southerly Buster. It doesn't get any harder than that. Thank you," she said again, and he smiled in return, moved by her words.

"Well, folks," Tom said. "It's time I justified my title as doctor, and we have some tidying up to do. May I suggest that the two drowned rats have a shower and get dry clothes on?"

"That sounds like a good idea." Finn realized he was feeling decidedly chilly now that the drama was over, and he could feel Juliet trembling with cold alongside him.

"I'll show you to the bathroom. Shower together if you wish – save water," Byron quipped, and Finn realized they were still holding hands. He glanced down at Juliet, and she gave him a shy smile as he reluctantly let go of her hand and they followed Byron out of the room.

He grabbed clean towels from a cupboard in the hall and handed them one each, then led the way to a bathroom. "I'll find dry clothes for you both in a jiffy."

"There's another shower in the guest room, I'll use that one," Juliet said, and disappeared around the corner.

"Bad luck, mate." Byron clapped Finn on the shoulder with a grin. "Enjoy the hot water. I'll chuck some clothes through the door for you in a sec, then I'm going back to Izzy and the bub."

As Finn climbed out of his clinging, wet clothes, he realized he was frozen to the bone. Teeth chattering, he eased his long body under the steaming jets of water and enjoyed the best shower he'd ever had in his life. He leaned his head against the tiles and sighed with relief that the day's drama had ended with such a happy outcome. It seemed to have brought him and Juliet together again too, erasing the awkwardness between them – hopefully for good, this time. He wondered how she was feeling, and he couldn't stop his imagination from picturing her dropping her clothes to the floor and sliding under the shower. She would be standing under the jets of hot water too – letting it cascade over her face and hair and . . . gulp . . . breasts. Dammit! It was impossible. The more he got to know her, the more she possessed what seemed to be his every waking thought.

*

Juliet woke up early the next morning basking in a haze of happiness. She stretched in her warm, comfortable bed, delighting in the euphoric feeling and letting her drowsy brain search for the reasons behind it. Of course – the baby! A picture of Isabella's tired but ecstatic face formed in her mind. She remembered the moments of Arlo's birth, when he'd slipped out with a rush of fluid onto the nest of blankets and quilts Juliet had arranged and into her waiting hands. She had been the first person to hold the new life as she'd gently lifted the baby, cord and all, and placed him into her sister's arms. He'd given a few shuddering cries; which Juliet was enormously relieved to hear as Izzy rubbed his chest and legs and they watched his skin turn from the bluish tinge of birth to a healthy pink. Feeling the solace of his mother's skin and heartbeat, the baby had settled immediately, and the two sisters had stared in wonder at the miracle of life.

Isabella had been entranced by him from the first second. "A boy! A beautiful boy! Hello, my darling. We meet at last," she'd whispered, cradling him on her chest and lightly stroking his cheek. The baby had stared up at her in quiet contemplation, with that manner some newborns have of looking like they've been on this earth before.

Isabella tore her eyes off him for a few seconds to smile at her sister, relief and happiness flooding over her face. "Thank you, Jules. You were a brilliant midwife!"

"I didn't do anything except catch him! You were incredible, Izzy; you did it all by yourself. And look at him – he's perfect!"

Juliet grabbed a soft, fleecy blanket and wrapped it around them, then helped Isabella prop herself up on the stack of pillows.

"Yes, he looks wonderful, and not at all worried about his early arrival. But I wish Byron was here to share this." She sounded suddenly tearful as she said her husband's name, but then Juliet heard a noise above the roar of the wind and stood up to glance out the window.

"He's here! That's Tom's boat. Finn is tying it up at the jetty and Byron and Tom are racing up the hill. Oh, I'm so glad to see them!"

"You and me both!" A couple of tears slid down Isabella's cheeks.

Byron had raced into the room then and Juliet saw the fear on his face, but it was replaced by utter relief as he saw his smiling, tearful wife cradling their baby.

"Oh, Izzy! My beautiful girl! Are you okay?" He dropped to his knees beside her.

"I'm fine, darling – just perfect, now you're here. We have a son. Look at him!"

They both had tears cascading down their cheeks, and Juliet's eyes had spilled over with emotion too. She struggled to get control, not wanting to take any attention away from the new arrival. Tom had followed Byron into the room, and he put his hand on her shoulder. "Looks like everything's okay?"

"Yes." She sniffed and wiped at her cheeks. "Izzy was amazing. I didn't have time to panic, because it happened so quickly. All of a sudden, there he was – right there in my hands. It was incredible!"

"Well done, Jules. Really well done." He patted her shoulder and then turned his attention to the couple.

"Looks like you have a gorgeous, healthy boy, you two, but I need to check a few things. Now, let's help you get up on the bed, Izzy."

Juliet remembered how she'd gone to find Finn then, realizing he didn't know what was going on. As soon as she'd seen his tall frame in the hallway she'd started to cry again. What was it about the sight of him that grabbed at her emotions like that? She'd reached for his hands, and the moment had overcome her, and he had gently pulled her into his arms. She'd never felt so comforted as she had during that blissful embrace. She felt like she'd come home.

She stretched some more in her bed, examining the feelings she could no longer deny. They were gathering more and more strength, like a wave ready to rush up on the sand. It wasn't just his physical appeal that attracted her, although he certainly had plenty of that, with his athletic build, and broad shoulders. They were shoulders that she loved to lean against, Juliet now knew. But – of far more importance than the mere physical aspects – there was this extra 'zing' between them that seemed to have a life of its own. A spark that ignited into something vivid and bright every time they were near each other.

She wondered again if she could be imagining the connection she and Finn seemed to share. Then her drowsy brain recalled the moments before he had left to run down to the boat. He'd touched the side of her face with his fingertips in such a tender and loving way. Juliet remembered the look in his dark eyes as they had gazed at each other, and everything else had momentarily fallen away – irrelevant in the face of that strong force. It was like a type of aura and, while Juliet lay in her bead and remembered the bliss of those moments, she pictured a light force of rich, beautiful colours swirling around the two of them as they stood together.

All of a sudden, something cold and wet nudged Juliet's arm.

"Argh, your nose is really cold, Roo! Go away!"

Ruby Roo wasn't going to take heed of that. In her opinion, it was well and truly time for the human to get up and play. She nudged her owner's bare arm again.

"Okay, you rascal. I get the hint," Juliet groaned, as her delightful visions evaporated into the morning air. "It's time to get out of bed, right? Well, good morning to you."

That was all the encouragement Ruby Roo needed. She loved boisterous cuddles in the morning, and she leapt onto the bed and pounced on her owner's prone form.

As Juliet's mind stepped into fully awake mode and she played with the happy dog, she dismissed her thoughts of swirling, mystical connections and auras. She'd obviously been listening to Zoot, her mother's hippy partner, for too long, or perhaps the miracle of new life she'd witnessed yesterday had made her thoughts go all mushy. She swung her legs out of bed as Ruby Roo leapt off it and thundered down the hallway and then back again. It was time to start the day and get practical, and to stop dreaming of fanciful things.

Once again, though, Juliet's fingertips returned to her cheek, where Finn had touched her face, and another unbidden jolt of attraction and longing shot through her.

"Oh Roo, this is ridiculous. I'm hopeless at the moment, aren't I? But we've got heaps to do today, and first of all, we're going for a walk."

Ruby Roo's enthusiastic reaction to the word 'walk', which included jumping on the bed and off again, then leaping in circles around the room and snapping her teeth like she was herding imaginary cattle, was so entertaining it made Juliet laugh out loud.

"Mad dog! Alright, give me a minute to get ready and we're out of here."

Chapter 19 – The Winter Solstice

It was time for the Winter Solstice celebration, one of Mirrabooka's biggest annual events. It involved a twilight market, a barbecue dinner and a dance, with Mirrabooka's own musicians providing the entertainment. If the weather was bad, they would all crowd into the mudbrick community centre, but everyone was hoping the night would be fine so they could use the outdoor stage and the partygoers would be able to dance beneath the stars.

Juliet loved the Winter Solstice party and was delighted to be home for it this year. She hadn't attended for a while but was hoping it would still have the same lively, friendly atmosphere that it always used to. She had another reason to be excited about the night too – her mother, Viola, and her partner were going to attend. Although they kept in touch regularly by phone and FaceTime, Juliet hadn't seen them in person for months.

The day had dawned clear and calm, with a heavy dew and a mantle of mist draped around the shoulders of the ranges. Juliet had arranged to help Byron with the Daisy-Belle stall at the market, as they had a lot of things to transport and set up. After walking

Ruby Roo, she met Tom down at the main wharf; he'd been enlisted to help too by using his boat to ferry goods and equipment across the inlet.

Tom had left his dogs at home, but Ruby was allowed to come with them in the boat, and she curled up on one of the back seats as they chugged slowly along the main channel.

"Roo-dog looks happy," Tom remarked, as he glanced around the boat to make sure everything was in order.

"She loves your boat," Juliet replied. "Cushioned seats – a luxury!" she grinned. "For both of us!"

She felt so happy being out in the boat with Tom on such a lovely morning, and on Solstice day too. Isabella and the new baby were doing well, the sun was out, and life seemed just about perfect. The colours of nature looked even more vivid that morning, and everything seemed tinged with a little bit of magic from the strange but beautiful half-dream that had been swirling on the edges of her consciousness all morning.

Tom rubbed his fingers together. "It's a bit chilly out here on the water, but I think it's going to be a good night for the party. It should be cool, but clear."

"Thanks, Mr Weatherman. Oh, that sounds perfect. I can't wait!"

Tom smiled at his friend. She'd always loved the Solstice party.

"Ready for some action?" he asked as they reached the end of the slow zone.

Juliet nodded, looking forward to the moment when the boat would surge forward.

"Hold on!" He pressed the throttle down, making the powerful engine roar and the boat rise up and flatten out again, and then they were zooming across the mirrorlike water.

Juliet glanced back at Ruby Roo, who had sat up and put her chin on the edge of the boat, where the cold wind was rushing past her nose. Her eyes were closed, and she looked completely blissed out.

Just how I feel, Juliet thought with a grin. She too closed her eyes for a moment and enjoyed the feeling of the fresh, cold air whizzing past, and the tangy fragrance of the ocean and the eucalypt forests.

Jayden was waiting to meet them at the farm as the boat chugged into the jetty. There were piles of boxes and some deck chairs neatly arranged on the grass. Tom threw a rope that was expertly caught by the boy.

"Good catch, mate," Tom said, and Jayden's face lit up with pride as he helped Tom tie up the boat.

"Do you play cricket?" Tom asked. "You'd be a good fielder, I bet."

"Nup. Never tried it."

"Well, there are a few delights in store for you, old boy, once the weather warms up. I'm seeing a few cricket lessons coming up. If you'd like to learn, of course," he added, settling himself back on the seat with arms crossed, perhaps already imaging the glorious future ahead for the town's cricket team with a talented new recruit.

'Sure!" Jayden said. "But I think we need to put all this stuff on the boat now."

"We do!" Juliet said. "Come on, Tom, we've got work to do." She climbed nimbly out of the boat. "Jayden can hand you the boxes and things and you decide how to stack them. I'll go up and find Byron, to see if there's anything else to be brought down. Back in a minute!"

Juliet ran up the hill with Ruby Roo racing ahead. Archie was fixing the fence of the home paddock and he straightened up at their approach.

"Mornin'. Nice day for it."

"Hi, Archie. Yes, it's a great day! Are you coming over for the Solstice celebrations?"

"Nah. Too hectic for my liking. Me and the goats'll take it easy over here. Hope youse all have fun, though." After what was, for Archie, quite a speech, he bent over and went back to his work.

"Thanks. We will!" She found Byron shutting the back door of the house. He gave Juliet a big hug.

"Good morning! Thanks for coming over to help."

"My pleasure. Is there anything else we need to take?"

"No. It's all down by the boat. Can Jayden go over with you?"

"Yes, of course. We'll all fit somehow."

"Good-oh. He'll be a great help getting all that stuff out of the boat and into your cars. I've just put Clemmie in the truck, along with the trestle tables and some more boxes, and we're about to head off. If you could get all your lot to the centre and start on the tent, that would be great. Jayden knows how to set everything up."

"Sounds like he's being really useful."

"Yes, he's learning a lot, and he's working extra hard lately. He says he wants to pay us back for all the hassle over the court case, even though I keep telling him there's no need – that's what friends do. I have to tell him to stop working sometimes and sit down. The kid's a dynamo!"

"Daaadeeee! Daaadeeee!" Clemmie's singsong voice could be heard through the truck's open window.

"Gotta go! See you later, alligator." He dashed over to the vehicle. "On my way, Clemmie-Clem!"

Juliet smiled. Byron was a big kid at heart, and he loved the Solstice party too. She turned to head back to the boat and paused at the top of the hill to look across the water. The mist had lifted now, and a few boats were speeding across the inlet, with the hum of their outboards drifting across to the shore. Tom and Jayden were putting the last few items in the boat, with Tom still talking cricket, she was amused to hear. The sky was wide and blue, with the few clouds that had been around drifting away to the west. Yep, it was simply a magical day!

*

The Winter Solstice party was in full swing. The evening stayed crisp and dry as predicted, and just about the whole town had turned out to browse the locally made goods at the market and share food, music and fun. Over-excited kids ran around squealing; there seemed to be a massive game of chasey going on. Juliet had watched them for a while, smiling as she remembered how she and Isabella, and Tom and his little sister, Amelia, used to be the ringleaders of such a game when they were kids.

Juliet was in the tent that had been the Daisy-Belle market stall, which had been a very busy scene during the twilight market. They had packed nearly everything up now, and Byron had taken Clementine to Mrs Mac's place, where she and several other small children were being put to bed. Mrs Mac had organised a tag team of local teenagers who were being paid to babysit for one hour each so that tired parents could have a night off and the youngsters could still enjoy lots of time at the party.

Juliet looked around the stall with satisfaction, thinking how well it had gone. There was very little produce that hadn't sold, so the dismantling of the displays had been a much quicker job than the set-up.

"Here you are, darling." A petite woman in a purple kaftan arrived and handed Juliet a plastic cup full of white wine. "I visited the stall with the organic wine while Zoot got us all lentil burgers."

The man beside her, who was wearing colourful baggy pants and a shapeless woollen top, put three plates carefully down on the trestle table.

"They're all the same," he said. "Lentil burgers with egg, cheese, beetroot and mayonnaise. Should be delicious! And there's plenty more of that wine in our basket, as well as some chocolate for later on."

"Oh, thanks, you two – I'm starving!" Juliet smiled at the two of them. "It's so great to have you here. Cheers!"

They carefully clinked their plastic cups of wine together and fell on the food with gusto, with Juliet thinking how extra-delicious food tasted when you'd been too busy to eat all day. They were wiping their fingers with paper serviettes and topping up the wine when Jayden arrived with a tall, dark-haired man in tow.

"You have to meet Finn," Jayden announced to Juliet's mother and partner. The boy had struck up an instant rapport with the couple as they'd worked together on the stall. "Finn saved me from going to jail. You should have seen him in that courtroom. He was ace!"

"Hello, everyone." He smiled first at Juliet and then reached out to shake her mother's hand, and then the man's as well.

"I'm Viola," the woman said, her kind eyes crinkling with pleasure. "And this is my partner, Zoot. It's lovely to meet you properly. I know I sold you some eggs earlier, but we were too busy to chat!"

"Finn! Byron said you're not to pay for anything," Jayden frowned. "He said we still owe you half a tonne of cheese and two goats in legal fees."

"Yes, but I got eggs, right?" Finn laughed. "It's fine, Jay, honest. Byron knows I'm insisting on paying for some things, so don't stress. 'Calm your farm', as you always say to me."

"Yeah, alright then." The boy's face relaxed into a grin.

Juliet noticed with pleasure how friendly and relaxed he was with Finn, whereas he could still be a bit shy with her and Tom. Finn was a great mentor for him. What a shame he wouldn't be staying in town. A shame for many reasons, she thought with a pang.

"Viola, it's lovely to meet you too. That's a beautiful name," Finn said. "And from a Shakespeare play, like Juliet, of course. Oh . . . and Isabella!"

Viola's face lit up with delight. "Well done! You're obviously a scholar; not many people notice the Shakespeare connection for all three of us. Yes, I'm a big fan of old Bill. My name used to be Valerie, back in the olden days, but I changed it when I was studying literature at university. I fell in love with the Bard and his work and was determined to name my children after his characters."

"And if you'd had a boy, would you have chosen Puck?" Finn raised his eyebrows.

"Well, he *is* a great character . . ." she said, and then smiled. "Oh no, I'm kidding. There are plenty of other lovely boys' names to choose from too."

"Just as pucking well," Juliet quipped, and everyone laughed, even Jayden, who had been looking mystified about the Shakespeare talk.

Finn had noticed. "You'll probably be studying a Shakespeare play next year, since you're going back to school full-time to do year ten, right?"

"Yeah. I said I would. Dunno if I want to, though."

"Hey, you're still working on the farm on weekends and holidays," Juliet reminded him. "And Byron has promised you a full-time job, but you've got to do year ten first."

"Yeah, I can't wait to work there every day!" The boy's face lit up.

"It's only one year at school and, if you're lucky, you'll get to read Shakespeare's most famous play, Romeo and Juliet," Finn said.

"Oh, right – Juliet! I get it now!" Jayden said.

"It's a beautiful play. The writing is amazing. Absolutely stunning." Finn continued. He was addressing Jayden, but he looked at Juliet as he said the last few words.

She felt the warmth of his gaze. It seemed to be creeping along her body, from head to toe and everywhere in-between. Her eyes met his.

Just then, the town's resident rock band swung into action with the classic Beatles song, "Twist and Shout". The line-up of the band tended to vary a lot, depending on who was in town and available to play at any given time, but they had a good turn-up for the Solstice party and their best singer was at the microphone. They sounded slick, professional, and full of energy.

"The band! That's so cool! I'm going to watch them!" Jayden said, and darted away.

"You've done marvellous things for that boy," Zoot said to Finn. "I only met him for the first time today, but Byron has filled me in on his background. Then Jayden told me this afternoon how scared he was about going to court. Well done."

"Thank you. I was pleased to be able to help him."

"Well, I think you should join us for a drink, and we've got plenty more organic wine here." Zoot picked up the bottle and found another plastic cup. "Can I tempt you?"

"That would be lovely, thanks," Finn replied. "And I think we should have a toast. Congratulations to you both, Viola and Zoot, on the arrival of your new grandson."

"Yes! To beautiful Arlo!" Juliet said, and they raised their glasses.

"Have you seen him yet?" Finn asked.

"We have," Viola beamed. "We visited the hospital this morning on our way down here. He is absolutely gorgeous! Isabella is feeling very well, and the doctors say little Arlo is fine, despite his hurry to arrive in the world."

"And a big thank you to you, Finn, for everything you did." Zoot raised his glass again.

"It was nothing. Juliet had all the responsibility, and she did a wonderful job. I just had a crash course in boat driving."

"And did a wonderful job," Juliet said, and then enjoyed the smile Finn gave her.

"So, whereabouts do you two live?" he asked Viola and Zoot, when he had finally shifted his gaze away from her.

Juliet sipped her wine and relaxed, sitting back in her deck chair with a happy sigh. She listened to the conversation as Viola and Zoot described their home and the commune they were establishing further up the coast, noticing with approval how courteous Finn was towards the pair. Zoot looked quite outlandish, by city standards, with his long grey hair and coloured patchwork trousers. His feet were encased in tatty leather boots he'd probably made himself, and he had a red silk scarf twisted around his neck below a lined and weather-beaten face, which housed shrewd eyes of emerald green.

Finn was completely at ease with the two of them and seemed genuinely interested in their alternative lifestyle.

"We get a lot of troubled people coming to the commune, looking for something to fix their lives," Zoot said. "They all have the same lost look about them – a look that says they are searching for their place in the world. I know that look well; I used to be a counsellor in the city, many years ago. Jayden has that expression sometimes too, when he's deep in his own thoughts but, with the help of all of you here, he'll be able to build a solid foundation for his life now."

"He's a good kid. I really like him," Finn said. "Bev and Eddie are wonderful, and they're doing a great job with him. And you know . . . I've handled, and won, some important cases as a barrister, but in the Children's Court with Jayden the other day – that was amazing. I've never felt a sense of professional satisfaction like that before, ever." He shook his head. "And it was great to stick it right up those arrogant parents and their lawyer, I have to say. They'd thought Jayden was going to be a handy scapegoat. Well, he most certainly wasn't!" He grinned. "I enjoyed that."

They all laughed, and Zoot slapped him on the back. "I bet you did!"

He'd never treated Ronan with such casual affection, Juliet recalled. Or any affection, really. Probably because Ronan was always looking Zoot up and down with disdain and referring to him as "that old hippy" behind his back. She was only just coming to realize how much stress she'd taken on board from Ronan's disapproval of her family and her town, and various other things. Under his civilized veneer ran a dark and negative undercurrent, which she could only truly recognise in its absence. In contrast, when Finn spoke about how it had felt to help Jayden, his face lit up with genuine pleasure. She looked with affection at the three people before her, happily perched on deck chairs, swigging wine from their plastic cups and laughing at some of the funny stories about the commune Zoot was telling.

"So, I said to this young guy, 'Mate, you can walk around holding your phone up to the sky until the cows come home, but you're not going to get a signal,'" Zoot was saying. "'There *is* no signal here. You have to go right back to the main compound!' He looked at me like I was speaking gibberish. No phone signal? That does not compute!"

"That sounds a bit like me when I first arrived in Mirrabooka," Finn laughed. "We city people are so dependent on our cell phones, it's a bit pathetic. But I've got it all organised now. If the signal drops out in the cottage, I go out on the back deck, stand on one leg with a fork in one hand and my phone in the other, and sing 'I'm a Little Teapot'. It never fails. Seriously!"

"I'd like to see that!" Juliet said as Viola and Zoot shouted with laughter. "Do you do the actions too?"

"Naturally. I must get Clemmie to join in one day."

"She'd like that." Juliet felt the warmth from his eyes once more.

"You two young people should go and watch the band. They sound terrific," Viola said. "Go on – scram! You always used to be one of the first ones on the dance floor, Juliet."

"Yes, go and have fun," Zoot said. "We'll tidy up a bit here and come and join you in a minute."

The band was playing "Moondance", one of Juliet's favourite songs, and the lead singer had a voice like velvet. Juliet could hear a hum of talk and laughter above the music.

She could still feel Finn looking at her.

"Sounds like a plan," he said.

"Okay. Don't do too much here, Mum. You come and have some fun too."

"Five minutes, I promise," Viola said.

"Let's go," Juliet said to Finn and, as they strolled away together, she felt like the stars above them were twinkling with a little bit of magic too.

Chapter 20 – The magic spell you cast

T rue to the words of the classic song, it *was* a marvellous night for a moondance. They walked towards the outdoor stage and Juliet was glad to see that the dance 'floor' – which was really a paved area with dancers overflowing onto the grassy surrounds – was crowded. There were coloured lights in the trees and the moon was shining bright. Everywhere she looked, people were laughing, talking, dancing, or just watching the band and tapping their toes to the music. It was a pity Isabella was missing the party, but Juliet knew her sister was happy to be having a well-earned rest in the hospital, with Arlo being thoroughly checked over after his dramatic arrival.

As they reached the dance floor, Byron swooped up behind them.

"Come on, you two! Time for a dance!" He grabbed their arms and pulled them towards the fray. "Clemmie's sound asleep at Mrs Mac's, and I'm off duty for a while. Woo hoo!"

He threw his arms in the air and leapt around the other dancers with abandon, to the amusement of everybody nearby. Not the most stylish of dancers, but definitely up there with enthusiasm,

Byron loved to strut his stuff on a dance floor, especially when his friends were playing in the local band.

The crowd applauded and whistled when "Moondance" was finished, and the band prepared to start a new song.

"This one is for Twinkle-toes over there – yes you, Byron – and for his beautiful wife, Isabella, who are celebrating their new arrival," the lead singer said into the microphone. "It's a boy! Congratulations, mate!" They launched into a rendition of "Hey Baby", and the crowd cheered, prompting Byron to dance with even more gusto.

They had no chance but to join in, and Juliet was glad – she loved to dance. They both had a style that was far more sedate than Byron's, and Juliet was pleased to see that Finn had a good sense of rhythm and didn't look too self-conscious. With the dance floor so crowded, and lots of people on it that they knew, they weren't really dancing *with* each other, it was more like they were dancing *near* each other. Juliet was glad, however, that he was never far away, and she could often feel his eyes on her. Tom was there too, and Sharon who worked at the pub, and she saw Jayden dancing with several of the local kids. Mrs Mac was jiving with Eddie while Bev danced with Byron for a while, and then Viola and Zoot joined in too, as promised.

Juliet felt so happy, it was like little bubbles of joy were building up and up inside her, filling her with energy. She wanted the music to keep going all night. She danced on and on, with Finn never far away, and they only stopped briefly for sips of water or the organic wine Zoot kept appearing with.

After a particularly energetic version of "Jailhouse Rock", the band regretfully announced that time was almost up, and they were going to play their last song.

"We're doing our take on Edith Piaf's famous ballad 'La Vie en Rose'," the singer announced. "But since we don't want to murder the beautiful French language, we'll go with the English lyrics."

"Oh! I love this song!" Juliet felt her breath catch in her throat as she heard the poignant refrain. She turned to face Finn, and he was standing still, staring at her with something unreadable in his dark eyes. She met his stare, searching for meaning in his expression, and then he stepped forward and held his arms out towards her. Somehow, a second later, she was wrapped in those arms, and they swayed to the music together.

Juliet wanted the world to stop so she could stay in that moment forever. The sensation of his arms around her, his strong shoulders under her hands, his body so enticing against hers – she knew right then that beside him was where she belonged. Woah! That was a big thing to realize! She felt dizzy for a moment and rested her forehead against his chest. Was she dizzy with wine? Life? Happiness? It was the thoughts of happiness that made her eyes glisten with emotion. The music, the moon, the precious new life she had held in her hands . . . seeing her mother again, being in the arms of this gorgeous man – she refused to think about suitability or non-suitability for those moments.

Finn steered her gently around the corner of the building, out of sight of everyone else, so that they were dancing alone, in their own private universe.

"Hold me close and hold me fast, the magic spell you cast, this is *la vie en rose*." The lyrics of the song and the true, smooth voice of the singer lifted from the earth and soared up through the tall trees towards the stars.

Then suddenly, Finn cupped her chin in his fingertips and kissed her, so sweetly, but so passionately too, and she responded as though she had been waiting for him her whole life.

The last few chords of the music hovered in the air and then the song was over, and the crowd was applauding, and they reluctantly drew apart. She found it hard not to stare at his sensuous lower lip. Had she really been kissing it only moments ago? She lifted her gaze to his eyes. His dark, passionate eyes.

He was looking at her as though he, too, wanted the world to stop and the moment to last forever. He wound a strand of her hair gently around his fingers.

"I suppose the others will wonder where we are," Juliet murmured.

"They will." He stroked her hair one last time and gave a sigh. "We'd better go back."

He reached down to take her hand and they walked back to the party together. Everyone was still milling around in groups, chatting and sipping their drinks, as the band members packed their equipment away.

"Ah, there you are." Tom grinned and raised his eyebrows at Juliet, and she felt her cheeks redden.

"We're heading back to our camper van now, so goodnight, darling. What a wonderful party it's been!" Juliet's mother swooped up to give her a big hug, and then she and Zoot kissed everybody goodbye and disappeared in a flurry of colour, leaving only the faint scent of incense.

"I'm off too," Tom said. "Early shift tomorrow, so I'll catch you later."

Byron finished chatting to the band members and wandered over to Juliet and Finn.

"Can we help you pack anything up?" Finn asked.

"Thanks, mate, but no need. It's all done, and Jayden and I will collect everything tomorrow. We sold such a lot; it will be an easy job. So, go home, you people! That way. Shoo!" He winked at them both and waved at Mrs Mac behind them.

"I'll be there in five, Mackie!" he called out.

"I think we should do what the man says," Finn said to Juliet. "May I walk you home?"

"You may indeed," she smiled.

*

The world was still and peaceful as they walked home. The only sounds were the occasional quiet rustle of a bush creature in the undergrowth, the rhythm of the ocean in the background, and the scrunch of their footsteps on the track. They hardly spoke, but Juliet felt completely relaxed walking alongside him, with their steps in time with each other.

He held her hand, and she couldn't remember another time when that simple body-to-body contact had meant so much. His touch was warm and strong and comforting, and exciting too – especially when she remembered their kiss and the feeling of his hands on her body, gently caressing her curves, awakening all sorts of delicious sensations in her.

All too soon, they reached her front door and stood at the foot of the steps.

"I'll say goodnight now." Juliet suddenly felt a little anxious, unsure of what expectations he might have. Was it a certainty with people who lived in the city that you would invite someone inside, in these circumstances? She hoped not. The night had been perfect, but she never liked to rush into intimacy, and now she needed to be alone for a while. "Thank you for walking home with me."

"Goodnight, Juliet. That was a very special evening." He didn't sound put out about not being invited inside, and her faint feelings of apprehension wafted away.

"Before you disappear . . . " His hand lightly touched her arm, and the sensation made her shiver. "I'd like to kiss you again. If that's okay with you." He sounded endearingly nervous all of a sudden.

She looked up at him and slid her hands around the back of his neck.

He needed no further answer, and they kissed again in the quiet dark, while the world seemed to hold its breath.

It was Ruby Roo, whining at the door of the cottage and eventually resorting to a bark, who brought the kiss to a reluctant end.

"I'd better go in to her," Juliet said, still in his arms and not wanting to end the embrace. "She's wondering what on earth I'm doing out here."

"You can tell her you're casting a magic spell, just like in the song," he murmured, his lips against her hair, and his arms still wrapped around her. "You've been casting that spell for weeks now. I don't want to let you go, but I know I should. Juliet . . ." He hesitated for a moment.

Ruby Roo barked again, sounding even more fractious. "I must go," Juliet said. "Goodnight, Finn." She kissed his cheek and slipped from his arms. As she skipped up the stairs to her front door, she felt like she was floating on air.

She gave one final glance behind her as she unlocked the door, knowing she was about to be set upon by an impatient dog. Finn was still there in the moonlight, waiting until she was safely inside, and he gave her a wave and turned towards his own house.

*

The next morning, Juliet woke early to walk the dog and settle her back home and then drive to the meeting point of the local bushwalking club. It was their weekly outing, which involved various destinations, but this time was going to be a walk to one of the neighbouring beaches and back. She often went on the club's walks, having been a member since she was eight years old when her father let her join him on the weekly outings in school holidays. He used to praise her determination to keep up with all the adults, even when she was quite small. If she got really tired, he'd give her a piggyback for the last part of the walk. Juliet had loved that, being perched on the back of her tall and gentle father, feeling special and protected.

The bushwalking club members had formed a guard of honour at Keith's funeral and had been a pillar of support in the weeks and months that followed. The girls would often answer a tap on the door to find a casserole left on the doorstep, or a bunch of wildflowers and a tin of homemade biscuits, while Betty or Bill or Norma – or whoever it was this time – drove slowly away with a wave from the open car window.

Juliet had never forgotten the kindness of the club members and, despite the difference in their ages, she counted some of them as her best friends. She didn't always join in with the weekly bushwalk but, the day after the Winter Solstice celebration, she knew she had no hope of concentrating on writing and decided to walk off some of her restlessness.

She couldn't get thoughts of Finn and what had happened between them out of her mind. What did it mean? The evening had been wonderful but, in the bright light of day, her reservations had come flooding back.

It hadn't been a good idea. Had it? Any liaison with a man from the city was doomed to fail . . . wasn't it? She would never leave Mirrabooka, and he would never stay. Why start something that had no future? It was madness. It probably hadn't meant anything to him anyway. Just a bit of fun, right? But the kiss . . .

Well, kisses – plural. She could vividly recall how she'd felt as she'd been dancing in his arms and then kissing him. No matter how firmly she tried to erase the memories by thinking about and doing other things, the feeling was unshakeable. Happiness. Damn happiness. That's what it was. She had to try harder to blot it all out!

She paced along the tracks with the bushwalking group at high speed, admiring the native heath coming into bloom with Norma, trying to spot rare native orchids with Bert, and listening to Catherine chat about her new granddaughter – and all the while in the back of her mind she relived how it had felt when Finn put his arms around her, when he touched her hair, when he put his lips on hers and it felt so right and so exciting . . .

"Did you hear me, Juliet? Look over there at that grevillea! It's a pair of White-eared Honeyeaters. I haven't seen any of those for a while. Aren't they pretty?" Bert was saying.

"Oh yes, I see them. How lovely!" Juliet tried hard to snap her mind back to the here and now.

*

When the group finished their walk, they went as usual to Sashi's Curry House and Coffee Emporium for refreshments.

Juliet was sitting at the big front table with the group, enjoying her post-walk coffee, when Finn walked through the door. He gave her a smile and a nod as he went past them towards the counter halfway down the room.

Her heart was pounding so hard it was like a drumbeat. She wondered if any of her companions might hear it or notice how distracted she was. She tried to interpret Finn's expression. What sort of a smile had that been? A special smile? How special?

Then she silently scolded herself for being ridiculous and reached for the jug to pour a glass of water. Honestly, she was behaving like a lovesick teenager. Finn had looked perfectly composed. See? Last night had probably just been a bit of a laugh for him. She could see him having a chat with Sashi and placing an order – no doubt for the homemade samosas he reckoned he was hooked on. Well, they were great samosas. That's what had brought him in here – not the chance of seeing her, surely.

But . . . there he was, looking totally handsome and kissable, and she felt light-headed and – she had to admit to herself – dizzy with happiness and anticipation. She downed her water with a gulp.

"Are you okay, dear?" Norma asked. "You look a little flushed."

"I'm fine. I need to get my walking fitness back, I think. Too much time in the city being indoors."

"Oh yes, it does take a while to get your fitness up," Norma replied, and launched into a long story of when she left Mirrabooka once to go on a cruise and it had taken simply *eons* to get back to her top walking pace.

Deep in a happy reverie while only half-listening to Norma, Juliet jumped when the door of the restaurant was flung open with a bang. She turned to see a tall, shapely brunette posed in the doorway, looking for all the world as though she was stage-managing a dramatic entrance. The conversation in the room stopped abruptly. It was like the scene in a Western movie when a stranger throws open the saloon doors and the card game stops – and all the cowboys reach for their guns. This wasn't a menacing stranger though. It was a stylish one in a curve-hugging outfit; the sort of outfit that had rarely, if ever, graced the streets of Mirrabooka. The fitted cream-coloured lace blouse had a plunging neckline, with plenty to plunge over too, and was paired with a tight red skirt. The red fabric – exactly the same colour as the woman's lips – was stretched around the top of her long, toned legs, which were clad in exquisite leather ankle boots.

Most of the dozen or so men in attendance sat up straighter, immediately wishing they were younger, as the glamorous vision sashayed through the room.

"Goodness," Norma said. "That's a fancy outfit for Mirrabooka. I wonder who she is? Does anyone know her?" The others shook their heads.

"No, but I'd like to *get* to know her," said Bert, wide-eyed.

"Oh yes, darls, and what would you do then?" asked his sprightly wife, Viv, who had been his one true love for more than fifty years.

"Well . . . not a lot, admittedly," Bert confessed, and the table erupted in laughter.

Juliet – like everyone else – watched the progress of the woman with curiosity. She walked with purpose through the long, narrow room, with her treacherously high boot heels clunking on the wooden floorboards. Rather than stopping to pick up a menu at the counter, she continued to the back corner, where Finn was sitting at the furthest table, waiting for his order. He must have been the one man in the building who hadn't noticed the woman's arrival, as he was sitting with his back to the door and was engrossed in a newspaper.

"Finn . . . *darling*! There you are! I thought that was your car outside – such a distinctive vehicle! Happy birthday!"

Chapter 21 – A wake-up call

Juliet clutched her glass so tightly; she was in danger of cracking it. She knew who this must be – Sophia, the ex-fiancée. Or was she, in fact, a current fiancée? Had he lied about the relationship being over? The possibility of that was horrifying. She felt numb with shock.

Hearing the woman's voice, Finn leapt to his feet, banging the corner of the table hard with his hip.

"Ow! Sophia? What on earth are you doing here?"

"That's not a very effusive greeting, darling, after I've been driving *all* day. I wanted to surprise you."

"Well, you've certainly managed that." He rubbed his hip.

Sophia leaned forward, and they kissed – cheek-to-cheek, Juliet noted through her dazed state.

"It's your thirtieth birthday, darling! I didn't think you'd find much to do in this dreary backwater, so I thought I'd help you celebrate in style. What have you got planned?"

"I see," he sighed. "Well, for starters, I thought I'd take these very nice samosas home and eat them. Then maybe go for a walk."

He collected his order from the girl behind the counter. "Thank you."

"That doesn't seem very thrilling. I insist on taking you out for dinner tonight. Where shall we go?" She began walking towards the door, with an assurance that said she was used to men trailing after her.

After a slight pause, he followed.

"Let's see, well . . . I think the bowls club might be the best option," Juliet heard him say as he approached their table.

She wasn't intending to look at him, but it felt like his eyes were burning holes in the side of her head. She glanced around to see he was looking straight at her with what seemed to be a tight, pained look on his face. Was it her imagination, or was this a telepathic apology?

"Do they have a jazz band or anything nice to listen to?" the woman trilled.

"It's bingo on a Wednesday night," Finn answered. "I think you'll like it."

"Bingo? How . . . quaint." Sophia linked her arm through his as soon as they were through the door.

Norma, sitting next to Juliet, looked at her closely.

"Are you alright, dear? Now you're as white as a ghost. And wasn't that the nice man you were dancing with last night?" She frowned, her eyes following the couple as they walked across the road, then swung her gaze back to Juliet. "I think your blood sugar must have dropped. Here, have some of my muffin."

"I'm fine, thanks, Norma. A bit tired, all of a sudden. I think I'll head off."

"As long as you're sure you're alright, dear. Make sure you go straight home and then have a nice cup of tea and a rest."

When Juliet had said goodbye to everyone and walked across the road, she could see Finn and Sophia still in the car park, having what appeared to be an animated discussion.

Good. I'll get home first.

She jumped quickly into her car and drove off, desperate to get inside her house, lock the door, shut the front blinds and stay there for the rest of the day. Apart from Ruby Roo's soothing company, she wanted to be alone.

Juliet took Norma's advice and was soon curled up on the sofa with a warm blanket and a book. Ruby Roo jumped up beside her and pressed against her legs. She patted the dog's fur, and sipped her tea, but she couldn't stop a couple of tears from forming in her eyes and spilling down her cheeks. Ruby Roo leaned closer, concerned about her human.

"It's not fair, Roo." Juliet patted the top of the dog's head and she licked her owner's hand, her eyes looking into Juliet's and showing pure love. Seeing the dog's steadfast adoration, Juliet felt a rush of emotion. She wrapped the blanket tighter around her and let the tears flow. They had been so lovely, those feelings she'd had about Finn, the deliciousness of being close to him, of breathing in his essence and feeling his warmth – and the happiness that had made her feel like she was soaring as high as the clouds. It had been like a beautiful dream.

But now, she'd been shaken violently awake. Whatever the arrival of Sophia did or didn't mean to the current status of 'Mirrabooka's Most Eligible Bachelor' – as dubbed by Mrs Mac – this was a massive, painful, wakeup call.

She wiped her eyes and resolved that she was over the shock now, giving Ruby an extra pat of reassurance. She had to get a grip. It was good that this woman had turned up, she reasoned to herself, even though she felt like her poor battered heart was twisting in her chest. It was a reminder that Finn belonged in the city; that he had a life there involving either Sophia or other sophisticated creatures like her. A life that was miles apart – and not just in distance – from the moments he and Juliet had shared in Mirrabooka.

She spent a restless evening trying to focus on cooking herself a light, healthy meal and then watching a crime series on TV, all the while trying to avoid imagining the dinner that Finn would be having. Even though she was tired from the bushwalk, sleep escaped her for a long time, and she lay in bed and listened to the plaintive calls of insomniac seabirds while she relived and processed Sophia's arrival.

Whether or not he had told her the truth about Sophia, Juliet could now see that she was the sort of woman he would end up with. And the sort of woman he *should* end up with – a tall, stylish woman from the city who said "darling" a lot and wore Italian leather boots and designer labels. A girl from the country who liked surfing, fishing, and watching the sun rise over the ocean was really not his type.

She'd been foolish to allow that scene to take place at the Solstice party the other night, and even more foolish to let thoughts of him sneak into her heart. She had to eradicate those thoughts and feelings, right now. When she saw Finn around town, she would be polite to him, but this ridiculous, fledgling . . . whatever it was . . . that been starting to gather strength and grow – like a tiny seedling pushing through the earth and reaching towards the sun – was ending. Right now. The seedling was nothing but a weed, and it was being ripped out and thrown away, immediately.

*

When Juliet went out fishing with Tom the next day, she was uncharacteristically quiet. Tom had a fair idea he knew why, since the town had been buzzing over the arrival of the glamorous woman with dark, exotic looks and amazing footwear. Sophia had appeared to be less than impressed with both the food and the ambience at the bowls club, and Tom knew this because he'd gone there too. Once the gossip about the new arrival had reached him, he'd had a sudden urge for a chicken schnitzel, a pot of beer, and a round or two of bingo.

"They're not together, you know." Tom cast out his fishing rod and reeled in the slack, then carefully propped it against the side of the boat.

He had two rods out and was hoping to catch some nice bream. Juliet had only bothered with one fishing rod, and she didn't seem to be taking much notice of it at all. It was so long since she'd cast it out, the bait had probably dropped off the hook by now.

"Who's not?" she said after a pause. "Stop being vague."

"You know perfectly well who I mean. Finn and Sophia are not together."

"Whether they are, or they aren't, it means nothing to me."

"Okay."

Tom reckoned it would be ten seconds at the most before she'd have to ask another question.

"And you know this . . . how?" she said at the eight-second mark. "Not that I care."

"No, of course, you don't care. You absolutely don't care even a tiny bit. But I can assure you that I know because he told me. He'd gone to the bar to get more drinks and I walked up, said hello, and asked how things were going. He told me everything was terrible, and Sophia had turned up out of the blue to try and patch things up with him, but there was no chance in hell of that happening. He said he felt he had to be polite since she'd travelled so far to see him, but he couldn't wait for her to go home. That was why he chose the bowls club. He reckoned that even if the food didn't make her want to leave town, the bingo surely would."

Juliet was again silent. "Their food's not that bad," she said eventually.

"Not exactly nouvelle cuisine, or east–west fusion, or whatever the hell people eat in the city though, is it?"

"I guess not."

Tom started counting to ten again.

"So, did you have a good night?" It was the six-second mark this time.

"Fantastic, actually."

"Oh."

"Yep. It was really entertaining. All the local boys were gazing at Sophia and trying to flirt with her. She's a stunning woman. She, meanwhile, was loving being the centre of attention, so she was flirting back, while still trying to charm Finn every second that she could. He, however, was trying to avoid conversation, which was awkward, since they were having dinner together and he's a polite sort of bloke. So, I could see he was gritting his teeth and enduring the night – and wishing for it to end – poor sod. I was mainly observing from the sidelines, but it was like having a minor role in a soap opera."

"Okay. You can stop talking now. I don't care what he did or didn't do, or what he may or may not have been thinking." She was facing away from him, with hunched-up shoulders, pretending to be staring at something in the water.

He couldn't stand it any longer.

"Look, Juliet, this is ridiculous. Let's stop mucking around. I know you like the guy and I know you were hurt when you found out he'd been dishonest – although he had reasons for it, we now know – but there's nothing in this, okay? She's making a play for him, but it won't work. Even if she hangs around here a bit longer, it won't matter. Nothing has changed."

"You're wrong. *Everything* has changed, Tom. It's true that I was starting to feel . . . something. And it's true that there was a 'connection', just like you were harping on about the other day. It was there, and it *was* special, but now it's gone. I've come to my senses and realized that nothing good could come of me getting involved with a man like that."

"He's a good guy," Tom said gently.

"Yeah, whatever." She shrugged. "He's a city guy, Tom – through and through. Whether or not he gets back with Sophia is of no consequence. If it's not her, it'll be someone *like* her. Someone completely different to me, and that's how it is and how it should be. I'm not leaving here, and he's not staying. End of story."

"He's been talking to people in Gipps Beach about a district legal aid job, you know."

"Oh!" She looked directly at him, shocked, and he noticed the shadows around her eyes. "He hadn't said anything to me about that."

"Well, you've hardly been talking to him, apart from doing baby delivery missions together and then kissing each other at the Winter Solstice party, that is."

"You saw?" her cheeks flamed red.

"I only saw you discreetly disappear around the corner, and I guessed the rest. But my suspicions are now confirmed!" he grinned.

She turned to face the water again. "Is he going to take the job in Gipps Beach?"

"I don't know. I haven't heard if they've offered it to him yet. But if he got it, that would be good, right? All those problems would be solved."

"No. It would be even worse. He wouldn't last living around here; it's too different to what he's used to. I don't want to fall for someone who thinks they're going to settle in here, but then a year or so later they realize they're bored to death and they miss city life, so off they go. You of all people should understand that!"

She turned back to face him again, and this time she had tears streaming down her face.

He handed her a clean handkerchief from his pocket. "Yeah, I do understand. You got me there. That's exactly what can happen and, when it does, you go through hell."

They sat in silence for a while, listening to the sound of water lapping against the boat hull and the plaintive calls of crows from the towering eucalypts on the shore.

"Let's try a different spot, Jules. We're not doing any good here."

She nodded, and wiped her face, and they busied themselves reeling in their fishing rods and bringing in the anchors.

The second fishing spot was much more productive, and they ended up being well-occupied and taking home a good haul of nice-sized fish, which appeared to be therapeutic for Juliet, Tom noted with relief. While not overly cheerful, she was at least more communicative for the latter part of their fishing expedition.

*

They were back at the boat ramp cleaning their catches when Juliet noticed two people strolling past the main wharf and heading towards them at the fish-cleaning benches. She realized immediately who they were.

Great, just what I need.

She noticed with some satisfaction that although Finn was strolling, Sophia was wobbling, since the current heels were even higher than the previous day's, and the ground's gravelly surface was uneven. Juliet wasn't in the mood to be charitable.

Maybe she'll fall in a pothole and twist her ankle and they'll have to go home before they reach us.

However, no such event occurred, and the pair stopped alongside the bench and greeted Tom, with Finn then introducing his companion to Juliet. My 'friend' Sophia was how he described her, Juliet noted with a smidge of relief.

"Hello. Nice to meet you," she muttered in reply to Sophia's offhand greeting.

"Lovely to see you again, Sophia," Tom said and went on to ask how she had enjoyed dinner.

While Sophia laughed about the basic food and Tom defended it, Juliet tried to not think about her and Finn being together, whether it was in the past, present or future. Instead, she concentrated on getting the knife in the right spot to cut the first fillet off a nice dusky flathead she'd caught. It would not be clever to be distracted and slice off half her finger instead.

"I meant to ask last night, Sophia, is this your first time in Mirrabooka?" Tom said.

"It most certainly is," she laughed. "And I should think it will be the last."

Juliet's knife cut through the abdomen of the fish, exposing its entrails, and Sophia recoiled in horror. "Oh! That fish is dead!"

"They kind of have to be, before you can eat them," Juliet said drily. "Don't worry, I killed it as soon as I caught it. I think that's more humane."

"Well, I don't know how you do any of it. It's quite awful." She pulled a grotesque face and shuddered dramatically.

"You don't eat fish?" Juliet asked.

"Oh yes, I love fish. I adore all sorts of seafood, especially at the top restaurants in the city. Finn takes me to all the five-star ones," she gushed. "But that's different."

"I see." Juliet continued her filleting.

"It's horrible to think of all the poor little fish swimming around out there worrying about being caught." Sophia gestured vaguely towards the water.

"I don't think the fish brain is that highly evolved," Finn said.

"Like some others around here," Juliet muttered, and Tom snorted with laughter then disguised it as a cough.

"Well, we'll leave you to it. See you later," Finn said.

Sophia had already begun walking away.

Juliet couldn't help but feel pleased when she noticed he was stifling a smile as well. He took a few steps then turned to look back over his shoulder, and again his eyes seemed to be trying to transmit a message to her. This time, however, she refused to consider what it could have been.

When the couple was further away, Tom turned to face his companion with a big grin on his face.

"Juliet! That was really snarky; I'm surprised at you! And it was also hilarious, I have to say."

"Well, seriously – it's alright to eat them but not catch them? Spare me."

"You certainly got the upper hand in that encounter. You have a couple of fish scales on your nose, though."

"Oh, that's just great." Juliet rubbed furiously at her face. "She's walking around looking like something from the pages of *Vogue*, and I'm all puffy-eyed and adorned with fish bits."

"Oh well. You win some – you lose some," Tom grinned.

Chapter 22 – A complete and utter disaster

When Sophia had turned up at Sashi's Curry House, Finn could hardly believe his eyes. He'd gone there hoping to see Juliet, knowing she sometimes went out with the bushwalking group and they always had afternoon tea at Sashi's. If they 'bumped into' each other, he thought it might provide an opportunity for the two of them to talk. When he'd walked in and seen her at the table, her face animated and happy as she chatted and laughed with her friends, his heart had danced a little jig.

The night of the Solstice party had been incredible. He still felt dazed with happiness at having been able to spend so much time with her. To talk, laugh and dance with her . . . and those kisses! He was a goner now, no doubt about it. There was no magic spell involved; it was love – just love. Pure, gripping, crazy, mind-altering love, like he'd never experienced before. He'd hardly been able to think straight since he had said goodnight to her outside her cottage. For a man who usually dealt with logic, facts and evidence, it felt slightly bizarre to be letting his feelings overrule his logical brain. Bizarre, but liberating! He couldn't exactly picture the practical aspects of what his future would look like, but the one thing he knew for certain was that she had to be in it. That was all that mattered.

Seeing her at Sashi's, he'd placed his order and was sitting in a happy reverie, his thoughts full of Juliet, while he pretended to read the paper. He hadn't wanted to intrude on her time with the group, but he hoped if he waited around for a while, he'd have the chance to talk to her quietly for a few moments, gaze at her lovely face and – all going well – ask her out for dinner. Dinner for two, somewhere private and quiet – if that was possible in this town – so they could get to know each other more without any interruptions.

It was uncanny that, as soon as the word 'interruptions' entered his head, he'd heard Sophia's loud and distinctive voice behind him and had leapt to his feet. He must be hallucinating. She couldn't really be right there in Mirrabooka, could she?

Seeing that she indeed was, Finn's heart had sunk all the way down to his feet and onto the dusty floorboards, where it flopped feebly around like a dying fish, ready to be stomped on by his ex-fiancée's boots. He had no desire to see Sophia, and even less desire to have dinner with her. However, since it really was his thirtieth birthday and she had travelled for seven hours to see him, he felt obliged to be civil to her.

It turned out that her claim of driving all that way had been exaggerated, since she'd hired a driver to bring her there and was paying for him to stay at the hotel. While thinking that was typical of Sophia – not wanting to make any personal effort but wanting the praise as though she had – Finn had been glad to hear it. It probably meant she'd be leaving soon; it would be too extravagant to pay the driver to stay long. Mind you, Sophia would have saved a lot of money by living rent-free in his apartment, Finn had mused.

He'd taken her out to dinner and put up with her incessant flirting, which became fairly desperate flirting when she'd realized the tactic wasn't working. He had driven her back to her luxury guest house and gone home, refusing her invitation of a 'night cap' and ignoring the look of fury on her face when he'd turned to walk back to the car.

He should have broached a serious discussion about what she was really doing in town but, if he had, it wouldn't have ended well. Disliking confrontation, he'd hoped she'd get the message that their relationship was over and would return to the city with the two of them still on good terms. That way things could end on a dignified note instead of more yelling and shouting. In other words, as he told himself several times during the mainly sleepless night that followed, he'd chickened out – like a cowardly fool.

She hadn't got the message. She'd insisted on him showing her around town the next day, then staying a second night, and having a second dinner, which had been much like the first but took place at the hotel instead. This time, he'd agreed to go inside with her after he drove her home, saying they needed to talk. He accepted the offer of the nightcap, hoping the alcohol might help as he faced up to the discussion that would inevitably become an argument.

After some prompting, she'd eventually dropped the flirty act and got to the point of why she'd turned up in Mirrabooka. It was – of course – that she wanted them to get back together and move on from "that silly tiff about nothing".

There was no way around it; Finn had to be blunt. He told her there was no chance of a reconciliation, as he'd had plenty of time to think about their relationship and to see how unsuited they were for the long term. He told Sophia that he wished her all the best, but this was definitely the end for the two of them.

When it finally registered that he really meant it, Sophia's face contorted with fury and she began to berate him for his failings, as she'd often done before. Although she was unpleasant and angry, he'd stayed calm – until she started talking about Juliet.

"You're not hung up on that blonde girl with the ratty hair, are you?" she said. "I noticed her eyeing you off while she was doing disgusting things to those fish. She's obviously plotting to get you.

You'd better be careful – tarts like that always manage to get knocked up so they can trap the rich guy."

He said nothing – shocked by her words. Even for Sophia, this was top-shelf nastiness.

"Oh, I see! You *are* hung up on her. I guess it's just a bit of fun before you go back to civilization. But that's really slumming it!"

She sat back, satisfied, sipping her liqueur.

He finally found some words. "No, Sophia, you're wrong. *Slumming it* is being here with you. This is the last time we'll speak. You are nasty and vindictive to the core, and I can't stand being around you for one more second."

It wasn't a clever response, but it was the best he could manage. With Sophia realizing she wasn't going to win him back, she had been deliberately provoking him, knowing he hated to lose control and give way to anger.

He had left then and managed to shut the door without slamming it, even though he felt like kicking it off its hinges. He hoped he'd managed to control his voice enough, so she wouldn't have noticed the gust of white-hot anger that swept over him. He didn't want her to have that satisfaction.

He drove to one of the further-away beaches, grateful there were no other cars parked there, and found his way by moonlight along the track and across the sand to the ocean. Then, knowing that there were no other people for miles around and the surf would drown out the sound of his voice anyway, he finally let his anger free. He yelled the words he would like to have said to Sophia into the cold, salty air, hearing them swept away by the wind. That made him feel better, somehow. He let himself drop the politeness and kindness that was so much a part of his personality, and he yelled, and he swore, and then he yelled some more. When he had let out the worst of his fury, he dropped down onto the sand and put his head in his hands.

It was a disaster, Sophia turning up in Mirrabooka. A complete and utter disaster. Fate was so cruel, with Sophia turning up just when things had come good between himself and Juliet. *Good?* That was the understatement of the year. Things had been incredibly, mind-blowingly brilliant, for those few precious hours. The thought that everything could now be ruined – blasted into smithereens by Sophia's manipulative behaviour – was too horrible to contemplate.

Finn groaned into his hands. Why hadn't he told Juliet how he felt about her when he'd had the chance? He'd walked her home and been on the verge of confessing his feelings, but he hadn't wanted to put any pressure on her. Even though he knew without a doubt how he felt, he'd sensed her natural reserve and wanted to let things develop slowly. He'd thought they had plenty of time. But they hadn't.

He stared up at the stars and listened to the rhythmic sounds of the ocean. He couldn't tell what the exact consequence of Sophia's visit would be but – given the delicate nature of the relationship, or non-relationship, or whatever the hell it was between him and Juliet – it wouldn't be good.

Well, there was nothing to be gained from hanging around on the beach, yelling and wailing like an idiot, therapeutic though it had been. He climbed to his feet and dusted off the sand, noticing – even in his cold, dejected state – the wild splendour of the ocean at night. It would be beautiful to come down here with Juliet sometime, all rugged up in coats and scarves, so they could walk together in the moonlight and admire the clouds scudding across the night sky as the waves crashed at their feet. A slash of almost physical pain tore at this heart. What if everything was completely ruined – beyond repair? He shook his head and started walking back to the car. He wasn't giving up, not by a long way. He'd start trying to sort things out tomorrow.

*

In the morning, Juliet's car was not under her carport. Finn had decided to walk over and invite her for coffee at his place, so he could have an honest talk with her about Sophia. He hated to think that she may have jumped to the worst conclusion and thought he'd kissed her when he was still involved with somebody else. He needed to set the record straight.

Finn felt a rush of foreboding when he saw the car was gone. He'd slept later than usual, as Tom was doing an early shift, so they hadn't done their swimming training, and he was exhausted from the Sophia-related dramas. Even so, she must have gone out early.

He worked in the cottage all morning, typing up information about shipwrecks he had found on some scanned documents, and searching online for more. It was hard to concentrate, as he was keeping one ear out for the return of Juliet's car, or for any signs of movement next door. There were none.

By mid-afternoon, Finn couldn't stand his own company and the repetition of his painful thoughts anymore. He drove around the inlet to Tom's place, pulling into the driveway behind his car. Tom's dogs came rushing over, and then he saw a red dog too. Ruby Roo! His heartbeat quickened. Was Juliet there? He couldn't see her or the car, but he couldn't stop anticipation and hope from flooding into his brain.

Tom walked over from where he'd been digging in the vegetable garden, as the three dogs milled around, wagging their tails at the visitor.

"Gidday, Finn."

"Hi, Tom. Sorry to interrupt your gardening. Hello, all you dogs." He patted Ruby Roo who was nudging at his knee, delighted to see him. "I see you have an extra one today. Is Juliet here too?"

Tom gave Finn a look he couldn't quite interpret. "No. I'm dog-sitting for a while. But anyway, I'm glad you've turned up. I need a break from the digging, and I reckon it's beer o'clock. Want one?"

"Sounds good."

Finn had plenty of thoughts churning around in his head about the events of the past few days, where Juliet could be, and how he felt about her, but he felt awkward about broaching the conversation with Tom.

Once the beers had been handed out, Tom took pity on him. "I see your ex-fiancée has left town."

"Yep. She's like a cyclone – blowing up a storm, causing chaos, and then blustering away and leaving a mess behind her. I'm relieved she's gone, but worried about repercussions. I was hoping to talk to Juliet, but I've seen no sign of her."

"She's away – gone to the city. I'll be looking after Ruby Roo for a while."

"The city?" Finn put his beer down on the table with a thud. "Why?"

"She's gone to the Writers' Festival to participate in one of the sessions. She was asked to join a panel for some sort of writerly discussion."

"Oh. Dammit! I wanted to talk to her. I guess you can figure out why, Tom."

"Yeah. Having Cyclone Sophia turn up the day after you and Juliet seemed to be getting closer to each other was not great, was it?"

"Nup. Worst possible timing. Look – I really want to talk to her and set a few things straight, but I don't have her phone number. Could you give it to me, Tom? It's really important." If he couldn't see her face-to-face, at least a phone call could help, couldn't it?

Tom thought for a minute and leaned down to pat Ruby Roo who was lying at his feet. "I'll need to ask Juliet. She's a very private person, sometimes."

Finn nodded, and felt his heart constrict. Tom obviously knew more about how Juliet was feeling and was – quite rightly – not breaking any confidences.

"I just want to know . . . Is she alright?"

Tom was silent for a few seconds. "You'll have to ask her that. If she'll speak to you."

"That bad, is it?" Finn gave a big sigh and rubbed his forehead. "I care about her, Tom. I really do."

"I know, mate. Look – I'll give her a call soon, and let you know what she says about passing on the number."

They chatted for a while about football and the ironman team, and Finn drove home, feeling better from having had Tom's company, but not at all confident about Juliet.

Tom's text, when it arrived, simply said:

Sorry, mate. She said no about the number. Hopefully you can sort things out when she gets back to town.

*

Juliet had driven to the city determined to make herself stop obsessing about Finn and focus on the rest of her life. Seeing him walking around town with Sophia, she'd realized she needed a change of scenery – immediately – even though the festival wasn't starting for a few days. It was good to get away and, by the time she got to the halfway point of the long drive, her spirits were definitely lifting. It was strange not having Ruby Roo in the car with her, but she knew the dog would have a great time playing with Tom's two and he didn't mind how long she stayed there. Juliet could easily repay the dog-sitting favour now that she was living back home.

She pulled up at one of her favourite towns on the highway and made a few phone calls. Having decided to leave Mirrabooka early for the festival, she didn't have accommodation organised for the next few days, but her girlfriend Zoe was delighted to hear she was coming back to the city and insisted Juliet stay with her.

"I want to know all about what's been going on since you left Ronan."

Zoe's house had been the one Juliet and Ruby Roo had fled to on the night of the massive and final argument. Zoe never liked

Ronan and had been glad to hear things were over, she'd finally confessed to Juliet.

Was Ronan really so bad that no one except me had liked him? Had I made up all those things I thought I liked about him?

Juliet had plenty of time to ponder these questions as she got back on the road, after buying all sorts of local cheeses and other delicacies to take to Zoe's.

She was going to be seeing Ronan at the festival, so perhaps that would provide some clarity. They'd been invited months ago to be part of the same panel. No doubt the organisers had thought it would be a nice idea for the literary couple to be together, and she didn't know if word had got around yet about them breaking up. Maybe Ronan had cancelled in the meantime, but she realized with relief that she honestly didn't care if he was there or not.

What will be, will be. Juliet shrugged as she drove. The fact that she didn't care was liberating. She felt like a different person now, with all the things that had been going on since she'd last been in the city. In addition, it would be great to catch up with Zoe, and she'd also arranged a meeting with her publisher to talk about progress on the next book. And there had been *some* progress, at least. Juliet was glad that when she hadn't been depressed, lovestruck, angry, delirious with joy, or crippled by writer's block, she'd done a fair slab of work and was marching towards the end of the first draft. Even better, the story seemed to be coming along nicely, she'd been relieved to find when she'd read over the new sections.

The only thing that disturbed her equilibrium was a conversation with Tom, later that afternoon. He rang just after she'd arrived at Zoe's and was putting her things in the spare room, and he told her that Finn had called around, looking anguished, and had asked for her phone number. Tom urged Juliet to let him pass it on.

"You've got to talk to the guy, Jules. You can't leave everything up in the air. The poor man's a total wreck."

"You're exaggerating," she had replied. "Blokes don't anguish over these things like us girls do. He was probably fretting because his share portfolio's taken a downturn, or he's noticed signs of rust in the BMW."

"Get real, Juliet. Don't talk clichés to me or do the bitchy thing. There was something between the two of you, but it all went wrong, the guy's worried, and you need to talk to him – end of story. Stop being so flippant."

"Sorry. It's a bit of a self-preservation thing, Tommy." Juliet allowed herself to think about Finn for a moment. And it hurt. It hurt a lot. Ripping out that seedling wasn't an easy job.

"I need time to think, and to do some other things for a while, okay? I'm not ready to talk to him yet, but I will – I promise – when I get back to Mirrabooka."

"Can I pass that on to him, at least?"

"No! Stay out of it, Tom. I need to get through this at my own pace, okay? And I don't want you giving him the wrong impression. Like I said, it could never work. But he is a nice person, and we do need to talk things over – to some extent," she conceded.

"Yeah, well, don't leave it too late," Tom had said.

Juliet shook her head when she ended the call. Too late for what? Too late to go on with something that had never really started and was doomed anyway?

She really needed to focus on work for a while. She was looking forward to the Writer's Festival, as this was her first one as a participating author. For years she'd longed to be a 'real' writer and had worked hard on different projects and manuscripts – eventually completing the one that had found a publisher. During those years, she'd dreamed of the day she might be deemed good enough to be part of a festival like this one and to be a peer of other writers she admired. Now that time had come, and she wasn't going to let anyone spoil it for her. Especially not a man. Either of them!

*

"Babe! Good to see you!"

Juliet would know that voice anywhere. Well, the owner of that voice could wait for a minute. She finished signing her name on a couple of paperbacks for a teenage girl and her mother, giving them her complete attention.

"There you go. Thank you so much for buying extra copies, and I'm very glad to hear you liked the book," Juliet said to the girl.

"It was ace! I can't wait for the next one," the teenager enthused.

"It's underway. I'll try to write faster for you," Juliet said with a smile. She loved knowing that people enjoyed her work.

"Thanks very much. We both think you're fabulous." The mother clutched her autographed book to her chest, and the pair walked away, looking at the messages Juliet had written for them and giggling together as though they were sisters. They reminded Juliet of the fun she and Izzy had together, and she felt a momentary pang of homesickness for Mirrabooka, but then banished it. She'd be home again, soon enough.

"Hello, Ronan." Juliet swivelled in her seat to face him. She was sure that he'd be looking impatient and sulky at having to wait for her attention but, to her surprise, he seemed to be perfectly calm.

"It's nice, isn't it? When people are appreciative." He gave her that smile she'd always thought was sexy. He was a nice-looking man, actually. And he could be very charming.

Phew! He wasn't all bad. She hadn't been completely deluded after all.

"It's great to see you taking part in all this," Ronan continued. "And you really deserve it. Everyone loves your book."

Wow! Ronan saying something nice about her work? Usually, he dismissed it as "an easy read" or some other back-handed compliment. Things had changed!

"Um, well, thanks," she stuttered.

"Are you nearly finished with this signing session?"

"Yep." She glanced at her watch. "As of now."

"How about we head for the bar and I buy you a drink, for old time's sake. We're going to be panel-buddies tomorrow, after all, and we can run through a few ideas about the discussion." He gave her that winning smile again. "I'll help you pack all this stuff up, if you like." He gestured to the piles of paperbacks that were waiting to go back in their boxes.

Juliet hesitated for a moment, remembering their ugly break-up scene. Why was he being so nice? She didn't trust him, and she hadn't forgotten what he'd done, but he did have a point – they were going to be working together. It would be better if they could be civil. Besides, she did have a lot of packing up to do.

"Okay, some help would be good. And a glass of wine would be nice."

*

The whole of the next week was excruciating for Finn. He'd looked up the Writer's Festival program and realized Juliet had left Mirrabooka days before it even started. Despite her dislike of the city, she'd obviously been keen to get away.

He jogged and swam himself to the point of exhaustion, read everything about shipwrecks that he could possibly find, and then started wondering what other things there were in town that he could do – things that wouldn't keep reminding him of Juliet. He couldn't stop worrying that this was going to be the end; that Sophia's arrival had caused too much upheaval and complication, and they would never work things out.

To add to his stress and confusion, Finn had been offered the legal aid job in Gipps Beach. He didn't know what to do about it, so he'd stalled them for a couple of days, saying that he had to talk to his current employer, which was partly true. The main problem was that he couldn't accept the job without talking to Juliet. He'd found out it would involve regular days working right there in Mirrabooka, in an office at the community centre, and he couldn't do that if it would make her uncomfortable. Things weren't looking particularly hopeful in that department.

He walked around town, deep in thought, and visited the few tourist shops on the main street, but there were only so many ceramic pelicans or toy kangaroos one could buy. Wondering what else he could do to kill some time, he spotted the hairdresser's and decided it was time for a trim. That would take care of at least twenty minutes or so.

The hairdresser was a chatty young girl who knew who Finn was and where he was staying.

"You're renting Juliet Cooper's cottage, aren't you?" she said, as soon as she put the gown around his shoulders.

He gave a brief nod. This was not a topic he wanted to discuss.

"She's famous, you know," the girl continued, not picking up on the cues. "She's at this writing festival thing in the city this week. Her picture's on the *Celebs About Town* website. Have you seen it?"

"No," he replied, resolving to immediately find it as soon as he got home. Even looking at a photo of her might be soothing.

The hairdresser saved him the trouble. She dropped her scissors onto the bench and picked up an iPad.

"Look! There she is! And she's with her boyfriend, Ronan Wittington," the girl gushed. "I was just showing it to the other girls. Ronan's really famous too, and he's *so* handsome. I met him once, you know. I cut his hair when he visited here. He promised he'd name a character in one of his books after me," she giggled.

Whatever she said after that, Finn didn't notice. He was too busy staring at the photo on the iPad. It was Juliet alright, looking stunning as always, and she was standing next to a smarmy-looking guy wearing a waistcoat, skinny jeans and cowboy boots. He had his arm around her, and she was smiling at the camera.

It was all he could do to stay in the chair and not bolt out of the salon and sprint home, with the hairdresser's gown flapping in the breeze behind him. But half-cut hair wasn't a good look, and it wouldn't take the girl long to finish it, surely, if only she would stop rabbiting on about how great Ronan-bloody-Wittington was.

He tried to block out the rest of her chatter about Ronan's attributes by thinking about getting organised for his tax return. A spreadsheet. That was what he needed. A really detailed, boring one.

Finally, she removed the gown with a flourish, and he was able to pay and escape.

Once home, he found the photograph, which was on the sort of website he would normally have to be bribed – with a substantial amount of cash – into looking at.

"Best-selling authors and literary couple Juliet Cooper and Ronan Wittington enjoy a reunion at the Writers' Festival," the caption said.

In the gushy article, Ronan was described as being ecstatic about being back with Juliet, saying she'd gone home to see her family and they'd been apart for way too long.

"I'm delighted to have Juliet back with me in the city, where she belongs," he was quoted as saying.

Wow. Finn was stunned. That couldn't be right, could it? But there she was – with him. He had his arm around her, and she was smiling. Whatever was going on in their relationship and, irrespective of whether a reunion was the right thing for Juliet, Finn knew he had to keep out of it. Feeling sick at heart, he tore his gaze away from the screen to look around the cosy cottage. It had Juliet's personality stamped on every part of it, and it made him feel alone and bereft. What was he doing in this place? It was time he went back to his normal life, his apartment, and his job, even though he couldn't imagine getting any shred of joy out of those things anymore. He'd thought there was something between him and Juliet – something rare and special – but he'd been wrong.

He rang the legal aid branch at Gipps Beach, thanked them for their job offer, and regretfully declined it.

Chapter 23 – The broken bridge

"Finn's leaving?" Juliet swung around to face her sister who was busy emptying the dishwasher. "Is that what you just said?"

Isabella straightened up and stacked a pile of clean plates on the bench for Juliet to put away. "Yes, that's what I said. He's leaving first thing tomorrow. But he's still paying for the cottage until the end of the month, so you should be pleased about that."

"Oh, right. Good."

Juliet was back in her own kitchen, chatting to Isabella, who was staying for a while with the children. Arlo was thriving, but she and Byron thought it might be wise for his first couple of weeks out of hospital to be spent in the relative civilization of Mirrabooka before they took him across to their remote farm. Juliet, of course, had been delighted at the idea and had loved driving back from the city to find them ensconced in her cottage.

Now, though, she tried to ignore the feeling of panic that welled up inside her, making her heart race and her hands clench into fists. He was *leaving*? She knew this would happen eventually, but she wasn't prepared for the feeling of loss that swept in like a southerly across the ocean. He couldn't leave now. That was unthinkable.

She turned away from her sister and looked out the window towards the sea, forcing her hands to unclench and tapping her fingers on the edge of the bench.

"I didn't know he was going back to the city so soon. Why tomorrow?"

"I don't know. I asked, but he dodged the question. He was offered that job in Gipps Beach, but he turned it down, apparently." Isabella looked at her sister quizzically.

He turned down the job?

She tried to seem nonchalant. "Oh, well. He was always going to leave sometime, wasn't he?"

He. Turned. Down. The. Job.

Each of those words felt like a stab to the heart, but she tried hard to ignore the pain. Her response was irrational. Everything was as it should be – and Finn was just living up to her expectations, after all.

Isabella was still looking at her closely.

"I'm sorry he's going, in a way." Juliet fidgeted with a pile of clean cutlery on the bench. "I was getting used to having him around."

"Well, maybe you should tell him that."

"Why?" She frowned.

Isabella sighed. "Just an idea. It would be a real shame if there were things left unsaid. But it's up to you, of course. Byron is sorry he's going too. They've become very close, which is funny, isn't it? The hippy guy and the barrister. And Tom . . . Tom's devastated."

"Devastated? That's a bit melodramatic."

"It's the football," Isabella explained. "The Mullets won their semi-final last weekend, and Tom is convinced they'll win the grand final on Saturday if Finn keeps playing for them. Then there's the regional ironman competition in a couple of months. Finn's on the team and Tom reckons he's the strongest swimmer they've ever had. He's promised to come back for the competition, but he won't have been training much, and Tom thinks he'll probably change his mind once he gets back to the city."

"Yes. He'll probably forget all about us."

"Some of us, perhaps, but not all, I'm sure." Isabella crossed her arms. "I saw him head down to the beach a few minutes ago. Why don't you go for a walk and catch him up? You might not see him in the morning to be able to say goodbye."

Juliet was on the brink of shaking her head out of childish stubbornness, but Isabella stared straight at her, using the 'I'm the oldest' expression that was not often produced these days but, when it was, Juliet knew was best to obey.

"Yeah, I suppose I could," she said. "Ruby Roo needs a walk, anyway."

The red dog pricked up her ears at the word 'walk' and then leapt up and wagged her tail furiously, dashing to and fro as Juliet dragged on her jacket and Blundstone boots. It had been raining hard most of the day, but the deluge had stopped about an hour earlier. Still, black clouds were circling the hills and the inlet, and a strong wind was making the surf boom and crash on the beach below. It was wild down there, but then the beach could be as appealing in stormy weather as in sunshine. Juliet loved the ocean in all its moods.

She opened the door and Ruby Roo charged outside. "Looks like we're off. I won't be long."

"I'll give Clemmie her dinner, and then start on ours."

"Okay. I'll be back soon to help," Juliet said with a wave, then followed the ecstatic dog who had bounded around the corner.

"Tell him how you feel, you beautiful, stubborn fool," Isabella said in exasperation as Juliet disappeared from view. "The whole world can see you two are right for each other. Why can't you?"

"Fool," Clemmie said. "Foo-foo-fooool, Mummy."

"Oh dear, forget I said that, darling. Now let's cook some eggs and vegetables, while your brother has a nice sleep. Googy eggs, right?"

"Goog, goog," Clemmie repeated happily, banging a toy car on the playmat on top of the coffee table, where she had been driving a wide assortment of vehicles and watching them drop off the edge, with peals of laughter every time one of them disappeared.

Life was simple, for a two-year-old, Isabella mused. Why do we let it get so complicated when we're supposed to be grown-up?

She dragged her thoughts away from whatever may or may not be discussed down on the wintry beach and began preparing her daughter's dinner.

*

Ruby Roo was loving being outside after having been cooped up in the car, and then inside the house because of the rain. There were all sorts of delightful new scents, and she dashed here and there, investigating fallen branches and eyeing off the little brown scrub wrens flitting from one bush to another. Even though she was itching to stretch her legs with a good run, the wrens were too small and too quick to chase, she knew that. Ah, but that thing there, further down the hill, that was a different story! She stopped dead, one leg poised in the air, staring at her potential quarry.

If Juliet had noticed Ruby Roo gazing at the rabbit, she would have called her to heel. It was dark and slippery on the bush track and the creek was in flood – not a great place for an over-energetic dog to go careering down the hill. But Juliet was deep in thought and looking in the other direction so, having glanced at her owner and then back to the rabbit, the dog figured it was time for some fun.

Mr Rabbit, sensing danger, made a run for it, with his white tail bobbing up and down in the gloom. He dashed down the hill and headed for a patch of thick scrub on the other side of the creek, which he knew would mean safety from red dogs that were fast, but too big to squeeze between a tight web of branches. Ruby Roo gave a single woof of joy as she took off after her quarry, alerting Juliet to the fact that her dog was belting full tilt down a muddy track and towards a slippery wooden bridge.

"Roo, come here!" She broke into a run, but the dog was too far ahead to hear her, especially with the roar of the surf in her ears and the churning of the creek adding to the din. Water was pouring down the steep slope between the rocks and through the gullies that were usually dry. The creek was many times its normal size and the torrent of water was racing down to meet the sea, carrying all sorts of debris with it.

"Ruby Roo! Stop!" Juliet yelled louder, and ran faster, reaching the corner in time to see her dog, propelled by the thrill of the chase, leap onto the bridge and scrabble to regain her footing on wooden boards slick with mould and water. Her momentum carried her to the side of the structure that the nimble-footed rabbit had already negotiated with ease, and the dog tried to slide to a stop, realizing too late that leaping onto the bridge hadn't been the best idea.

None of this would have mattered, of course, if the bridge's broken railings had been fixed that morning as had been scheduled. But the shire's council workers had taken one look at the rain pouring down and had immediately invented a reason to reprioritise, finding a job that kept them in the nice, dry workshop instead.

So, the rails were still down and the side exposed, and the rabbit had already hopped out of sight when the red dog slewed around and skidded off the edge, haunches first. She had no hope of regaining her footing, no matter how much she scrabbled her paws and adjusted her agile body. Juliet saw the flash of red go over the edge and thought firstly with annoyance about how wet the dog would be. Ruby Roo had swum in the creek many times. Not when it was in flood like this, though.

Running across the bridge herself – carefully – she noticed with dismay how big and swollen the creek was, and how fast the water was pelting down the hill. She could see Ruby swimming along in the current and trying to head for the side, but the water was flowing too fast for her to get a foothold anywhere. Juliet ran faster along the track, around the final turn where she could see the beach below. The creek – more like a river now – had a fifty-yard stretch across the sand where it was flowing faster than she'd ever seen it, and the area where it met the surf was a churning mass of sea foam, brown creek water, and debris that had been carried down the hill and the into roaring, dumping waves of the ocean.

She had a sudden vision of the dog being carried out in all that chaos and tumbled over and over in the breaking waves. Sick panic stabbed at her. "Ruby! Ruby Roo!" She was screaming her name now, running as fast as she could and pushing her strong legs to propel her across the wet sand as she sucked more air into her lungs.

The dog was a third of the way to the surf, still paddling like crazy with her head above the water. She was a fit dog and a strong swimmer, Juliet knew. She just had to get in there and help her. She drew level with Roo at last, pulled off her jacket and dropped it on the sand, then plunged into the creek, boots and all.

Even the second it took for Juliet to get in the water meant that the dog had been swept further on by the strong current, and her jeans and boots were heavy and holding her back. She gasped for more air and threw herself forwards, so close to the dog now that as she stretched her arm out as far as she could, she desperately hoped she might touch her.

Instead of wet fur, however, her hand hit something solid, and with a shock Juliet realized a big branch had swept into her, whacking into her shoulder and now entangling her in its spiky grip. She fought it with fury and frustration and wrenched herself over it.

"Roo!" she screamed again. The dog was being carried further away, and they would both be in the surf soon.

Ruby Roo didn't much like being swept along in the water. She could hear the roar of the surf and she swam towards the sand as hard as she could, even though she was tired, and the water was so cold it was sapping her strength away. But she was a red heeler, an Australian cattle dog, with a proud history of ancestors of various breeds – including the dingo Finn once mistook her for – and the traits of all those dogs had come down through the generations to make up her strong and loyal personality. The main trait, and the essence of a true heeler, was that it never gave up – no matter what. Ruby Roo heard Juliet scream her name and she struck out gamely for the shore once more, her paws kicking and pushing through the water over and over again.

*

Finn saw the drama unfold from the lookout further along the ridge.

He'd been admiring the wild beauty of the crashing surf, genuinely sad to be leaving this remote, unspoiled place, as well as the woman he adored. Then above the roaring of the wind and waves, he heard what sounded like someone yelling, and then he saw Juliet burst out of the gloom of the bush track and sprint across the sand, heading for a dark shape he could see bobbing along in the swollen creek. The dog!

He started running then too, but as his shoes pounded the muddy track his adept mind was quickly assessing the situation. He saw Juliet plunge into the water and figured she was about to reach Ruby Roo, and he would be best to position himself on the point where the creek met the surf, in case they both needed help to get out of the raging water. He dropped his warm, heavy coat onto the sand, kicked off his shoes, and stripped off his track pants, knowing that if he ended up in the sea, he'd be better off without them. It was surprising how heavy clothing was in the water; he'd learned that as part of his training at school, when he'd had to jump fully dressed into a swimming pool. With that memory, he quickly pulled off his sweatshirt as well.

At that moment, he saw a large branch sweep into Juliet, and he changed direction and headed towards her, worried she would be dragged under.

"Roo!" she screamed again, sheer panic in her voice.

He could see why. The dog was only yards from the surf now. Seeing in an instant that Juliet had extricated herself from the branch, he raced to the edge just ahead of the furiously paddling dog.

*

Juliet caught a glimpse of something out of the corner of her eye and then realized it was Finn, and he was heading straight towards Ruby Roo. Relief swept across her but, although he was a strong swimmer, she knew that the surf in storm conditions could be brutal. Would he really go in there and risk his life for her dog?

"Get to shore," he yelled, gesturing with his arm, and she did as he said, too far behind to catch up to Ruby Roo now. Finn, running on the sand, was in a much better position.

Even in her distress, she was impressed with his shallow dive into the water. Not so foolish that he'd dive headfirst when he didn't know the water depth, he'd taken a few steps until he was thigh deep and then used his strong legs to propel his body forward in a graceful arc. His arms, with hands joined to make a V shape, cut through the water and when he pushed his head up Ruby Roo was only a few yards ahead of him. After a few of the strongest, fastest strokes of freestyle Juliet thought she'd ever seen, he caught up to the dog, grabbing the scruff of her neck with one hand and wrapping his other arm around her body as the first of the waves churned around them. They were in the surf.

Juliet saw them both shrouded in spray, and hovered knee-deep in the shallows. She would wait there to see what happened and where the current might take them before she went in again too.

The relief she felt knowing Finn had got hold of Roo was indescribable. He was standing up now, in thigh-deep water, straining against the current and cradling the dog. The waves were so big, even compared to Finn and his tall frame – if Ruby Roo had been in there on her own . . .

Juliet clenched her fists. She wouldn't think about that. Finn was with her, but they weren't safe yet. She could see a huge wave bearing down on them and, after it had broken with a crash of churning, white foam, they were gone from her sight.

Chapter 24 – Time to dive in

Finn glanced around to see the wave rearing up behind him and braced for the impact. His legs were pulled from under him as the wall of water came crashing down. Dammit! This one was too strong; they'd just have to go with it.

His fingers gripped Roo's collar and he held her close with strong arms as the wave tumbled him over. He knew it was best to relax as the churning water roared above them, then get a footing once it was past. The dog seemed to sense that too. She'd been struggling and scratching at his body with her paws, but as they went under, she stayed still, seeming to realize she had to trust in the big human who held her close.

The wave surged towards the shore, dragging them along with it as Finn straightened up and fought for a foothold, his arms still full of red dog. At least they were heading in the right direction – for now – but he knew they'd only have a second or two at most before the backwards drag of the water and the pounding of the next wave. He propelled his body forward as fast as he could. The next wave was smaller, and he was able to keep his feet, and then with two more mighty strides he was in the shallows, feeling receding waves drag and tear at his legs, as if the ocean was angry that they'd been able to escape its clutches.

Ruby Roo wriggled in his arms as he waded towards Juliet, impatient to be put down.

"Look what I caught!" He took a couple more steps and then lowered her gently into ankle-deep water, and she bounded towards the sand and gave a great big shake.

"Roo!" Juliet had dropped to her knees.

Ruby Roo headbutted her owner and then ran away a few yards, feeling a bit funny. She coughed and gave a big retch, vomiting up sea water and coughing some more. Feeling much better after that effort, she shook herself again and raced around in a circle, then went back for another headbutt.

"Oh, Roo," Juliet wrapped her arms around the wriggling, jumping animal. "I was so scared, but it looks like you're okay, you crazy dog. Good girl, Ruby Roo – you're a good girl."

The dog licked Juliet's arm. Her owner was emotional, she knew, and needed some cheering up. She tried to climb onto her lap, wagging her tail furiously, and Juliet fell over backwards, half-laughing and half-sobbing with relief. Job done; Ruby Roo scampered away. She was cold and needed to run around so her thick fur would start to dry.

Finn held out his hand to Juliet. "Time to stop rolling in the sand, I'm afraid. We need to grab those coats before we freeze to death. Oh, excuse my lack of clothing, by the way. I knew I'd be able to swim better if I stripped off."

She looked up at him, wiping tears from her face. "Well, I'm glad you didn't lose your undies in the surf. That can happen when it's rough."

"I know! And I couldn't have let go of your dog, so I would have had to walk up the beach totally starkers! That would have been embarrassing."

"I think it would have been okay, in the circumstances," Juliet said with an impish smile.

She was standing now, still holding his hand, and she put her other hand on his arm.

"Finn. How can I ever thank you? You saved Ruby Roo's life." Her eyes filled with tears again.

"Hey, no crying now. I hate it when women weep all over me with gratitude. Happens all the time, you know. Besides, you were doing a great job of saving her yourself, until you got whacked by that branch. Are you okay?"

"I think so. I'm probably a bit battered and bruised, but I'm so numb from the cold I can't feel it. I'll survive – but look at you! You're all scratched from Roo's claws."

"A mere flesh wound," he grinned. "Manly men like me can swim in icy seas and wrestle savage dingoes without even messing up our hair, didn't you know? I don't think poor old Roo knew what was going on when I grabbed her. It's not her fault she went a bit wild with her footsies."

Finn realized he was starting to babble again, light-headed from the adrenalin rush. He was saying whatever silly thing popped into his head, and Juliet probably thought he was a bit mad, but he was enormously relieved that the dog was safe. He'd grown to be fond of Ruby Roo, that was true, but he was far more fond of her owner. He didn't want to contemplate how distraught Juliet would have been if her beloved dog had drowned.

But she hadn't. She was leaping around in the dunes now and rolling in the sparse reeds, looking as though she'd already recovered from the ordeal. Tough creatures, those cattle dogs.

He led Juliet up the beach, only letting go of her hand so that he could gather up their discarded clothing. He put her jacket around her shoulders, then rested his own big coat on top of that.

"Let's sit here for a minute and catch our breath. At least the sun's come out now. Probably our last glimpse of it for the day."

They lowered themselves onto a log that was lying on the edge of the dunes.

"This is your coat, Finn. You put it on."

"No, keep it. You're probably in shock after getting such a fright. You need to warm up."

"We'll share. It's big enough for two." Juliet wriggled closer to him and pushed the thick woollen coat over his shoulders as well.

Finn only noticed how cold he really was when he felt her body heat and the shelter of the coat. He reached his arm behind her, making sure the coat was still in place on her shoulders, then realized she was shaking with cold.

"Here." He handed her his dry track pants and sweatshirt. "Take off your wet clothes and put these on. I'll look the other way, I promise. No . . . go on!" he insisted, seeing she was about to refuse.

"Oh, alright, thanks. I really am very cold, and wet jeans aren't that comfy."

He swung his gaze away from her and she clambered to her feet. This time, he was too concerned about her to be imagining anything sensual as she undressed; he just wanted her to warm up.

"Oh, that's better, thank you. You can look now."

She sat down beside him again and he put his arm back around her.

"Why is it that whenever I have any adventures with you, Juliet, I end up dripping wet and freezing cold?"

"That's the way we roll, here in Mirrabooka," she said with a grin.

Finn produced a bottle of water from his coat pocket. "Want some? It'll be better than that creek water you probably swallowed."

"Oh, great! Thanks." She drank a couple of mouthfuls. "You have some too, and then I'll give Roo a drink. I bet she'll be glad of it."

She called Ruby Roo over and he poured water into her cupped hands. They watched as the grateful dog lapped at the fresh water.

"Luckily, us city people always walk around clutching bottles of water. You never know when you might die of thirst during a half-hour walk," he said, imitating Mrs Mac perfectly.

"You do that so well!" Juliet laughed, as Ruby finished her long drink and flopped down on the sand beside them, panting happily.

"But I'm never going to listen to anyone say that again without pointing out how *this* city boy saved my dog from drowning and then revived her with his bottle of water."

She reached out and rubbed Roo's head. "She is one lucky dog. I am so grateful, Finn. I can't believe you risked your life to save her. That surf is treacherous today."

"It's wild, alright." He looked at the churning water he'd just emerged from, and the line of brooding clouds along the horizon, almost black in some parts and slate-grey in others, the edges tinged with pink from the sinking sun. A sea eagle soared above them, banking and wheeling as it looked for prey, being carried along effortlessly in the gusts of wind. He'd be leaving all this soon, and city life was going to be very dull in comparison.

He contemplated how open to be with the woman by his side. His natural reserve was lowered by the drama they'd just been through together. To hell with it – who cares about stupid pride? This was real life. It could have ended in tragedy, but it didn't. The three of them were sitting safely together on the sand, and for that he would be eternally grateful.

"I did it for you," he said quietly. "I wanted to save Roo, of course, but really – I did it for you. I'd do anything for you, Juliet. Don't you know that?"

"No!" she stared at him, frowning. "I don't, actually. You're leaving! *Tomorrow*, I've just found out. You could have taken that job and stayed here, but you're leaving!"

There was anguish in her voice, but she quickly extinguished it. "Of course, that makes sense. Your career is in the city. And Sophia, of course. I hope you've enjoyed spending time in Mirrabooka, though. It's a lovely part of the world."

She was sounding like a tour guide. Any minute now and she'd whip out a feedback form for him to fill out.

So, what did you think of Mirrabooka, sir?

Very nice, once you get used to being in a small town.

Scenery?

Stunning.

Favourite attraction?

The most beautiful, brave, amazing woman I've ever met.

He studied her face. She was staring down at the sand and her expression looked tight and closed off but, before she'd slipped into tour guide mode, there had been pain in her voice – and he wanted to know why.

"Sophia? That chapter is well and truly over, I can assure you. She won't be turning up here again." Was he imagining it, or did her face seem to relax a little? "You've got it all wrong, Juliet," he continued. "I turned down the job because I realized I couldn't bear to be around you, of course. I care about you, but I know you don't feel like that about me. You're sorting things out with Ronan, and I wish you all the best, I really do. But I can't stay here and see how happy you are with somebody else. I couldn't bear it."

"What? No—"

She tried to say something, but he kept talking. The words were so painful, he knew he had to get it all out in one go. "You know what? I've just realized what true love is really like." He stared again at the brooding clouds and churning water. "It's when you think of the one you adore being with someone else, and the physical pain that causes makes you want to stab yourself in the guts while jumping off a very high cliff and landing in a river of snapping crocodiles."

He paused and then looked straight at her gorgeous face, as she gazed at him with wide eyes. This was the face that was always in his thoughts – first thing in the morning and last thing at night. The face he would never forget. Talk about jumping off a cliff – well, it was time he took the plunge and bared his soul. This beautiful woman had taken hold of his heart. He didn't want to spend the rest of his life regretting the fact that he'd never told her how he felt.

"I love you, Juliet. That's what I'm trying to say, and it would tear me apart to be around you with those feelings not being returned. I love you, I love this place, and I even love your mad dog. I mean, look at her. What a clown!"

Ruby Roo had got bored with all the talking and had found a flock of seagulls to play with. She was trying to round them up by running around them in a semi-circle and dropping to the sand, then dashing closer up – at which point the nearest seagulls would fly away and she'd drop down and wait for them to land before starting all over again.

Finn turned his eyes from the dog back to Juliet. He'd switched her attention to Ruby Roo on purpose, to save them both some embarrassment. He steeled himself for her polite rejection and hoped she wouldn't look too appalled.

She didn't – not at all. In fact, she looked more confused than anything else.

"Ronan? What do you mean, sorting things out with Ronan? Why would you think that?"

"I saw the two of you together in a photo. On the *Celebs About Town* website."

"You're a *Celebs About Town* follower? Wow, I really am learning all sorts of things about you today." Her face lit up with a grin.

"Yeah, thanks." He gave her a wry smile. "I was having a haircut, and the hairdresser kept talking about it. She showed me the photo on her iPad. You were standing together, and Ronan had his arm around you. You both looked happy, smiling together." He winced, remembering the image and how he felt when he saw it.

"Huh! Natalie has a massive crush on Ronan. She always wants to talk about him. I saw that photo too, and I think my smile was more of a shocked grimace. The whole article is complete rubbish. I'd had a drink with Ronan the first day of the festival, and then we did the panel together, which was all fine. I figured it was best if we could at least get along. But then, at that cocktail party, he changed gears and was all over me, and kept talking to everyone as though we were still an item. The photographer missed the best bit, which was what happened around the corner, when we had a brief conversation out of sight of everybody else. That was when I threw my red wine all over him!"

"Really? That's pretty feisty!" Relief flooded through his body. They weren't back together! She probably thought he was a fool for rushing in like a crazy person and saying he loved her, but at least she wasn't back with that scrawny, pretentious weasel! He felt like doing cartwheels down the beach.

"It's a long story but, basically, I wouldn't have anything more to do with that slime-bucket if he was the last man on earth *and* offered me a billion dollars and a life-time supply of chocolate. He'd been unfaithful to me, Finn. It went on for months, but he only admitted it when I had proof and confronted him. Then he turned nasty. That man is a lying, cheating, low-life scumbag of the highest order."

"Okay, well, that seems a thorough summing-up."

"And, there's more!"

"More?"

"The night we broke up, he kicked Ruby Roo. We'd argued, and I'd told him it was over. He grabbed my arm and wrenched at it, making me cry out, and Roo ran between us and barked at him, so he kicked her as hard as he could in the ribs."

Finn frowned. "That's assault. Against both of you."

"Yes, and after all that, when he insisted we go around the corner at the cocktail party for a talk, which I thought would be an apology, he had the nerve to tell me he'd *forgiven* me for the dog attack and was willing to resume the relationship – if I got rid of the dog! So, I laughed hysterically and told him he needed treatment for his rampant self-delusions. Then I said some extremely rude words, threw my shiraz all over his best hipster waistcoat, and walked away."

"I like your style." Finn hugged her closer, feeling almost giddy with happiness. They weren't together!

"But, hang on – what dog attack?" he asked. "Was there one?"

"There may have been a few moments when Ruby Roo's teeth were clamped onto Ronan's ankle, I will admit. But it was in self-defence, Your Honour."

"I see. Well, the judge needs a moment to consider this and discuss it with the accused. Ruby Roo! Come here, girl."

He whistled to the dog and she left the herd of disobedient seagulls and trotted towards the couple on the sand. She liked this tall man with the low and pleasant voice and was happy to see him snuggled up with her owner. She stopped in front of him and obediently sat down.

"I have heard a grave allegation about you, Miss Ruby."

The dog looked at him and tilted her head to one side.

"Do you have any feelings of remorse about the afore-mentioned incident with that man's ankle and your sharp teeth?"

Ruby Roo shook her fur, sending sand flying in all directions.

"The accused says no. Good dog!" Finn reached out and ruffled the fur on her neck and she leapt forward and gave him the headbutt she reserved for people she really liked.

He laughed and patted her again. "You have permission to bite that man if he ever mistreats your beautiful owner again, and that goes for anybody else who is mean to her too. You're a *very* good and clever dog!"

Pleased with the praise, Ruby Roo wagged her tail, gave Juliet a swift lick on the arm, and bounded away to resume the seagull game. All sorts of exciting things were happening today!

Chapter 25 – A very busy day

Juliet's head was spinning, with a host of thoughts swirling around in circles. He loved her? Despite the sensible part of her brain erring caution, a delicious tingly feeling seemed to be radiating through her body.

"So, Finn . . . what you said before. It's going around and around in my head. I knew there was something between us. I have feelings for you too . . ." She hesitated, playing with a shell on the sand, concentrating hard on smoothing the grit off its pearly surface.

"Go on," he said gently.

"But I didn't want to fall for you. I kept trying to hold things back. I knew I was starting to care for you, but that it could never work. You would go back to the city, and I can't live there. I'm not going to make the mistake of changing my life for a man again – not when I know it won't be right for me. This sort of life is the one I want. Right here, all this." She gestured to the sea and the sky. "The ocean and the rain and the sun, the birds and the kangaroos and the space – the way you can look across the water at dusk and know there's nowhere else you'd rather be. This place is in my blood. It's part of me."

"Yes. I can see that now," he said. "It's got to me too, you know. Byron told me to be careful. He said that once the Mirrabooka magic got hold of you, you were a goner. And that's exactly what's happened, just like he predicted. He's a smart guy, that Byron," he smiled.

"I've grown to love the place, and the town and the community too. I feel peaceful here and involved, like I never was in the city. I love Mirrabooka – but I love you more, Juliet. Like I said, if you don't care in that way for me, or if you still think it's all impossible, I can't stay here. That's why I turned down the job."

"You really would have moved here?" Her heart was beginning to do little flip-flops of either joy or anguish, or possibly both.

"Firstly, I'd move to the North Pole if I could be with you. But secondly, I think that job and this town would be the sort of thing I could find really satisfying. Helping Jayden made me realize that's what I want to do. I want to be involved in a community and work with people who need someone on their side. I know they won't all be good, innocent folk, or victims of unfortunate circumstances, but some will be. And most of them who've gone wrong will have done so from disadvantage, and they need guidance and another chance. Everyone deserves good legal advice and representation, and providing that for the people who live in this area sure beats the hell out of working for crime gangs in the city."

Juliet heard the regret in his voice as he talked about the job that could have been his. How she responded now could change everything. She had a decision to make – head or heart? If she followed her heart, would it turn out to be another foolish mistake? Allowing herself to love again meant taking a huge risk. Was she brave enough to do that?

Then she imagined him leaving and felt again the chill wind of loss. Her decision was made, just like that. She could not choose any other way.

"I don't want you to leave." Their eyes met and, all of a sudden, the world seemed alive with possibility.

"It might not be too late. He scrabbled around in the coat pocket and grabbed his cell phone. "There's a good chance they don't have anyone else yet."

He looked at her, then the phone, then back to her. "But I need to know, before I do this . . . Do you care, Juliet? Really care? Is there a chance for us?"

"Yes,' she said simply. "I love you too, Finn. I've fought and fought against all these feelings I have for you, but now I surrender. There is a chance for us. Are you seriously saying you want to stay in Mirrabooka . . . with me?"

He gazed at her, his earnest, dark eyes holding a promise.

"I'll show you how serious I am." He tapped a few times on the phone and put it to his ear. A few minutes later, that call was finished, and a second one had been made and completed too.

"I don't believe you just did that," Juliet shook her head, amazed. "You've accepted one job and quit from another while you're sitting in your jocks on a deserted beach, practically freezing to death."

"That's me, Mr Impetuous," he grinned. "And we really should go home soon. Before that, though, I'd really like to kiss you again. Would that be okay? Also, you should know that I've been entranced by you from the first moment I saw you, even when you were shouting at me and calling me hurtful names. 'Dog-botherer', was one, if I remember rightly." He smiled at her and his eyes crinkled at the corners. "Maybe 'sadistic city psycho' was another, do you recall?"

Juliet put her hand across his mouth. "No wonder you make a good barrister. You sure know how to talk. Why don't you just shut up and kiss me?"

So he did, wrapping warm arms around her and pulling her to him so their bodies were fused together, and his lips were exploring hers with exactly the right balance of passion and tenderness. Ruby Roo tilted her head and stared at the humans, then sighed. She wanted to go home now, but they appeared to be busy. She would just have to sit and wait.

*

Voices echoed across the beach. "Jules! Where are you?" Tom shouted.

"Finn! Juliet!" Byron joined in.

"Over here!" They waved their arms at the two men who were stepping off the track and onto the beach in the gloom of approaching night.

Ruby Roo ran to greet them, tail wagging, and Byron leaned down to pat her as they reached Finn and Juliet. "You're all wet, Roo . . . Good grief, so are you, Jules! What's going on?"

"Whoa!" Tom looked at Finn and noticed his lack of clothing under the draped coat. "You barristers really know how to bust a move! Are we interrupting something?" he grinned.

"It's a long story." Juliet smiled up at Tom, looking cold but radiant – and happier than he had seen her look for a very long time.

"We need to hear it, but firstly, I'm glad we found you!" Byron said. "Izzy sent us down here. She said you'd gone to look for Finn ages ago, and she was worried because you hadn't come back."

"You were coming to find me?" Finn looked pleased.

"Yes, so this whole drama is your fault, actually," she teased.

"Well, you can tell us all about it soon," Tom said. "But right now, as town doctor, I'm ordering you both to go home and get warm. You're insane sitting here in this weather – and if I have to treat either of you for pneumonia, I'm going to be very annoyed!"

"Yes, Doc," Juliet climbed to her feet. "Oh, I think I've stiffened up in the cold." She wobbled a bit and Finn reached out to steady her, slipping his arm around her waist.

"As a quick summary," Juliet said, "Ruby Roo fell in the creek and got swept out to sea, and both of us went in after her. It was

Finn who saved her, though." She looked up at the tall man beside her with a smile of dazzling intensity.

"How on earth did she fall in the creek?" Tom's eyes were wide.

"The broken bridge. The council is certainly going to hear about this!" Juliet said.

"Leave it to me. Your lawyer is going to point out a thing or two about public liability," Finn said with a frown.

"You mean she fell in up there and got carried all the way to the surf?" Byron's face looked pale in the gloom. He adored Ruby too.

"Yep. I thought she was a goner. I really did. I thought I'd lost her." Juliet's voice broke a little, and Finn held her tighter.

Byron knelt down to hug the dog. "Man, I'm not surprised – poor old Roo-dog. Good job, Finn. You did well, mate." He nodded up to him.

"Right, we're going up to the house. Come on." Tom's voice sounded emotional too.

It had dawned on both men what the ramifications could have been, and not just for the dog.

"I hope you'll read the riot act to that bloody council," Tom said to Finn, who nodded as they headed back towards the hill.

*

The full account of the drama was told over dinner in Juliet's cottage, with an open fire roaring in the living room, and Clementine tucked into her cot in the spare bedroom. The baby slept there too, snug in his bassinet, and Ruby Roo was curled up in her basket near the fire.

Tom had ordered the two of them to go and enjoy long, hot showers, insisting he would be in charge of dinner. He put chopped-up potatoes and pumpkin in the oven to roast, marinated some steaks and chopped more vegetables and then, clad in several layers of warm clothing, took them out to the deck to grill on the BBQ, while Isabella and Byron bathed and settled the children.

Juliet was setting the table in the open-plan living area when Finn reappeared with a bottle of red wine. Her heart leapt at the sight of him.

"We're drinking this tonight." He placed the bottle on the table and produced a corkscrew from his pocket. "It's a special one, but we've got a lot to celebrate."

He stood behind her, slipping his arms around her waist and kissing the back of her neck, and she leaned back against him, feeling his warmth and pressing against his desire.

"You're driving me crazy," he murmured into her hair, tightening his arms. "I'll have to stop being a gentleman if you keep behaving like this."

She looked up at him with a slow, languorous smile. "Since Byron's staying tonight too, he and Izzy will be in my room with the baby and Clemmie's in the other room. So, I was wondering if maybe I could bunk in at your place? Save me from sleeping on the couch."

Finn nuzzled her hair, and Juliet breathed in his masculine fragrance.

"Mmmm, let me think about that." His hands felt the contours of her hips and waist.

"In the guest room, of course," she teased, loving the feeling of his hands becoming more insistent.

"Oh, sure. The guest room, the living room, the kitchen . . . all around the house is fine with me," he grinned. "I just hope you're not expecting to get any sleep."

The door banged as Tom headed in from the deck to the kitchen, and Finn released Juliet from his embrace, sneaking a kiss on the side of her neck first. He turned his attention back to the wine bottle, carefully twisting the corkscrew into it, and Juliet continued arranging the cutlery on the table as they exchanged private smiles.

Tom's head appeared through the doorway. "Is that Grange Hermitage I can see? Wow! That's a top drop. Is this a special occasion?"

"Something like that," Finn smiled. "There are a couple of things we need to be thankful for, I think."

Juliet left him in charge of the table and went to help Tom in the kitchen.

"This meal looks brilliant," she said. "Thank you, Tom."

"My pleasure. And by the way – remember that conversation we had round at my place? I really like Finn, and I think we could be great friends for a long, long time. Does that seem significant to you?"

"It does. It certainly does. There are a few things I need to tell you about soon."

He put his arm around her shoulders and gave them a squeeze. "Good. I look forward to it."

Isabella and Byron emerged from the bedroom where they'd settled the children.

"Both asleep. Hooray!" Bryon said with a grin, so Tom and Juliet carried the plates to the table and Finn poured the wine.

"It tastes pretty good," he said. "I was worried it could be past its best, as it's quite old, but I reckon it's fine. What do you think, Tom?"

"Excellent," Tom confirmed. "Even better than Byron's home-made beer. Probably a smidge more expensive too."

"Just a bit," Byron nodded.

"Right, time to charge our glasses," Finn announced. "Who else is having some of this plonk?"

Even Isabella said she would have a tiny glass. Her doctor confirmed that two or three sips of excellent red wine would not do any harm.

"They used to recommend stout, you know, for mothers."

"Well, that was some time ago," Isabella laughed. "And Arlo seems to like his feeds just as they are, thanks very much, but I'd like to have a little taste of this fine wine."

"Time for the toast," Finn said. "We need to raise our glasses to the endurance and fortitude of a brave cattle dog. To Ruby Roo! The nicest dingo impersonator I've ever met!"

"To Ruby Roo!" they repeated, laughing, and the guest of honour heard her name, lifted her head sleepily and thumped her tail in reply, and then went straight back to sleep.

*

"So, suddenly, there was Finn . . ." Juliet resumed her telling of the long version of the story, which was becoming more embroidered with every sip of wine. "He appeared – whoosh! – like Superman, just when I was wallowing around in the creek with a big branch. He sprinted across the sand like an ironman then dived in the creek like an Olympic swimmer. Seriously, is there anything this man can't do?" she said happily.

"He's a great swimmer," Tom said. "And footy player." He shook his head regretfully. "You know I'm broken-hearted, mate, that you won't be here to play in the grand final on Saturday. Of all the times to leave Mirrabooka . . . My man-crush is finished. It's over, I tell you." He put his head in his hands and pretended to sob with grief.

"Well, actually . . ." Finn glanced at Juliet and she nodded.

"You can stop crying, Tom, you big sook," he said. "I'll still be here, so I'll play on Saturday if you want me to."

"Seriously?" Tom lifted his head and looked at him with the beginnings of a grin that threatened to split his face in two.

"We have a couple of other things to tell you too."

Juliet's heart did a happy dance as Finn used the word 'we' for the first time. It sounded so right.

"I've taken that job in Gipps Beach after all," he continued. "And I quit my other job as of today, so I'm going to be around for a while. As long as Juliet wants me to be, anyway. And that's a promise." Finn took her hand.

"I should think he'll be here a long time, Tom, so don't worry. You can start planning next year's sporting program as well," Juliet said, having to drag her gaze away from the man beside her, whose steady, warm eyes held the assurance of everything she'd ever wanted in life.

Tom pushed back his chair and leapt in the air. "Yes! Victory is ours!"

"Shush!" Byron said. "Don't wake the children! Hey, I love saying that. Children! We have two now."

He leaned over and kissed his wife, who stroked the side of his face and said, "Oh, I'm just so happy – about everything!" and then burst into tears.

Juliet leaned over and hugged her and started to cry too.

"Well, that was quite an announcement, mate," Byron said to Finn, as Tom continued with his victory dance around the room, quietly chanting the footy club theme song, and the two women half-cried and half-laughed on each other's shoulders. He reached across the table and shook his hand. "Welcome to Mirrabooka!"

The guest of honour and cause of the day's drama was oblivious to most of the celebrations. In fact, she was snoring quite loudly, on and off. Ruby Roo knew the humans were having all sorts of discussions, but she only woke from time to time when she heard her name. All the people she loved were right there in the room with her, she'd had special treats for dinner, and her basket was near the fire, where she was warm and snug. All was right with her world, and she dozed peacefully in the cosy room. It had been a very busy day.

About the author

Maggie McGuinness has always been fascinated by people and the ways they relate to each other. Now, after years of observing and experiencing life in all its wonderful, messy glory – it's time to write about it!

Maggie lives in a corner of Australia in a remote coastal town called Mallacoota, which is surrounded by the ocean, inland waterways, and beautiful native forests. Her housemate, best buddy, and constant shadow is a very cute rescue dog called Tilly.

Currently working in bushfire recovery and doing freelance writing and editing for a living, her vision for the future is to be able to spend her days wearing PJs, drinking tea, and writing fiction. Maggie's hobbies are walking Tilly on the beach, learning the art of wood splitting, and perfecting her own extreme sport of combining Zumba dance moves and cooking.

Instagram: https://www.instagram.com/maggiemcg_author/
Facebook page: www.facebook.com/MaggieMcG99
Website: www.maggiemcguinness.com

Planet Single

Looking for love – take two! A romantic comedy

"The night I landed on Planet Single, I had no idea I was about to blast off from the familiar married landscape. If I'd known, I could have packed a few essentials like some nicer undies, a dating guidebook and a much thicker skin, but I didn't have the chance. I was dumped – defenceless – into a strange new world."

Meet Katerina – mother- of- two, chronic daydreamer, and soon-to-be ex-wife. After losing her marriage and reclaiming her name in one surprising night, Kat realizes that being single again is a whole new learning curve. Things have certainly changed. You can shop online for men now, with a bewildering array of choices, but there doesn't seem to be a refund policy. Was looking for love always this complicated?

Determined to create a better life after the train-wreck of her marriage, Kat sets off to find out who she really is, meeting a succession of dodgy dates, two contrary inner voices, and a handsome detective along the way – as well as a whole tribe of young and sexy colleagues. Who knew selling stationery could be so much fun?

Relatable, quirky, and seriously funny, *Planet Single* is an Australian romantic comedy about starting over. Get ready for an emotional rollercoaster ride of dating adventure, laugh-out-loud humour, and heart-wrenching moments. Will Kat ever find what she's looking for?

** Sexual references, some sex scenes (not explicit), and lots of 'colourful' language. **